DANCING ON KNIVES

DANCING
ON KNIVES

Joanne Rush

[signature: Joanne Rush]

HONNO MODERN FICTION

First published in Great Britain in 2025 by Honno Press
D41, Hugh Owen Building, Aberystwyth University, Ceredigion, SY23 3DY

1 2 3 4 5 6 7 8 9 10

A catalogue record for this book is available from the British Library.

Published with the financial support of the Books Council of Wales.

ISBN 978-1-916821-12-5 (paperback)
ISBN 978-1-916821-13-2 (ebook)
Cover design: Ifan Bates
Text design: Elaine Sharples
Printed by: 4Edge

This is a work of fiction and no resemblance to persons living or dead is
intended or implied.

For Pip and Sof

But what shall I do in Illyria?
  – William Shakespeare, *Twelfth Night*

You will keep your graceful movements – no dancer will ever glide so lightly – but every step you take will make you feel as if you were treading on a sharp knife, enough to make your feet bleed.
  – Hans Christian Andersen, *The Little Mermaid*

Wednesday 4th December, 2011

There are ghosts in Baščaršija, so they say. Well, there would be. I remember the shells squalling down from the hills round Sarajevo, eighteen years ago. Back then these narrow streets were a death-trap, all rubble and brick dust. But the war ended, and builders smothered the debris in wet cement. The ghosts, too. Surely I'd have seen them otherwise.

I am sitting in Café Illyria, wearing fingerless gloves and a coat that's tight over my breasts. On my head is a red bobble hat, which someone in the audience left behind tonight. The heating has gone off. Even gloved, my hands are cold.

I should go home: it's long past closing time. The market will be empty at this hour, though soon fresh slabs of meat will slap against the trestle tables, and pop-eyed fish will arrive on trays of ice, like frozen memories of shoals. If I hurry, I'll catch the last tram.

But I want to tell my story. I know it will be subjective, and warped by memory. Stories, after all, are only what we bring to the surface. Under the surface are dreams and monsters.

1

ENGLAND

2008-2010

CHAPTER 1

I was on my way out of the Map Room, unpinning the ASSISTANT LIBRARIAN badge from my shirt, when I saw the sign.

> A talk by Ivan Tabak
> Bosnian poet and activist
> 7 p.m.
> St John's College
>
> (WRITER IN RESIDENCE PROGRAMME)

It was typed on ordinary A4 card. Nothing about it glowed or sang. Perhaps I should have ignored it, averted my eyes. A year ago I had come to Cambridge for a fresh start. I had fallen in love with the skies and stones, the way the punts slid downriver like puppet boats in a paper theatre, the calm scholarliness of the courts. Even my job stacking shelves at the University Library had its upside: I got to read hundreds of books. But today was the anniversary of Mama's death. I found myself longing for a face from home.

That was how I ended up standing in the doorway of a small lecture hall. It was crammed with students, so I might have left, even then, if a girl in the back row had not turned round and smiled at me, moving her scarf and coat to make room. As I slid gratefully into the seat beside her, a man who could only be a Bosnian poet walked onto the stage. He was wearing black-and-white chequered trousers and an orange shirt. 'My name is Ivan Tabak,' he said. 'Eee-fan. If it is hard for you to pronounce then call me Joe or something. No problem.' The tell-tale Sarajevan growl of his consonants made my heart race.

Ivan Tabak began to talk about a literature festival he was setting up next summer. 'In Sarajevo,' he told us, smiling from under his soft brown moustache. So I was right, he came from my hometown. I let myself remember the steep path from my house to Baščaršija – the old Turkish bazaar – and the slippery cobblestones, blotched red by fallen plums. But I caught my thoughts there, before they got to the body in the river.

'We need volunteers,' Ivan was saying. 'I am one month in Cambridge, if you wish to know more. Or you can sign up for the newsletter.'

When the time came for questions, the girl beside me raised her hand. 'Will the festival have a theme?' She had a lilting accent I couldn't place.

'Vilas,' Ivan told her. 'You know of vilas? Bosnian water spirits. The first one was swan – our word is labud. Or else it was goose. Guska.' Startled, I gave him my full attention. 'Goose and swan are water birds,' he explained, twisting the ends of his moustache. 'They are migrants, but always they come home. In ancient Slavic legend they bring us gifts, such as spring.'

I thought about this all through the vote of thanks and the burst of clapping that followed it. My neighbour wolf-whistled. As the applause died down, she introduced herself. 'Roisin Clery. Are you a student?'

I shook my head, blushing.

'Good,' she said frankly. 'Me neither.' She tapped a forefinger on her chest. 'Singer by night, songwriter by day. But Adam, this boy I live with, he smuggles me into some of his classes. I got hooked on Tabak's poetry – not to mention his gorgeous dark eyes.' Her own eyes sparkled at me. 'What brings you here?'

'I'm Bosnian,' I said. 'Laura Guska.'

'L-our-a Goos-ka,' she repeated. 'You're a homeward-bound spirit?'

'Well—' I laughed. 'A migrant, anyway.'

Roisin laughed too. 'I'm fresh off the boat from Belfast. I

brought two guitars and a suitcase full of Barry's tea, because the tea here is just dishwater, isn't it?' I was about to agree when she grabbed my wrist, turning it so she could see my watch better. 'Oh shite,' she said. 'I've got to run – I'm so sorry.' Snatching up her belongings, she dashed for the door so fast her scarf flew out behind her. I watched it swing wildly open, bang loudly shut. So that was that.

Disappointed because I'd liked her, I buttoned my own coat, and as I left I signed up impulsively for Ivan Tabak's newsletter. Then I retraced my steps through stone cloisters and dark courtyards until I emerged into the lamp-lit street.

The dark yellow leaves on the linden trees reminded me of Sarajevo again. It used to be lovely at the end of summer: hot by day, when the tables in Baščaršija filled up with men and laughing girls; cool at night, when a mountain wind blew down into the kitchen of our house on Gnijezdo Street, with its blue Ottoman tiles and the bulky, grumbling oven, dubbed by Mama 'that communist stove.' I did miss it. But my most vivid recollection of the city was of Kalashnikov rifles, grey rubble and death. That was why thousands of Bosnians were still as far from home as the shape of the earth permitted, in America or Australia, while others, like my dad, made new lives across the border, where the food and the language were familiar but the names on the gravestones were not.

I was just turning downhill when Roisin veered towards me on a bike, a guitar across her back, her cheeks pink with cold. She braked abruptly, skewing the bike crossways in the road. 'Laura!'

I felt my mood lift. 'Zdravo,' I said.

'Zdravo.' She grinned at me. 'How's my pronunciation?' A taxi honked as it swerved round us, and she waved after it so airily that I started laughing. 'Are you busy tonight?' she demanded, turning back to me. 'I've got a gig at the Red Bull. It's out in Newnham village, but you could ride on my pannier.'

I had planned to go home and make a pot of dishwater tea. Ed might drop by when the library shut – poor Ed, hoping for some home-cooked baklava. But I felt a sudden, leaping desire for change. That's the Slav coming out, my dad would have said. So I told Roisin, 'Okay, yes!'

Her guitar pressed my cheek as we wobbled off. Another taxi honked at us and I grabbed hold of her waist. 'Jesus, it's a one-way street!' Roisin shouted.

'If the police stop us, pretend to be Bosnian!' I shouted back. 'Cyclists do what they like there!'

'Is it legal in Bosnia to ride the same bike?'

'No idea! It's so windy, I can hardly hear you!'

'Are you all right?'

My hair was whipping across my eyes. 'Yes!'

We swooped down King's Parade, where the gargoyles loomed above us, their mouths open in eroding screams, then over Silver Street Bridge and out across the dark fenland. 'Hold tight!' Roisin said, standing up on the pedals.

When she stopped with a squeal of brakes outside the Red Bull, I saw my wind-stung cheeks and tangled curls reflected in the window. The pub was dark inside and smelt of vinegar. The band was tuning up. 'Beer?' I asked.

'Lovely,' said Roisin. A guitarist with a ragged black beard stooped to kiss her on the mouth. I went to buy us each a bottle of lager. As I leant on the bar, Roisin blew me a kiss across the room; then she caught hold of the guitarist's hands and I heard her ask, 'Will I turn up the PA?' The alcohol was going to my head, making colours glow and haze.

By the time Roisin returned, the pub had got crowded. 'Come meet my housemates,' she said, grabbing her beer. We squeezed a path to three people by the stage. 'This is Laura,' she told them. 'I kidnapped her from town. Laura: Adam, Mim and Rupert.' She looked at the band. 'Shite, we're starting in a second. I'd better go.'

Rupert cupped his hands to my ear. 'What are you drinking?'

I held up my bottle, and I took in Adam's overgrown hair and his

Sonic the Hedgehog T-shirt. He's a video game player, I thought. A geek. But when he smiled lopsidedly at me, from the left side of his mouth first, I found myself smiling back.

On the stage Roisin spoke into the microphone. 'We're The Vagrant Revolution – we'll be playing you some soul classics tonight.' The guitars pulsed and thrummed. As the lights dipped lower, she seemed fragile. Her brown hair had been unevenly cut, giving her a ravaged, metamorphic look, like a girl frozen in the act of turning into a boy. But then she began to sing. First she sang "Son of a Preacher Man," her voice rising huskily above the guitars. The lyrics grew strident and hot, and the man who had kissed her leant into them as if into a wind, his guitar held low over his crotch. 'He was, he was,' she crooned, her eyes on his. 'Ooh, yes, he was.'

When Rupert came back with his hands full of drinks, the band was playing "Ain't No Sunshine" and Roisin's voice ached against the sax. I was aware of Adam leaning his shoulder into the wall beside me, his T-shirt dark and wet because Mim, turning, had spilt her pint over him. At the end of the song, he said, 'Loura,' the way Roisin had, making an experiment of it. 'Loura what?'

'Guska.'

'You're from the Balkans?' He laughed at my astonished look. 'I'm studying for a master's in Slavic politics.'

'My family are from Bosnia.' I remembered now what Roisin had told me about him smuggling her into Tabak's class. 'But "Laura" is fine.'

The band started playing again and we stopped talking. I kept my eyes on the stage, though I knew he was looking at me. He smelt of hops, of Mim's beer. Roisin sang "Use Me," a song I'd never heard before, dancing with her feet, holding the mic close to her lips. Everyone else was tapping a foot on the floor or over their knee, and the bass seemed to come from inside me, an extra heartbeat. I could feel Adam's gaze between my shoulder blades, like a hand touching my back.

We walked home through the centre of Cambridge after midnight, Roisin wheeling her bike. The guitarist came too. Was he hers? I thought so. 'The boy I live with,' she'd said, meaning Adam. But the guitarist had kissed her. A few undergraduates were straggling back from clubs or burger vans, and somewhere near the river we heard a group of them shouting 'Drink! Drink! Drink!' and singing a song about lions. I felt excited, as if I was leaving the everyday world behind. We passed the singers on Magdalene Bridge, dressed in football shorts and dinner jackets, and pouring champagne into a stiletto.

In a house on Portugal Street, four or five people wearing pyjamas joined us at the kitchen table. Roisin rolled a spliff. Adam went to change his beer-stained shirt. My chief memory of that night is of everyone smoking and talking about music, getting drunk on cheap red wine, waving their arms and breaking things. I thought at first they were all graduate students except Roisin, but Rupert told me they were a mix of what he called town and gown. There was a skinny actor who complained about the breakages, and a Chinese physicist named Jiao Ting, which was pronounced *Shou-ting*. This seemed funny in English because he couldn't raise his soft voice. He told me he'd just got home from his college library, where he was reading his way through banned books.

When Adam returned, wearing a faded blue top with RUN, JUMP & BLAST! on the front, he sat down next to me. 'So, Loura-Laura. I like your accent. Did you grow up in Bosnia?'

I took a sip of wine. 'I was born there, but we left in '92.'

'When the civil war began?'

'Yes,' I said, too surprised by his knowing the exact date to point out that the war was far from civil. Internal armies rose up, but external armies also invaded – Serbia from the east, Croatia from the north. I remembered the Chetniks with their blue uniforms and Russian guns, the Šokacs fetching out old rifles from World War II. I said, 'The Red Cross gave us asylum and we ended up in Coventry. I was nine. I got British citizenship, but my dad took me back to

10

the Balkans straight after the peace agreement. Not to Bosnia – we moved to Croatia. My family has a café near Dubrovnik harbour now.' Why did I tell him so much? I never talked about my past. But there was something charming about his nerdy T-shirt, his warm brown eyes.

'Your family,' he said. 'Seven younger sisters in case I mess things up with you?'

That made me laugh. 'You read Slavic fairy tales?' I teased him. 'No sisters. The café belongs to my dad and my aunt.' I took a breath and said it fast. 'My mum died in Sarajevo, during the siege.'

'God. I did say I'd mess up. I'm so sorry.'

'That's okay. It was a long time ago.'

There was the short silence I never knew how to fill. Adam ran a hand through his tangle of sandy hair. He said, very gently, 'I'd like to hear about your café.' And he gave me his lopsided smile.

'It's only small,' I told him. 'Tata – my dad – he's a genius with fish.' Glad of a chance to change the subject, I described the harbour market, where we'd buy red mullet to roast over charcoal: the charcoal made the skins crackle and taste smoky. Also, octopuses and bulbous shrimps, and kapuni.

'Kapuni?'

'It's a big white fish. It means sea rooster.'

'Let me guess – it tastes like chicken?'

Rupert nudged my shoulder. 'If he's started telling bad jokes, he's trying to impress you.'

The interruption made me blush. I had almost forgotten anyone else was in the room. I couldn't help smiling, though. 'Is that true?' I asked Adam.

'It's a reliable tactic.' He reddened too. 'It fails every time. So, listen –' he lowered his voice, shutting out Rupert – 'do you miss the sea?'

'I'd reach it in the end,' I said, 'if I swam downriver.'

He raised a quizzical eyebrow. 'Are you planning to?'

'No!' I felt my face get hot again, and took a deep breath. 'I went to a lecture by Ivan Tabak. Roisin said he teaches you? He was talking about water spirits.'

'What's the Bosnian for a water spirit?'

'Vila.'

'Vila,' Adam repeated, flattening his hand in a short glide. 'Linguist's habit,' he said, when he saw me watching. 'I thought my Bosnian was pretty decent, until last week I tried to tell Tabak that Rosh writes song lyrics. Only I said pišati, not pisati. Apparently it's rare to pee in verse.' I laughed, and so did he. 'Tabak was in the siege too,' he added thoughtfully. 'He wrote some powerful stuff about it.'

I avoided modern books about Sarajevo, especially those about the war. But I was saved from saying so by Roisin, who dropped her hands on Adam's shoulders. 'You're monopolising Laura,' she told him. He leant back and smiled at her, and I felt a surge of jealousy, an unreasonable possessiveness. *Let go.* Even though Roisin's hands fell everywhere, on any shoulder. She had caressing hands.

Much later, when people started going to bed, I saw her lying on the sofa with the guitarist bent over her like Dracula. The kitchen clock showed three in the morning. I said, 'I should go,' and Adam stood up at once.

'Can I see you home?'

So we walked down Portugal Street together. Silent. Not yet touching. Then down Magdalene Street and onto the bridge, stopping over the Cam. After the tobacco-fragrant warmth of the house, the night felt as cold as water.

I turned to Adam and he kissed me. I kissed him back and he drew me closer. He still smelt of hops, and underneath was his own smell, which is hard even now for me to describe. Resin perhaps, and smoke. A hint of the smell that rises from charred pine needles and scorched earth.

CHAPTER 2

I didn't think about Ed until Monday morning. Then I checked my work email and found a message in his quirky telegraphese.

SORRY ABOUT FRIDAY NIGHT STOP HAD A LAST MINUTE ONLINE DATE STOP WILL BUY YOU DINNER WEDNESDAY STOP

I called his mobile at once, and he picked up on the ninth ring. 'Laura. I'm in the West Room. It's not a good time.'

'I've got some news,' I said. 'I'd like to see you.'

Ed and I had been friends for a year almost to the day. We met at the library, where he also worked. 'I have autism,' was the first thing he said to me. 'Why are *you* here?' That made me laugh. It was at once sincere and clumsy. The other junior librarians were women with names like Beatrice, who did yoga on Mondays and gave me cold looks. 'It's your clothes,' Ed said. 'You're meant to wear more. The English like buttons.' In Dubrovnik my dresses had been chic. But with my first pay slip I bought two black cardigans and a pinafore. I thought: if that's all it takes. And the Beatrices did get nicer to me. Ed asked my buttons out on a date. I said no thank you, and he said that was probably wise. We still spent a lot of time together. I listened to his girl troubles; he lent me books. Until yesterday he had been the only person in Cambridge who knew my mum was dead.

Ten minutes after I phoned him, we met in the tea room, which had grey plastic tables and a smell of old mushroom soup. Ed was standing by the urns, wearing a duffle coat. He looked cold all the time – even indoors. As soon as I walked in, he said, 'You've met someone?'

13

I felt myself blush. 'Yes.'

He turned away from me, pushing a lever on an urn. 'Yes. Well, let me just, just, just pay and I'll join you.' He didn't often stutter, but when he was upset he sometimes fumbled a catch.

I found a free table, to which Ed brought his tea and a cheese scone. 'How was your date?' I said.

'Vapid.' He began buttering his scone. 'Do I know yours?'

'You might. He's a graduate student, so I expect he's here a lot.'

Ed remembered every person who came to the West Room, right down to the books they ordered. He said, 'What's his name?'

'Adam Quin.'

'Of course I know Quin. The Balkanist. Don't date the readers, Laura. It never works.' When I didn't reply, he flicked away a crumb that had fallen off his plate onto the table. 'You and I match,' he said sulkily. 'We're both too smart to be stacking shelves. But I'm neurodivergent and you got educated in a second-world country.'

'Ed,' I said. I hadn't expected him to mind so much.

'When did you even meet?'

'Friday.' I was blushing again. It was a habit I wished I could shake, a treachery my skin was prone to.

'You slept with him, didn't you?' Ed picked up his scone and glared at it. 'You woke, woke, woke up with him on Saturday.'

Adam had walked me back to Chesterton Road. The neon sign glowing over the kebab shop: SHISH HAPPENS. Bloody smears of ketchup on the pavement. 'Murder victim?' he said, and then looked horrified. 'Sorry. I forgot about your mum.'

We both knew he was coming up to my room. I saw him noticing the chipped walls and the single bed on its iron frame. He went to my bookshelf. '*The Art of Translation*,' he said, with real interest. 'I read this last year.'

'I studied it at Dubrovnik University.' I was glad of the chance to tell him that. 'Croatian qualifications are no use here,' I explained. 'I'm saving up for a master's – I want to translate fiction.' Then I turned off the light. In the dark it was easy to kiss him again.

14

The next morning I made coffee and toast. Adam sat on the edge of my bed in his boxer shorts, looking tousled and awkward. I apologised for the plain breakfast. He said it was fine. 'I had you pegged as a chocolate-bread girl,' he said. 'What's it called, buhtla? Piano practice before school. Hair in a ponytail.'

'We didn't have a piano,' I told him, uncomfortably aware of how little he knew about me. 'We lived in a council flat after we left Bosnia. The sofa folded out for me to sleep on.' I was perched on a chair, my feet drawn up as if there was a mouse, or a flood. Beyond the toast, I didn't know what he would expect. 'I don't—' I swallowed. 'I don't normally do this.'

Adam gave me a rueful smile. 'Nor do I.' Then he came over and put his coffee cup on the table beside me, touching my shoulder a little awkwardly, as if he wasn't sure of a welcome. And we ended up back in bed.

I felt bad now, for Ed's sake, but I didn't regret it.

'I knew this would happen,' he complained, putting down his scone. 'My therapist always said you'd sabotage your own happiness.'

'Your therapist hasn't even met me.' I hated psychoanalysts. I stirred salt into Ed's tea once and she told him it was passive-aggressive behaviour. But he kept his salt next to his sugar, in the same colour jar. Who *does* that? Well, now I was living up to all her worst expectations of me.

'There's something odd about Quin,' Ed said darkly. 'Why is he studying Slavic politics?'

I paid no attention to this. It was nice that Adam spoke my language, but what I liked most was his steady Englishness. It made me feel safe. 'I could lie here forever,' he'd said, when we woke up again, at midday.

So I recited a poem I remembered from university. '"This bed our centre is, these walls our sphere. Nothing else is."' Curled up against him, his arm under my head.

He laughed. 'You're very beautiful,' he said. 'And very strange.'

The Cambridge I'd known up to that point was a city as cold and unfriendly as a winter sky. It reminded me of how I'd felt about England during my first months in Coventry, fifteen years earlier. Back then I kept thinking I heard bombs: the shuddering thud of howitzers, the distinctive *eeeooow* of mortars. I lay awake and listened for Tata's shuffling tread on the stairs, then the lurch and creak as my brother, Tarik, snuck up in his socks, drunk or high. Tarik was my hero for a while. He bought me a pair of Doc Martens because a boy at school laughed at my 'refugee' shoes. 'May your mum find you in sausage meat,' I snarled at the boy, which only made him laugh harder. Tarik taught me *sod off* and *swivel*. As my English improved, I got to know some girls from my class; we visited each other's flats to watch *Top of the Pops*, and I tried to forget about sneaking off with my friends from Gnijezdo Street to sit in the bombed-out car by the bakery, all of us singing Take That at the top of our lungs, pretending to be the radio.

I had just turned fourteen when the war ended and Tata moved us to Dubrovnik. I was furious with him. Tarik, who was eighteen, refused to come, so I was furious with him too. But I set out to reinvent myself again. From my new classmates I learnt how to drink beer and dance with my hips. I went through high school like that. And then, at university, I found something I loved. Translation. I leapt into it the way a bird leaps off a windowsill. There were no jobs in Dubrovnik, though – certainly not if you wanted to translate stories. Tata thought I would write tourist brochures or work in his café when I graduated. He didn't understand why I had to leave. So at first I took the inhospitality of Cambridge as a kind of punishment. And I did wonder if I'd made a mistake, that's true.

But after I met Adam I lived brightly. *Žustar*. It means radiating joy, or glowing. On Saturday afternoons I would walk down to Sidney Sussex College after I finished my shift at the library. More often than not the porters would tell me that Quin & Co., as they called them, were in the table tennis room. 'Less sexy than rugby,' Adam admitted, laughing. But I liked how he got everyone together

16

to play. He wasn't a leader exactly, but he was good at making people feel welcome.

At night we sat round the table in Portugal Street, talking, drinking, breathing second-hand pot. One time the tobacco was too strong and Roisin got ill. 'You can't believe daylight out of these dealers,' she complained. 'Either they sell you dried basil or they're poisoning you.'

She threw up in the toilet while I held her hair back. All at once I had a memory of Mama being violently sick during a television report about the attack on Ravno, maybe half a year before the war began. I had held her hair too, a nervous first aider in my Razija Omanović Primary School uniform. Afterwards she told me it was her medicine which made her ill, and perhaps it was partly that. There was a dark streak in Mama. She could be wonderful, fired with enthusiasm over a craft project or racing me to the river. At other times she tipped over an unseen edge and sat alone for hours, silent and blank. For several years she had been taking antidepressants. They helped, for a while. Then Ravno came on the screen – bodies just lying in those not-far-from-us streets, all bloody, with bits missing. Tata said she was unwell again, but I had seen her seeing ghosts, her gaze so fixed and terrible I'd closed my eyes in case I saw them too. She was under siege. That's how it seemed to me.

'Did you *smoke*?' Roisin said. 'My love, you look like hell.'

'You smoked,' I told her dizzily. 'I was just breathing.' This was why I never did pot. I couldn't control what memories came seeping out of the cracks.

'Laura?' Adam called from the corridor.

Roisin began to laugh. 'Ah, go and see what he wants.'

So I went out to Adam and put my head against his chest, without saying anything. 'Hello,' he said, resting his chin in my hair.

There were things I would have to tell him. But for now I cocooned myself in red wine and music. Words, too. I read the Slavic folk tales I was hoping to translate into English one day – stories about magical spirits of marshes and lakes, about fish-women and frog-women and bird-women. Just once something modern slipped through: Ivan Tabak's first newsletter landed in my inbox. *Rebuilding Sarajevo: The Poetry of Forklift Trucks.* If I had not bumped into Roisin on her bike that night, I might have gone back to see him before he left Cambridge. He would have poured two cups of black coffee, smiling at me through his moustache as we talked about vilas and poems. Instead, I skimmed his email at the kitchen table in Portugal Street while Adam researched his master's thesis on British-Balkan diplomatic relations by my side. 'Happy?' he said, leaning over to kiss me.

'Concentrate!' I protested, laughing. 'You know I'm happy.'

When he was done with work, one of us would get dinner. By his own admission, Adam was a disastrous cook, so he brought home characteristically British things for me to try. Crumpets, for instance, and Scotch eggs. If it was my turn, I made the Bosnian dishes I loved – the ones Tata had taught me. Grah with white beans and smoked ham. Vanilla-flavoured krempita. Giving him the crumbly edges of pastry as I cut them off. 'Eat this,' I was always saying. 'Bite that.' He stood behind me and lifted my hair in his hands, burying his face in my neck. 'You taste of the Balkans,' he said, and I realised that for him my nationality had its own appeal. But then, didn't I feel the same way about his safe and solid Englishness?

At night we slept tangled up in each other. In the morning we would go back to the kitchen, where I would brew apple tea in a bright red teapot, while the Kaiser Chiefs sang "Ruby" on the radio. Adam would take my hands and spin me round the room. When I was about to leave, I would stop at the door to kiss him and we would end up back in bed.

Just once, that first month, an odd thing happened. As I was moving the post off the table, I found a letter for him with HMG: CONFIDENTIAL stamped across it in bold red ink. 'Why is the British government writing to you?' I asked, mainly because I was pleased with myself for working out what those letters stood for. In Sarajevo, painted on wooden crates that arrived from America, they used to mean *Heavy Machine Guns*.

Adam took the letter out of my hand and put it hastily in his dressing gown pocket. 'If I told you,' he said, 'I'd have to kill you.'

He had a bottomless supply of bad English jokes.

CHAPTER 3

I remember the exact date of the second odd thing. It was the fifth of November and I had just received my first British passport, which I'd applied for at Adam's suggestion. He had brought a form home from the post office. 'You should make the most of your dual citizenship,' he'd said, with a seriousness that surprised me.

When the passport arrived I felt strange. The cover was burgundy, not blue like my Bosnian one. My face inside was surrounded by a hologram of British birds, yet it remained stubbornly alien – the sharp cheekbones and my long untameable hair that would never be Anglo-Saxon, no matter what a piece of paper said.

Adam seemed happy, though. He said we should celebrate by cooking a classic, like toad-in-the-hole. At first I thought he was teasing me. In the siege Tata had invented flown-away-chicken pie, and if it didn't make us full, it made us laugh. But who would give sausages a name so disgusting? I told Adam I would cook pašticada, with bacon and red plums and garlic simmering round a side of beef. I was not a dual citizen when it came to food.

'A glass of wine for the stew and one for me,' I said, reaching for the potato masher. 'And boil the kettle, please.'

'What's a sous-chef in Bosnian?'

'A slave.'

He laughed, bringing the wine over to me. 'You said there's something else we're celebrating?'

'Yes – Saul promoted me to the Rare Books Room today.' The potatoes I was mashing made soft sounds. 'I'll get a bit more money,' I went on breathlessly. 'It can go in the pot for my master's degree.'

Saul Hafler was a senior librarian. A mournful man, with a dark widow's peak and an accent, he was always wrong-footing me –

tripping me up. 'Happy Christmas,' I had said to him at the end of last year. 'I'm Jewish,' he'd said. And a few months ago I told him, 'Happy fourth of July.' He was Canadian.

This morning, however, he had called me into his office, a room with oily landscapes on the walls. He gave me bitter coffee and ginger biscuits. I was doing well, he told me. It took real grit to start over. I said thank you, politely, although I didn't know what *grit* meant: there were still a few gaps in my English. When I got home, I looked it up. An abrasive stone. An indomitable spirit. And also – I liked this – a small, sideways-moving crab.

Adam slid his arms round my waist. 'You know, most librarians wear horn-rimmed glasses and pencil skirts.'

'Only in your old comic books,' I said, rolling my eyes as I began to make potato dumplings. Those comics were relics of his schoolboy collection. He kept them on a shelf in his room, along with an old Sega Genesis console. Like his vintage gaming T-shirts, they seemed to be largely, but not wholly, ironic.

Roisin came through the back door at that moment, in a whirl of cold air and cut grass. 'Let's see you!' she said to me. 'Oh yes, you definitely look more British than you did yesterday! Sorry I'm late – it was my first shift at Indigo. The boss kept saying, "Stop singing, girl, and make more coffee."' She kissed my cheek and lifted the lid from the pan of stew. 'They've lit the bonfire on Midsummer Common. No Guy this year, I checked.'

Adam poured her some wine. 'We've given up burning Catholics – luckily for you.'

'Ah, Laura and I are heathens anyway.'

'I was raised religious,' I objected. 'My dad used to take me to Sarajevo Cathedral, till the priest caught me staring at the naked angels.'

'Deviant *and* distractible,' Adam said, making me laugh.

Roisin smiled. 'I liked the superstitious bits. A spider at night means money coming. Never give a handkerchief as a gift.'

'It's the same as giving tears,' I told Adam. My childhood had been full of such lore. There were still things I did, or didn't do. 'Don't pass a knife from hand to hand,' I said. 'Wear red knickers on New Year's Eve if you want to be lucky in love.'

He laughed, and Roisin said, 'I'll try that one.'

Mim came in, then Rupert. Adam set the food on the table: the pale dumplings, the dark steaming stew.

'If you get wet doing the dishes you'll marry a drunk,' Roisin called out, fetching five plates from the draining rack. 'That's an Irish superstition for you.' Soon I was serving second helpings and she had tussled the cork from the last bottle of wine. 'I have a date tonight,' she said. A firework exploded outside the window, in a burst of yellow and white stars.

'Who is he?' asked Rupert, holding out his glass.

Mim said, 'He pole dances.'

'Of course he pole dances.'

'For exercise. He has one of those telescopic poles that shoot up and screw into the ceiling.'

'Behave,' Roisin told them serenely. 'He's a comedian. He's got a late gig at the Junction and he's dropping in on the way. In ten years you'll both wish you had his autograph.' She rose to clear the plates, touching Adam's shoulder as she passed.

He leant back in his chair. 'In ten years I'll be a big-bellied tata with hordes of fat babies.'

Roisin said, 'Getting a little ahead of yourself, Adam Quin?'

I let my hair fall forwards to hide my smile.

At that moment his phone rang. He looked at the screen and his whole face changed. 'Dad?' He rose abruptly as he put the phone to his ear. Then he left the kitchen, banging the door. I was startled by the violent slam. We had spent almost every day of the last month together and he had barely talked about his parents. All I knew was that he didn't see much of them.

A few minutes later I heard a noise in the corridor, but the door was opened by a man in low-slung jeans and a wife-beater shirt. Roisin's comedian. The wine was finished so she poured him a glass

22

of sambuca. Gunpowder was going off all over Cambridge, as if everyone wished the Houses of Parliament had blown up after all. I watched the door. *Dad,* he had said. He meant, *What do you want?* No. *What is it now?*

'It's nearly eleven o'clock!' Roisin exclaimed. 'Laura, chuck me that coat!' She jumped off the sofa. 'Hurry up, love. Are you not coming with us?'

'I'm going to wait for Adam.'

She shook her head at me, but I pretended not to notice.

As soon as they had all gone, I went down the corridor to his room. His voice was coming through the door, low and loaded. 'They've taken my references ... No. I told you. I've made up my mind ... Look, I've got to go.'

I returned to the kitchen quickly, as if I'd been spying on him. My first feeling was one of pure alarm. References for what?

He joined me a few seconds later. 'Sorry,' he said. He poured himself a glass of sambuca from Roisin's bottle and drank it down, grimacing at the taste of it. 'My dad wants me to be a lawyer. Join the family firm.' He moved his shoulders as if to shrug off his father's expectations. 'We don't get on – or it's truer to say I hardly know him. Guess what, don't put a nine-year-old in boarding school.'

I had met two of his schoolfriends just the week before – Knuckles and Tails. Adam was Sonic, of course. And me they called 'Amy Rose,' which I found mystifying until they explained that she was Sonic's pink hedgehog girlfriend. In England, a nickname is a badge of honour.

Now I said, 'You didn't like boarding?'

'It wasn't that bad,' he said quickly. 'I mean, you lived through a siege.'

I laughed. 'So you lived in heaven?'

'Well, a fairly strict and overcrowded heaven. I think I played video games so I could control a story for once.' He smiled and shrugged. 'The teachers were good. They got me here.'

23

'What do you want to do next? I mean, if you're not going to join your dad's firm?'

He reddened. 'Last summer I applied to the Foreign Office. I got through the interviews – I'm just waiting for my vetting clearance.'

'Oh!' Suddenly I understood that letter, the one with HMG on the top. It was easy to picture Adam at a government desk in London – writing reports on the Balkans, perhaps, and eating toad-in-the-hole during his lunchbreaks. But I wasn't sure what that meant for us. 'Congratulations,' I said quietly. 'Why didn't you tell me?'

'Nothing's certain until I get my vetting. That doesn't stop my dad from going on and on about it. According to him, I'm letting the firm down.' He had turned a darker shade of red, the colour spreading right to the roots of his hair. 'Do you mind if we talk about something else?'

Though I was both startled and curious, I said, 'Of course not.'

Adam poured two shots of sambuca and passed one to me. 'I don't want to stir up bad memories, but I'd like to know more about your family. I mean, how did you get out of Sarajevo?'

My curiosity left me at once, replaced by dread. I hated talking about this. Still, I had to tell him sometime. I picked up my glass and swallowed the shot, its aniseed burn. 'We left the day after Mama died.' I closed my eyes. Took a breath and let it go again. 'Tata had been planning it for weeks, paying a fixer to get us out. My brother and I—'

'You have a brother!'

'Yes.' I reached for a matchbox someone had left on the table, twisting it between my fingers. The matches inside rattled. 'Tarik.' Just saying his name was hard. I still missed him. 'He's somewhere in Eastern Europe,' I said, 'working as a chef. We don't talk anymore. He didn't move to Dubrovnik with me and Tata and my aunt after the war – he went off on his own. He was doing a lot of cocaine by then, among other things.' I put the matchbox down beside my glass. My hand was shaking.

24

Adam said, 'How did your mum die?' His voice was gentle and serious. 'A sniper?'

I shook my head. *I found her.* That's what I meant to say. But I couldn't get the words out. All the spaces inside me had gone icy and silent. Mute. I picked up our glasses and took them to the sink. 'Let me just—' I had to swallow to steady myself. 'I need a moment.'

'We don't have to do this now.'

'I want to,' I said softly, not trusting myself to turn round.

Tata used to love telling the story of how he met Mama. I gave Adam his version, in which a beautiful raven-haired girl had followed him out of a Political Sciences lecture at Sarajevo University and asked to borrow his notes. 'She was top of our class,' he'd boast, 'she just wanted a date with me.' Two years later they got married and both of them ended up working for the municipal government, though at weekends Tata brewed beer in their kitchen and forgot to pay the bills. Mama said he was in disguise as an adult. She also said he had a good heart. Tarik was born in 1977, followed, in 1983, by me. And in 1992, war broke out in Bosnia.

Leaving Sarajevo was illegal, especially for Tata, who was of army age. But by the summer, Mama was in a bad way. You couldn't get antidepressants anymore. You couldn't get an aspirin. He planned it all for her, although she didn't want to go. 'Even supposing your sister can get us visas,' she said, 'what will we do in England?' She was Bosnian through and through.

The day before we were due to leave, Tarik and I went to school as usual. Tata went to work. The fixer said we must stick to our routines. That afternoon, though, Mama didn't pick me up. I knew it was dangerous to hang around in the streets, so I walked home alone. She was not in our house. Nor were the water canisters, though she never fetched water – only Tata did that. I waited two hours. Then I went looking for her. I wasn't allowed out by myself but I didn't know what else to do. I walked down the hill, past the sweet-smelling viburnum bush and the sign that said SNIPER, DAY

AND NIGHT, and when I got to the Miljacka I turned left for the bridge to the brewery, where the water taps were. I never got there. I saw a lot of dust and a new shell crater, and then I saw Mama. She was lying in the shallow river, with her Walkman on the bank beside her playing Dvořák's "Rusalka" – an opera she loved. The first thing I did was turn the Walkman off.

The river was a cloudy crimson where one of Mama's wrists lay in it. Her other wrist, across her chest, was glossy with blood. The shell blew off both her poor hands, though what killed her was the shrapnel buried in her skull.

We didn't need water. That still haunts me. We were leaving. We were leaving, and I think she found a way to stay.

'Laura?' Adam said. 'You've washed that plate three times.'

I dropped it into the sink, splashing my shirt. How long had I been talking? My throat felt raw.

He came to stand next to me. 'It was an accident,' he said. 'Your mum couldn't have known there'd be shelling that day.' The smell of his aftershave was becoming as familiar to me as the smell of my own skin. With his thumb he smudged out the tears where they ran down my face, as if he was an artist of pastels and chalk, as if he would remodel grief. But he didn't understand. The shelling had been relentless. It never stopped for long.

I rubbed eyes, my fingers coming away black with mascara. 'I don't look back,' I said fiercely. 'I don't do this.'

Adam gave me that crooked smile of his. 'Maybe you need to,' he said. Then he put his arms round me and I rested my head against his chest. We stood for a long time like that.

CHAPTER 4

In January, when most of what was lovely about the south of England had died of cold, Adam took me to meet his parents. The road signs flashed past the hire car's windows. Royston, Baldock, Stevenage. Welwyn Garden City. He said, 'Hanging in there?'

'Yes,' I said. Then, 'What if they don't like me?'

'I'd drive straight back to Cambridge. They will like you.' He rubbed his hand through his hair. 'I'm the one they're gunning for.'

St Albans, Watford. As we reached the western edge of London, I wondered if that was the whole truth. Families could be complicated. 'My soul, have you met anyone new?' Tata had asked, when I went to Dubrovnik for Christmas. He was a man still full of nervous energy, with unruly grey hair and black eyebrows. His voice had the awkward tenderness in it that he reserved for me. On the plane I'd been excited to see him, but over the week we spent together I said nothing about my new life. I helped my aunt make božićni kruh, a fruity loaf, like stollen, and I got home to Cambridge as soon as I decently could. I didn't want my past and my future to touch. You see, something happened after Mama died that I hadn't even told Adam.

It was Tata who found me on the bank of the Miljacka. Crouching. Numb. He said a hospital van would come for Mama. I remember his sobs, a world-ending sound.

We left at dawn: me, Tata and Tarik. There was no time to bury her. A Bosnian soldier at the Alipašina checkpoint had been bribed for us. His shift ended at noon. It began to rain as we passed the charred trams in Titova Street. We got through the checkpoint all right, and in Serb-controlled Iližda the soaking wet officials barely glanced at our fake papers. The walk into free Bosnia took nine

27

hours in the pouring rain. At last the mountain road bent down through fields of green corn to Kiseljak, where our connection picked us up and drove us across the border to Croatia. He left us at Split airport and we slept on metal seats – or Tata slept, worn out with adult fear and grief. Tarik saw me pinching myself to stay awake and put his arm round me. 'She's bloody dead,' he said. 'She's not coming back.' But in the dark she did, with open, unmotherly eyes and doughy skin.

Our flight was the next morning. The small plane shuddering, banking sharply. The Balkan peninsula below us bleeding a short trail of islands. Then British passport control. Immigration. Hours spent waiting while they scrutinised our refugee visas, which my aunt had got us – Tata's sister, who had fled here at the start of the war, six months earlier. And then a train from Heathrow to Coventry, and a bus to her house. I read a book of Bosnian fairy tales the whole way, trembling with tiredness. The one I liked best was about a water spirit who had her wings stolen and got locked in a prison far from home, but she stole her wings back and turned into a cloud of butterflies and escaped out of the chimney. Tata tried to make me put the book down, but I said I didn't want to see England. I did look up when I smelt burning. A fish-and-chip shop was on fire. The bus crawled for the last mile and the driver made us close all the windows.

We arrived at my aunt's house to find the front door ajar. Tata put our bags down in the dark hall. He said, 'Eno vatre.'

'What does he say, Laura?' she called from the kitchen, speaking English as she did on the phone to me, but with a heavy accent. 'Tell him he's late.'

'He says there's a fire.'

She appeared in the doorway wearing a checked apron. Kissed Tarik on both cheeks, kissed me. 'Dinner is burnt,' she grumbled. 'When it comes to this family, there's always fire.' She knew Mama was dead because Tata had called her from Split airport, but that was my aunt all over; a kindly and childless woman, her affection took the form of pies and puddings. Her answer to grief was food. So there she was, soft and liquorice-breathed, making a path for me through the stray cats that hovered and arched at the kitchen door, making sweet clove biscuits, making bread.

After dinner she went up to the first-floor roof to check on her washing. I followed, being careful at first to stay near the wall. Many of the houses around us were derelict, so there was a lot of rusty iron and broken glass. My aunt turned and saw the place where the fish-and-chip shop was still burning, the orange glow in the west that was like no other sunset. I heard her say, 'Sweet Mary, look at those flames!' But after that I stopped listening, because on the far end of the line, above the roof gutter, was a yellow cotton dress like the one Mama had been wearing when she died.

I pushed through the damp clothes towards it. As I did so it turned translucent orange, lit through by fire, and a gust of wind filled the sleeves, which moved to embrace me. I saw her face again, wet with river water, and heard her soft voice say my name. I jumped away in terror and my foot caught a broken tile, unbalancing me, so that I was flailing on the very edge of the roof, my arms like frantic wings, and then I was falling and twisting in an upside-down scream towards the scrubby ground, where the pain of landing knocked out my breath and spilt like paintbox colours through my chest and head. Dark reds. Shiny blacks. 'Mother of Jesus!' That was my aunt shrieking. 'Oh my dear god!' More red. Then black, black, black.

I came to briefly in an ambulance. 'No spinal injury.' In hospital. 'Two broken ribs.' When I woke up again, Tata was holding my hand. My aunt was there too, and Tarik. An English doctor in a white coat asked me what had happened.

We'd done English at school, but Bosnian was my mother tongue – my mother's tongue. It was what came easiest when I was tired or hurt. So I answered the doctor with care. 'I saw Mama.'

There was a pause. Then Tata said, 'My soul, Mama's dead.'

I wanted to tell him that she dripped on me, to share my horror

29

at her wet arms, her dank touch. But I couldn't say any more words. I couldn't scream, or whisper. I turned my face to the wall. My throat hurt. Mama's unmendable deadness hurt too, worse than anything.

Because he couldn't get me to speak, Tata told the doctor in halting English about Mama's death, and how I found her. My aunt said, 'The child jumped! I saw her!' The doctor tapped my knees with a small hammer and tried to make me push against his hands. Then he started talking in long words. 'Post-traumatic stress ... hallucinatory episode ... reactive mutism.' I said nothing. I had gone deep inside myself. I was lost in the silence I found there.

'In hospital she is safe,' Tata said, unhappily.

'Fuck off,' said Tarik. He stepped forwards. 'We're taking her home.' He was shaking with anger and exhaustion, both of them were. They looked so similar in their travel-stained clothes, their dark unwashedness. Yet it was Tata who won. He shouted Tarik down and made him go outside.

I see now how vulnerable Tata was. He didn't speak good English, or know the system. In that hospital, though, I felt abandoned by him and my aunt – by everyone except Tarik.

The doctor took me to an adult psychiatric ward because they didn't have one for children. On this ward he tied a plastic bracelet round my wrist and took away my shoes. My memories of that time are muddied by the drugs he gave me. Antidepressants, I was told later. I didn't see Mama again. The old woman in the next bed kept wailing, and for a while I heard other, more extraordinary sounds. Bleak, freewheeling voices, guttural wisps, black noise. I kept my book of fairy tales in my hands and read it over and over: the boy whose witch-mother pulled out his heart and ate it while his aunt held the candle; the girl locked in a tower who hissed like an angry snake. The doctor told Tata I was not reading, just turning pages. But he got it wrong. I was wandering deliberately if also helplessly in those more luminous worlds, where loss and trauma were part of the story, and so had meaning, which did not seem true of that chaotic ward.

When I looked up again, the sun was low and orange. Adam was driving through Guildford, beneath a brick cathedral on a hill. 'Surrey,' he said, rolling his eyes. 'The only county that sounds like an apology.'

'It's nice,' I managed to say.

'Decent landscape,' he admitted. 'But it's full of accountants. And lawyers.' He kept the car in fourth gear on a narrow lane with banks that rose steeply above us, tapering down occasionally to show the mist-wreathed fields. 'My primary school was off this road,' he said. 'Did I tell you my best friend there was Bosnian? Aldin Stupac. He came over with his mum after his dad was killed in the massacre at Srebrenica.'

Oh god. Suddenly I felt very tired. But I also felt a rush of love for Adam, the way his hands had tightened on the wheel. He said, 'I guess that explains why I study Slavic politics.'

'Do you need an explanation?'

'My parents do.' He moved his shoulders as if they were stiff. 'Have you ever thought of going back to Sarajevo?'

'No,' I said quickly.

The look he gave me was curious.

'I left it behind me. I want it to stay there.'

At that moment something plunged off the bank above us and hit the road. Long twisting neck, lots of flailing legs. Adam braked sharply and there was a shriek of tyres that threw me forwards, my seatbelt catching me with a violent jerk. The instant the car stopped he had his hand on my shoulder. 'Are you okay? Laura?'

'Is it dead?' I asked, my voice thin with shock. 'Did you hit it?'

'I didn't hit it.' I could feel him trembling. 'We could have crashed.'

'We didn't.'

'No. My god. It came out of nowhere.'

I undid my seatbelt and fumbled for the door handle. 'Wait—' he said, but I was already out of the car. The crumpled body lay strewn across the tarmac. The huge, leaf-shaped ears, the delicate hooves. A young deer, startled by the noise of the car and clumsy in its panic. Wake up, I willed it. Don't be dead. I could hear Adam

31

behind me, reversing to the side of the road. As he switched on our hazard lights, the deer opened its eyes. They were a depthless brown, with no emotion in them that I recognised – not pain or fear, but only a kind of dazed awareness. At that moment a flash of headlights rounded the curve of the road ahead, a white Land Rover coming straight for us. I didn't have time to move. I stood near the fallen deer, completely frozen. The Land Rover slewed to a stop just a few metres away from me, its tyres screech-growling, and a bearded face erupted through the driver's window – bug-eyed and purple. 'What the bloody hell?' it shouted. 'Get out of the road!'

A fierceness rose unexpectedly out of my fright. 'It's *alive*,' I said.

In the mountains around Sarajevo, I knew an animal hurt like this one would be hauled into the back of a trailer, knocked on the head and turned into stew by some hungry farmer. I stood firmly in front of the Land Rover, glaring at the driver as if at any moment he might whip out a rifle. It was in the reflection of the windscreen that I saw Adam hurrying out of the hire car towards me. Then I saw him stop, stock still, as the deer staggered to its feet.

I pivoted to face it – all bone and sinew, the most elf-like of animals. For the longest time it just stood there in the dim light, trembling with the effort of resurrection. Then it began to walk down the road, gingerly, as if the very earth might buck and falter.

Afraid of what another car might do, I walked after it. I was close enough that I could see its sides heaving – every shivering breath a kind of miracle. The bug-eyed driver leant out of his window, reduced to silence, and Adam followed right behind me. At last we came to a place where the bank lowered, dipping down into a field, and the deer broke into a stumbling run. It passed through a hedge and birds flew up off the bare branches – a flock of tiny sparrows rising like a magician's sleight of hand.

Then it was gone.

I turned to Adam, who had come after me into the field. 'Did you see it?' I meant the mystery of it, as it stood on thin legs in the road. A thing so alive that alive was all it was.

'Yes,' he said quietly. 'I saw.'

He put his arm round me and I rested my head against his shoulder, breathing in the smell of wool and aftershave. The sun was just above the hedge, blood-red and grainy, and the long grass was rich in noises – creepy with small, scuttling things that filled me with a guessing wonder. After a moment Adam said, 'My Foreign Office clearance came through yesterday. I start in July as a Balkan Research Analyst.' He stepped back to see my face. 'We'll be okay when I move to London, won't we? I mean, we'll stick it out?'

I smiled at him. 'Just try unsticking us.' For a while the words seemed to hang in the frosty air, an avowal of shared intent. Then I said, 'What will you be doing? Do you know?'

'There's a big drive to help Balkan governments crack down on organised crime. I think I'll be involved in that, initially.'

In some muffled village across the fields, a church clock began to strike the hour. All my life I'd heard stories from Tata about the mafia: sawn-off noses, ritual scarrings, bodies dumped in shallow graves and covered up with plaster. At the start of the siege he'd taken me to visit an injured friend, splitting our UN aid packet in half – for some reason I vividly recalled a tin of sardines in tomato sauce – and we'd seen a procession of mafiosi driving armoured cars on Sniper Alley. Now, in Surrey, the sun slipped below the hedge and I asked Adam, 'Will you be in danger?'

'No,' he said, 'I'll be at a desk in Whitehall. It's not glamorous.' But there was a gleam in his eyes: it was glamorous enough. I smiled at him and he took my hand. Neither of us spoke as we walked carefully along the edge of the darkening road, past the skid-marks left by the departed Land Rover and the scuff of earth and leaves where the deer had fallen. As we got into the car, Adam said, 'Your turn next. Laura Guska – world famous translator.'

'Touch wood,' I said.

He leant over, carefully, and touched his knuckles to the side of my head.

CHAPTER 5

Adam's mother met us outside her house, sleek and perfumed, two cats slithering over her. British shorthairs, I learnt later. She kissed him and held out her hand to me. 'Please call me Naomi. Would you take off your shoes before you come in?'

The cats eyed me over her shoulders all the way down the hall, unblinking. In the living room she shook them off, and they twisted bonelessly to land feet first on a large rug. Adam's dad, much older than I had expected, rose from an armchair with the help of a cane. He touched his son on the shoulder, then shook my hand. 'Charles. Adam tells us you're Bosnian?'

'She grew up in Coventry,' Naomi corrected him. Her lips pinched together, as if the word tasted of factory smoke.

Charles wafted this detail away. 'Gin and tonic? Sherry?'

I said, 'Gin, please,' and smiled my best smile, trying to look like the sort of girl who was offered sherry regularly.

While the drinks were being poured, Adam went off into the depths of the house with our coats, while I looked curiously round the room. It was all glass and leather, with a dining table at one end and an open fireplace at the other, an oar above it in his college colours. I hadn't known he rowed. Over the table, unexpectedly, there was a painting signed by Ernst Kirchner – a bright pink naked dancer, upside-down on a circus horse. The other pictures were all photos of Adam. A blond child holding a hedgehog in the garden of his cupped hands, his lips wide with delight. A skinny teenager in his boarding-school uniform. A young man in a black gown and a white fur hood, kneeling down to receive his first degree. They seemed more like a shrine to an idea than a scrapbook of family life.

'I noticed you looking at the oar.' Charles held out a glass of gin, which trembled in his fingers like air over fire. 'I was bow seat for

34

Sidney Sussex, back in my day. My son isn't much good at water sports, unfortunately, or we might have had a pair.' He turned round as Adam came back through the door and his voice hardened. 'Have you given more thought to joining the firm? I presume Laura's nationality rules out the Foreign Office.'

'Oh Charles, they just met.' Naomi gave a fluttery laugh. 'They're not thinking like that.'

But Adam said, 'I told my vetting officers about Laura three months ago.' I felt a glow of pleasure, mixed with alarm. Who were those people? What had he told them about me? 'You won't change my mind, Dad,' he went on. 'My vetting's come back clear.'

'Well, that *is* good news,' said Naomi. 'Darling boy, are you eating enough in Cambridge? You've got thinner.' Adam shrugged off her concern as she had shrugged off the cats. He and Charles faced each other irritably across the rug, so maybe it was in the interest of peacekeeping that she turned to me. 'You're a librarian, am I right?'

'Yes.' I took a sip of gin. 'An assistant librarian.'

Her smile started from the left side of her mouth, like her son's, but it reached less far. 'Does that sort of work suit you?'

'I want to be a translator,' I said, holding her gaze. 'I'm saving up for a master's degree.'

Adam said, 'Croatian qualifications aren't recognised here, Mum. I told you that.'

She dropped her eyes. 'It was just a question.'

Later, when she invited us to the table, he put his hand on my shoulder and I rested my cheek briefly against it. His knuckles smelt of soap.

Naomi brought in a joint of beef on Portmeirion china, bleeding dark juices. The thin garland of painted narcissi gave it the look of a sacrifice. She said, 'Charles, will you carve?'

'Perhaps Adam?'

'Don't expect straight lines,' Adam said wryly, as he picked up the knife. His white-haired father sat and watched, a cat in his lap – like that villain in James Bond, I thought, charming and caustic. Over his head was the Kirchner print, and my eyes kept turning there. To a casual observer, the girl on the horse looked helpless. But it was *her* the crowd was staring at. She had a defiant grace. All the rest of them had were clothes.

Charles uncorked the wine. 'You must tell us what you think of this,' he said to me. 'I believe I first drank it in my early years as a lawyer. The Inns of Court have some very fine bottles. And it's a fine profession, I'm sure you'll agree.'

Adam said, 'Leave Laura out of it, Dad.' He was carving the roast as if it had mortally offended him. 'I'd make a fucking awful lawyer, you know that.'

'There's no need for language,' Naomi said. 'Your father's disappointed about the firm, we both are. But we're also very proud that you'll be serving your country.' She glanced at Charles, but he gave no sign of conceding this, so she held out her hand for my plate which she filled with roast beef, pink and tender, then roast potatoes, parsnips and carrots. 'I'm glad you're not a vegetarian,' she told me. 'His last girlfriend was. A vegan. Don't scowl like that, Adam, it's true. She wanted me to buy Quorn, and soya milk. It reminded me of a cult.'

I said, 'This looks lovely.'

'If it's too much, just leave what you can't eat.'

The evening wore on a little more easily after that. Adam spoke to his dad, with wary courtesy, of his college and his grades. I managed a second portion of beef. Then we helped Naomi carry out the plates, and she produced from the oven a dish that smelt fragrantly of toasted sugar. 'Queen of Puddings,' she said. 'There's cream in the fridge if you want it.' She smiled at Adam. 'Remember when you used to sing to the pudding? "Thy choicest gifts in store, on her be pleased to pour..."'

Adam coloured. 'An old joke,' he explained to me. 'Not even a joke, really. Just a family thing.'

Without warning I felt sad. We'd had things too. Mama would say, 'What's for dessert?' And Tata would pick me up and growl into my hair, because he was making šape, also known as bear's-paw biscuits. Us just laughing because we could.

Soon after supper, with a glance at his own quiet dad, Adam said we would call it a night. 'I made up the double bed in your old room,' Naomi told him, causing a moment of embarrassment to us all. She pressed my hand and kissed his cheek. So did Charles, rising from his chair. Can a kiss be cold, and reproachful?

As we climbed the stairs, Adam gave me a strained smile. 'Family politics. Sorry.'

I smiled back at him, but my mind was full of the new things I'd learnt. This huge house, for a start. It was a long way from Hillfields Estate in Coventry, where the joke was that the local cats went missing and the curry house owners got fat, and even further away from my old poured-concrete home in Sarajevo. I could act like I was perfectly comfortable. 'Sherry?' 'Not tonight, thank you.' But I couldn't stop thinking about the queen's pudding, or whatever his mum had called it. 'You wanted me to get a British passport for a reason,' I said slowly. 'The Foreign Office doesn't like me being Bosnian.'

Adam got to the top of the stairs before he answered. 'They're a bit funny about it,' he admitted, rubbing the back of his neck with both hands. 'Don't worry. If I can cope with my dad, the rest will be easy.'

For the first time, I wasn't sure whether to believe him. I had come here as a refugee: I knew how much this government loved its red tape. What if his dad was right, and one day my nationality got in the way of his career?

That night we made love soundlessly beneath a Sonic All-Stars quilt, and afterwards I dreamt that I was Kirchner's naked dancer, tossing on the muscles of the great horse. I woke up covered in sweat, as if I had been riding round a circus ring.

CHAPTER 6

Everything ended too quickly after our visit to Surrey. Spring came early and was unusually warm. Summer began in April. Birds flickered through the sky like hot light, while cyclists raced past on the kind of bikes that dogs chase through parks – bikes for dreamers and fools, with wicker baskets and leather saddles and brakes that don't work in the rain.

In May the undergraduate engineers hired a punt which they climbed into one by one, to see how many it would take before it sank. It took twelve.

In June Roisin got dumped. I bought her a box of Chelsea buns and we ate them in front of *Gone with the Wind*. Roisin had smudged eyes, but she tilted an imaginary Panama hat between her fingers and said, in Clark Gable's smoke-scarred voice, 'Frankly, my dear, I don't give a damn.'

In July we sat round the kitchen table in Portugal Street for the last time.

Mim lit a joint, and Roisin sang Irish songs that made me want to cry. "The Fields of Athenry." "The Last Farewell." I leant into Adam's shoulder. 'Say cheese, lovebirds,' Rupert instructed. He took our photo with a polaroid camera from which the pictures came out wet and glossy, but also blurred, already looking like the past. 'I don't get why you're not moving to London with him,' he told me.

'I'm waiting until he learns to cook,' I said.

Of course, that was a lie. If we wanted to live together, a vetting officer would have to run checks on me and it would be more fuss than usual, Adam said, because I was Bosnian. We were in bed when he explained this, his fingers tracing a scar on my palm that I got cutting fish in Tata's café. 'You don't want the *fuss*?' I pulled away from him.

38

'I don't want it *yet*,' he said steadily. 'Let me get through my probation first.'

That made sense, though I didn't want to admit it. Moving in together was not a plan, just a dream in broad strokes. Where would we live? What work would I do? Saul Hafler had been pessimistic when I asked him about library jobs in London. 'Your degree is next to useless outside Croatia,' he'd reminded me, his eyes severe behind steel-rimmed glasses. 'My advice is to stay here.'

The Portugal Street household was breaking up entirely. Even Roisin would be singing at the Edinburgh Festival until September. We drank shots of vodka and some people made toasts. Rupert said, 'It's the end of an era,' and Mim said, 'We'll all stay in touch.' Adam didn't say much. He kept his arm round me, tightly, as if he didn't want to let go.

After he left, I went back to my room above the kebab shop on Chesterton Road. For a while a blackbird woke me every morning, singing its heart out from the roof of the job centre. 'More tuneful than you in the shower,' I texted Adam.

In the University Library every window lay open; warm breezes shuffled the pages of books, and Saul Hafler taught me to spot paper lice and the larvae of deathwatch beetles. I took dutiful notes, but in my lunch breaks I did sums about London living costs and searched for jobs online.

When the library shut, I read in my room.

That first week Adam rang me every night. 'Hello,' he said. 'Hello. Hello. Hello.'

He was living with a colleague from his new department, he told me: a Peter Abbott, or Peter Rabbit, as everyone called him. And one night he said, 'The Lyons have just left.'

I got up from my desk and crossed to my bed. 'It's a zoo now?'

He laughed. 'Martin and Katy L-y-o-n. He works with me and Peter, she's an art teacher. Martin used to rent my room, actually. Big Dave – that's our Head of Section – doesn't like us to have unvetted housemates.'

'I remember,' I said dryly.

'There's something I need to tell you,' Adam went on. 'Dave wants me to do eight weeks of immersive language training, starting next week. The course is in Belgrade.'

It had never occurred to me that his job might take him to the Balkans, let alone to Serbia – a country I still associated with shellfire, tanks and snipers. But I didn't say this out loud. 'I'll have a blue rinse by the time you get back!' I complained. 'I'll have a Zimmer frame!'

The day after he came home from his language course, I took a train to London. I was so impatient I could have got out and pushed. I wanted to go straight to dinner – in a restaurant where our bodies would angle helplessly towards each other across the tables, across the cutlery and glass. Or I wanted him to rush me home, to take my suitcase and my clothes off me in hurried hunger. But the train stuttered through the suburbs, stop-starting, and rain slashed the windows.

When I finally got to King's Cross, Adam was on the concourse, pacing up and down. I noticed at once that he had cut his hair short, in a military style which made it look darker – a dirty gold. I liked this, though it drew attention to his bloodshot eyes, the skin beneath them smoke-coloured with tiredness. Then he saw me. It wasn't a decent kiss for a railway station.

He drew back first, with that crooked grin of his. 'God, I've missed you. These last weeks have been brutal.' He reached for my hand. 'Are you ready to be thrown to the Lyons?'

'The lions?' I said, frowning, as we walked to the escalator. 'Martin who works with you, and Katy the schoolteacher?'

'That's right. They're coming round for Martin's birthday – Peter told me this morning. Katy's bringing karaoke. And Big Dave said he might drop in.'

'Oh Adam, let's go to a hotel!' I said. 'Right now. Let's just find ourselves a bed!'

He laughed and kissed my hair. 'I know it's bad timing.'

At the bottom of the escalator, we ran for a southbound train, ducking through the closing doors. As the carriage lurched forwards he said, 'They're keen to meet you.' And then, as if to reassure himself: 'They're a good crowd.' We got off at Stockwell and he led the way through the rain to the downtrodden end of a red-brick terrace. Tempted to hang back, I lifted my chin into the air.

Adam's housemate opened the door for us. Peter Abbott – or Peter Rabbit – was tall and skinny, with forgotten cycling clips round his ankles. 'I saw you from the window,' he said. His face twitched when he smiled, so that he did look a bit like a rabbit. Maybe, over time, he had grown into his nickname.

'Hello! I'm Katy,' said a woman with yellow hair and a paisley scarf, pushing past Peter from the hallway. 'You must be Laura. This one's talked about you a lot.' She reached up on tiptoe to kiss Adam's cheek. 'Come in!' She swept us down the hall, and Peter bent awkwardly out of her way again. All his limbs were too long. 'It's as if he got stretched on a rack,' Katy whispered to me. I didn't know what that was, but it sounded painful.

In the living room, her husband Martin rose from an armchair with Union Jack cushions on it. He had a dry handshake and bitten nails. 'Beer or prosecco?' he asked me. Adam sat down at once on a cracked leather sofa, and I spotted his old Sega console nesting on a nearby bookshelf.

'Prosecco please.'

Martin poured cautiously, letting the froth go down. 'So, Laura. You're from Bosnia?'

Before I could answer, Adam said, 'She's British too.'

I took the glass that Martin held out. 'I'm Bosnian first,' I told him, surprising myself. 'My family are from Sarajevo.' I saw Adam stiffen. But my burgundy passport couldn't change where I was born.

'What ethnicity are you?' Martin asked.

'A mix. My dad's Croat. My mum was half Muslim, half Serb.'

41

'You have British citizenship?' He dried the bottom of the prosecco bottle on a tea towel – a dabbing, pedantic process.

I said shortly, 'I'm a dual citizen.'

'Since when?'

Peter smiled at me. 'We work in the Balkan Department, with Adam. You're our first Bosnian girlfriend – I'm afraid we're a nosy lot.' I knew right away that I liked him best. Martin's questions reminded me of the fighting dogs in Coventry, the ones that never let go.

'I got citizenship when I was fourteen,' I told him. 'I learnt all the names of Henry VIII's wives.' Turning to Adam, I said, 'I haven't seen your house yet. Can I have the grand tour?' He looked surprised, but he rose to his feet.

When we got upstairs, I shut his bedroom door and kissed him urgently. 'This isn't sociable,' he pointed out. But he was already unbuttoning my top, unzipping my jeans.

'I don't care.' I wriggled out of my bra. 'I didn't come here to be interrogated. Do they think I'm a spy?'

And then we heard Peter cough, apologetically, right outside the room. 'Katy sent me to tell you the cake's ready.'

I could feel the doorhandle digging into my spine, Adam's fingers inside my knickers. To Peter, he called, 'We're on our way.' And he put his mouth to my ear and whispered, 'Fucking cake.'

What could I do except laugh?

He left first, while I tidied myself in his mirror – cooling my flushed cheeks, smoothing my hair. I opened the door to the sound of him joking around downstairs. He was good at managing atmospheres. Peter, however, was still in his own room, which had half-made kites all over the bed, gaudy and fragile as a brood of dozing dragonflies. When he saw me looking, he told me he owned sixteen of them. 'China has a huge kite festival on the Weifang salt flats,' he said.

'Have you been?'

He shook his head. 'My best festival so far was in Bristol.'

The gangly structures seemed to brighten the room with their own light. I would have lingered, asked more questions, only Katy shouted for us to come down right away. She had set Adam to work lighting thirty candles, with HAPPY BIRTHDAY MARTIN written inside the circle of flames. Her husband was pouring more prosecco, his shirt tail hanging out beneath his shabby blazer. I'd have thought an art teacher might smarten him up, but perhaps she liked the contrast they made. Or perhaps he couldn't be smartened. He put all his sharpness into his cross-examinations, so there was none left over for his clothes.

'Rabbit invited David Focket,' Katy told me, once the rituals of singing and candle blowing were over. 'He was hoping to meet you, but something came up at work.' She took in my blank look. 'Hasn't Adam told you about Big Dave? He runs their department.' She giggled. 'Martin's always coming home with stories about him. When they visit the Doughnut – that's GCHQ – he has to use the disabled entrance, because once the airlock tube registered him as two people and locked down to prevent a security breach.' Handing me a slice of cake, she said, 'He thinks a lot of Adam. He rated him top of his cohort on the torture course.'

Adam cleared his throat as if to cut her off, but I said, 'The torture course?'

'You know – the one where the army teaches them how to resist it.' She shrugged. 'A bunch of soldiers turn up and put sacks over their heads.'

I stared at her, fascinated and horrified. It was dawning on me just how much I did not, in fact, know. I said, 'What happens then?'

'Oh, they get made to sit in stress positions. Kept awake all night and shouted at if they fall asleep.' She rolled her eyes dramatically. 'They all say they're waterboarded, but I think they're boasting.'

'Katy,' Adam protested, with an uneasy glance at me. 'How about some presents for Martin?'

When I asked him later about that course, he seemed embarrassed. He said Big Dave had offered him the chance to do it, and the thing to hang on to was that none of it was real. The ones who came unstuck were the ones who started to believe in it, the ones with too much imagination.

I would have too much imagination. Or not enough – I would not be able to imagine how it was fake.

Martin's present from Adam was a box of cigars which filled the air with the toe-curling scent of rich tobacco. From Peter there was a bottle of whisky and a fridge magnet that made him laugh. 'Where did you find it?' he asked.

'I came across it on my last trip,' Peter said.

Katy made a little show of boredom, crossing to the sink with our plates, but I picked up the magnet. It had a joke on it in Bosnian. '"How many types of country are in Europe?"' I translated. '"Three. EU membership countries, EU candidate countries, and Bosnia-Herzegovina."' I could feel them all looking at me to see how I would take this, Adam in concern, the others curious. 'Our famous black humour,' I said lightly, to hide a feeling of hostility that caught me by surprise. I remembered my brother coming home late one night and showing me a tattoo on his arm of the British flag in flames. As the war went on and nothing was done to help our country, Tarik had grown angry, a rebel with a cause by the age of fifteen. I didn't like the idea of Peter buying the magnet: it was not his joke to make.

'How well do you know Bosnia?' I demanded.

He blushed. 'I used to ski in Sarajevo every winter as a kid. We moved countries a lot, so it was a bit like home for me.'

I said, 'I grew up near Baščaršija.' Now I felt shy, my anger faltering. 'I haven't been back since the war.'

'It's still very beautiful. Of course, it got badly shelled. And you can't ski there now, because of the landmines.'

From the sink, Katy said, 'Oh, not landmines again. Sorry, Laura. If you get him started, he'll go on all night.'

In Dubrovnik we'd have called her a kuja. I'm not going to

44

translate that. But Adam got hold of my hand and gave it a squeeze. He wanted me to like them all, I could tell.

Next Martin said, 'Should we have a smoke?' So the men took the cigars out to the garden, as if it was the sixties. I would have gone with them, only Katy drew me into a corner.

'It's such a boys' club, isn't it?' she complained. 'I'm glad you're here. Not that I'll be in London much longer – we only got back from Kosovo last year and Martin is already being sent to Serbia. At least we'll have embassy accommodation this time. Living on an army base was the pits.'

'What do you do while you're away?' I asked her politely.

'Oh, international schools always need art teachers.' She refilled her prosecco glass, splashing bubbles up the sides. 'It felt like my real work in Kosovo was the embassy parties,' she confided, pouring the last of the wine into my glass. 'David Focket asked me personally to keep my ears open. It's amazing what people say over cocktails.'

I was uneasy. If the Foreign Office extended beyond its formal edges, as she seemed to be suggesting, would a day come when I was taken aside by Adam's boss? I spoke Bosnian, after all, and therefore Croatian and Serbian. Before I could ask Katy more questions, she changed the subject to watercolours and offered me a wooden easel from her loft. 'You're going to need hobbies,' she said. 'David keeps them late.' I think she enjoyed being the expert for once. All the same, she kept checking the mirror on the wall, to see if the others were coming back. She was dissatisfied with just me.

Peter returned first, looking for a cardigan. He glanced at the mirror, touching his hand to his receding hair, but met Katy's eye and shied off in alarm. When he had gone outside again, she said, 'Has Adam told you about the time Rabbit got picked up in a bar?'

'I don't think so.'

Katy giggled. 'A woman started him asking questions about his job. Just ordinary small talk. You know, who did he work for, what did he do, what were his colleagues like? Rabbit panicked. The next day he told Martin he'd been caught in a honey trap!'

Poor Peter. I found myself hoping he'd make it to his Chinese kite festival one day.

Last thing that night, Katy brought out the karaoke machine. I can't sing to save my life, but she and Martin did a duet of "Don't Go Breaking My Heart," and Peter sang "Angels" in a clear tenor. And then Adam took the microphone. He had a gravelly baritone that surprised people because it was deeper than the way he spoke. Roisin used to call it his sex line voice. 'Adam,' she'd tease him, 'say, "What colour underwear have *you* got on?"'

Winking at me, he chose "Ruby" by The Kaiser Chiefs, the song that always used to be on the radio when he lived in Cambridge. I forgot all about army bases and overheard secrets. I just wanted to go upstairs with him again.

CHAPTER 7

In August I'd sellotaped newspaper over the sash windows of my bedroom to keep the temperature down. By the end of October I was stuffing silver foil into the cracks to stay warm.

Adam and I tried to meet every other weekend. One time I baked jabukovača, which means I cooked apples in cinnamon, rubbing flour and butter together to make pastry. The rain was so constant that we barely got out of bed. When he left, my sheets smelt of sex and cinnamon for days. At other times, though, a fortnight felt like a year. I found myself bitterly jealous of that room with the Union Jack cushions where everyone sat round the karaoke machine, drinking and laughing. 'Our boiler's broken,' Adam said on the phone. 'Katy says to tell you she's knitting me a scarf.' And I felt like snarling. Like wolves do, not like wool.

Siberian winds blew through Cambridge all November. There were no mountains between us and Russia, so in the library I kept my coat on, and sometimes my hat and fingerless gloves. The news that month did nothing to warm me up. It was full of the trial of Radovan Karadzić for crimes committed during the Bosnian war. I read these stories in the Rare Books Room, while old manuscripts dried out in the humidor. They reminded me of headlines in Coventry when I was fresh out of hospital, the war still raging.

KARADZIĆ DENIES MASSACRE AT SREBRENICA

MLADIĆ'S SHELLS KILL 43 IN SARAJEVO MARKET

Tata used to sit in stony silence, the newspapers crushed to his chest. As for Tarik, he began to set fire to things. The letterbox of the town hall – that was the first time he got arrested. The second time was when he burnt BOSNIA into the putting green. I would catch him at the window, swinging his leg over the fire escape. Sometimes he touched my hair and said, 'Goodnight, little sister. Sweet dreams.' Once he let me come, riding on the pannier of his bike. In a dark street he made me get off. 'Don't move,' he said. A door slivered open as if on a chain. I scarcely breathed. When he got back, he said, 'Well done. Where do you want to go?' So we went to the park. He helped me climb over the gate and I slid down the other side, cutting my legs on the brambles. Then I stood on one leg in the centre of the children's playground, among the rusty slides and swings, lifting the other leg above my head with both hands, while he spray-painted names on every possible surface. KARADZIĆ: the president behind the genocide at Srebrenica. MLADIĆ: the general who ordered the siege that killed our mother. Tarik said, 'We'll make the Brits fucking care.'

Now, in Cambridge, I stared at the BBC web page until it dissolved into meaningless dots. Karadzić might be on trial, but Mladić was still free. What I found hard was to care the right amount – enough, but not too much.

One day I bumped into Ed in the library. His lips were blue with cold. He said, 'I've been meaning to call. There's a Croatian choir singing evensong in King's College chapel on Saturday and my date has dropped out. Are you free?'

Ah, Ed. I felt a glow of affection for him. But we never did hear evensong together because the next morning he texted to say he had flu.

Roisin had it too. On her first day back from Edinburgh, she'd turned up outside the kebab shop in a battered black Nissan, leaning out of the window, hammering the horn. 'Laura! Jump in, love, there's a bus coming!' In the car I hugged her. The bus honked madly at us, so Roisin slammed her foot on the accelerator, bouncing forwards with a screech of rubber. She'd made a road trip of the journey home, she told me, raising her middle finger at the bus driver in the rear-view mirror – she came back with the bassist of a Cambridge rock band she'd met at the festival.

'Has he got dreadlocks?' I teased her.

She laughed. 'Long ones.' It was his car. She drove it badly, breathing in as she squeezed through tight spaces, shutting her eyes. 'Shite, did I scratch that?' she said, as she parked next to a Bentley.

'Not even close.'

'Liar. Right, let's crack open some wine.'

The bassist wasn't home that afternoon, but there were photos of him with his band all over his flat. He looked like a wire string, spasming metallically, like he might snap under the violence of his own music. Roisin chose men with a craving to damage themselves, the world, other people – they glittered with the joy of devastation. I had tried to say this to her and she'd laughed. 'I'm leaving the grand love affair to you. I just like how this one plays the guitar. Sure and the sex is great, too.'

But now they were fighting. 'He gave hash brownies to the trick-or-treaters,' she told me, when I went round to visit after Halloween. She was wearing his pyjamas and she'd lit his log fire.

I had to laugh. 'He's a budalo,' I said.

'Remind me what that means?'

'It's like an idiot, or a fool.' Beside the fire was a basket of wood in different sizes, which the bassist had stolen from skips. I put a table leg on the grate. All of a sudden, I felt – not homesick exactly, but homeless, displaced. 'Alo budalo,' Mama used to say, when Tarik kicked a football through the Sarajevo Youth Centre window, or if I was kept after class for daydreaming. Hey fool!

Roisin crouched down on her heels before the fire. 'Being ill makes me all Gaelic and despondent. Say something silly.'

So I said, 'Those builders by the Corn Exchange are budale. But Cambridge girls don't talk back. They roll their eyes and cross the road.'

'Not me,' Roisin objected. 'I give them a wink and I blow them a kiss.'

I laughed, and she laughed too. But our laughter came out fractured, glassy.

A few days later I was on the sixth floor in the north wing of the library, looking for a misplaced book. I didn't feel well at all. When I found the book, it was water-stained, the pages brittle. I stood up dizzily. In the darkening library I heard Mama's quiet, familiar laugh behind a row of shelves. With a fluttering heart I rounded the corner. No one was there. But the fire door at the end of the corridor was sliding shut, and I looked up just in time to see the disappearing hem of a yellow cotton dress.

By the time Adam rang that night, I was huddled in a blanket – hot and shivering, with the honey and lemon drink Tata used to make when I was ill. I had a high temperature, I told myself. Nothing more.

'Sorry it's so late,' Adam said. 'Big Dave and I went to the pub after work.' He was opening his front door; I heard the key turn. 'Can you come next weekend?'

'I have flu. Didn't we say the week after next?'

'The army's invited me to spend a few days at Sandhurst. I'm going to learn to strip down a gun.'

I had a chilling memory of escaping through Iližda – the Serb soldiers with water dripping from their rifles. I said, 'Why do you need a gun for a desk job?'

'I might have to fire someone.' He laughed. 'Sorry, I've had a few beers. I don't need a gun. Dave arranged it as a sort of reward – for doing well on that course Katy told you about. Are you okay to wait an extra week?'

I could think of some names for his boss. But I gave a shaky laugh. 'I'll be the old lady with the purple rinse.'

'I thought it was a blue one?'

'That was last decade.'

'Point taken,' Adam said.

When I did go to London, three weeks later, I found him pan-frying lamb chops. That was unusual. Adam never cooked: he unwrapped things. He had also opened a bottle of Mauro. It wasn't a wine I'd heard of, but I could tell it was expensive from the label. 'We should do this every night,' he said, clinking his glass against mine.

I picked up a spoon to stir the lamb. 'One small problem. I live sixty miles away.'

'What if we got married?'

Just at that moment the oil spat out of the pan and burnt my hand. I went to the sink and ran the cold tap. My pulse was beating hard under the flow of water, but I said, 'We could buy a plane – that would work too.' I didn't believe he meant it. I thought he was joking.

Adam came to the sink and turned my wrist over to see the burn, possessively, as if I had scalded his own skin. 'We'd rent our own place,' he said, his words coming out in a rush. 'Somewhere really cheap. Then in a year we could afford your master's. Translation, if that's what you still want? Or cheese-making, beekeeping. Anything at all.'

I think I forgot to breathe. Etymologically, the Bosnian word *paradajz* means both paradise and tomato, perhaps because it's the small good things that make a heaven. To sit in a lecture hall every day, and fall asleep next to Adam every night? That would be paradise. I said, 'Don't you want to finish your probation first?'

'No. I want to live with you.' His voice turned gruff. 'I want you to be my next of kin, in case anything happens.' I just looked at him. What might happen? But from his pocket he was fumbling a gold ring. It had a flying bird on it – a goose, I thought, with broad wings and garnet eyes. He said, 'Is this too soon?'

The odd little ring, so characteristic of Adam, made it thrillingly real for me. 'You have to ask properly.'

'Laura Guska,' he said 'will you be my wife?'

'Yes,' I told him. And with growing certainty, 'Yes, yes, yes.'

He kissed me, then he kissed me harder. I wrapped my legs round him, and as he carried me into his room I bit his neck. Laughing, he dropped me down on the bed. We broke zips and buttons. Afterwards our breathing slowed together. I was half asleep when the fire alarm went off. 'Fuck,' he said, leaping up and pulling on his boxers. His exit filled the air with the smell of burning.

After a moment I walked into the bathroom. Stepping under the shower, I turned the temperature low, the good coldness making me gasp. I was going to live a tomato-paradise kind of life – simple and safe and very, very English. Shivering now, I got out of the water and towelled myself dry. People would say I was getting ahead of myself, moving too fast. Which people? Roisin. But I didn't care: what mattered was happiness. I put the ring on my finger before I put on my clothes.

The kitchen was full of the smell of burnt lamb, the air black with it. Adam had found some spare jeans and a shirt. 'The frying pan's ruined,' he said. 'No great tragedy. I ordered a Chinese from up the road.' When the doorbell rang, he glanced in the mirror and pulled his collar up. 'You vampire,' he said. But he was smiling.

We sat on the sofa to eat our dinner, dipping plastic chopsticks into pots of chow mein. Adam said, 'I'll tell my boss on Monday, so he can start the vetting process.'

I put my chopsticks down. 'How long will that take?'

'A few months, I think. They're fiercer with dual citizens.'

'In case I'm a honey trap,' I said, trying to smile. I didn't know what fiercer meant. Had no idea how thorough they would be. 'Do they tell you what they find out?'

Adam cupped his hand gently over my skull. 'Why? Are you keeping dark secrets from me?'

'Two murders and a bank robbery,' I said. He laughed, but I rose from the sofa and turned to face him. 'My brother used to take cocaine. I think he might have sold cannabis. Would he get in trouble?'

Adam shook his head. 'Big Dave doesn't care about drugs – it's not a criminal investigation. Are you related to the mafia? Do you have any history of Islamic radicalization, or mental illness? Those are the only major concerns, so far as I know.'

Mental illness.

For a moment I froze. It felt like my heart forgot to beat. Fifteen years ago I had spent four weeks on a psychiatric ward, twelve months on antidepressants. Did that make me an unfit partner for him, according to the British government? My pulse came back, fast and shallow. If I told him the truth, he'd have to disclose it. I reached for a chopstick and bent it between my hands until I felt it about to snap.

A line of worry had set in between Adam's eyes. 'Are you okay?'

I'd been *nine*. Surely my hospital records were long gone? But I knew he wouldn't stay quiet if I told him about them. Rule-breaking wasn't in his nature. Even the old video games he liked to play were linear: he ran along pixelated tracks, trying not to plunge off sideways. 'I'm fine,' I said at last.

I hadn't met Big Dave yet, but he felt like my enemy.

I travelled back to Cambridge early on Monday morning. The train went through farmland, passing long open fields that were winter brown. The scarecrows looked crucified. I phoned the hospital in Coventry the minute it opened. 'Medical records were not the patient's property,' a smooth male voice told me. The patient could read them, but was forbidden by law to remove them. So that was one hope gone. But did my records still exist? A more difficult question. I spent half an hour on hold – by the end I could have hummed "Greensleeves" in my sleep. Then the smooth voice returned to say that the folder was proving hard to find. I had been a patient fifteen years ago? And I was not, at the time, a British citizen? Well – here the voice wrinkled slightly – even so, it *ought* to be in the storeroom.

Squat East Anglian houses dwindled past my train window, smoke rising from quaint chimneys. My records must have been destroyed. That was the case I made to myself. If they had not been destroyed then surely they were lost beyond Big Dave's ability to find them.

I called Adam. 'What if I don't get clearance?'

He must have gone back to sleep after I left, because he sounded groggy. 'You will.'

'But if I don't.'

'I guess I'd have to leave the Foreign Office.'

'Or leave me?'

'Stop worrying,' he said. 'We'll be fine.'

When I got to Cambridge the sun was shining. The smell of chip oil came from the Pickerel Inn, and punt touts shouted by the river. People walked past me as if it was just an ordinary day.

CHAPTER 8

Roisin said, 'Laura, you didn't!' I met her coming out of Fitzbillies, two days after I got back to Cambridge, and she nearly dropped the paper box she was carrying. 'You put the heart crossways in me,' she complained. 'Do you want a Chelsea bun? I had a horrid week, I'm about to get sticky and fat.' Then she spotted the engagement ring with the red-eyed bird on it and seized my hand. 'Shite, that's sinister! Are you pregnant?'

'Of course not!' I linked my arm through hers as we walked into town along Trumpington Street. 'It's not sinister, it's a guska. Adam chose it.'

'Oh, it's Adam's ring,' she teased me. 'I thought that librarian of yours had popped the question.'

I smiled in spite of myself, stopping by the new clock – the one with the grasshopper crawling over a bright gold dial, blinking its crazed eyes – to show her the text Ed had sent me that morning.

CONGRATULATIONS STOP ABANDONING HOPE STOP I'LL BE IN THE WEST ROOM IF YOU EVER CHANGE YOUR MIND

Roisin put her hands on her hips. 'You told *him* before *me*?'

'I didn't tell a soul! Someone at the library must have seen the ring. Anyway, *you* don't approve.'

'I don't see the rush.' She reached for my arm again, twirling the paper box from its ribbons. 'But let's get some bubbly to go with these buns.'

Tata said, 'Who is this Adam? Bring him here for Christmas!' I could hear him striding back and forth in his hallway, brought up short each time by the cord of his old-fashioned phone.

'I can't. He'll be with his family.'

'You want to get married to an Englez? For sure?'

'Yes, I do.'

'It's very romantic,' he said doubtfully. 'Your mother would have said you're too young.'

I thought Mama would have asked more questions. Is he tall? she'd have wanted to know. (Tata was tall, for a Bosnian.) Is he a good cook? Are you happy? But until my clearance came through, my happiness was far from certain. 'Do you have a way of contacting Tarik?' I said.

There was a long pause.

'He rang your aunt last month from the landline at his latest job – he's working somewhere called Café Illyria. He didn't leave a phone number.'

'I want to invite him to the wedding.'

'My soul, of course you do.'

Naomi said, 'Twelve months is a good length for an engagement. And winter weddings are so chic. Fur stoles and glühwein.' She was making the best of me, I could tell.

Adam said, 'We've decided on July, Mum.'

'If my vetting goes well,' I added. Each time the wedding came up I repeated this. I was superstitious about it.

His mother had paused in her selection of champagne flutes, her hand on the dresser door. 'Charles and I got married in the chapel of his old college. Adam's college, that is.' She put the flutes on the table and fetched out a photo album – to show me the wooden pews, the hallowed, sepia light. I found Naomi difficult. This was such an ordinary problem that I almost welcomed it.

Once we were alone in his childhood bedroom, under the Sonic All-Stars quilt, Adam said, 'I know you wanted a quiet wedding. But going back to that chapel will make her very happy.'

'It's okay.'

'She says to tell you Oliver Cromwell's skull is buried under it.

56

He started out in Westminster Cathedral. Then they dug him up and hanged the corpse, and someone swiped his head.'

I laughed. 'That's not disgusting at all.'

But I owed Adam the chapel, and even Cromwell's skull, because he was helping me to look for Tarik.

'I don't understand how you lost touch,' he said, reaching across me to turn on an old lava lamp by the bed.

'Things just got sour between us. Tata used to ask him to Dubrovnik every Christmas but he never showed up. The one time he did, I was horrible to him.' I recalled it vividly, though it was nine years ago. I had opened the front door, noting at once the cocaine in his eyes, all black pupil, and the tremor of his hands. He said, 'I've come to see you, little sister,' and I said, 'You're three years too late. Go away.' I was full of self-righteous teenage anger. When he took me at my word, I shut myself in my room for hours, refusing to cry. We hadn't spoken since. During his years of absence and addiction even my guilt had grown precious to me, the closest I got to having a brother.

Adam rolled onto his back, making the bedsprings creak. 'I thought of a way to find him,' he said. 'He's working somewhere called Café Illyria, right? There's a Shakespeare play – *Twelfth Night* – where a brother and sister get shipwrecked and wash up in Illyria. We did it at school.' He pillowed his head on his arms. 'I had a look on the internet and it's a real place. The Illyrians were one of the first tribes on the Balkan coast. Croatia, Bosnia, Serbia and Albania.'

I watched the lava bubbles in the lamp drift and bulge. 'Tarik would never go to Serbia,' I said. 'Not after what they did to us in the war. And if he was in Croatia, he'd have told Tata. But Café Illyria is just a name – it could be anywhere.'

'I think it's worth checking.' Adam leant over to kiss me. 'I know some people who travel in Bosnia and Albania. Shall I see if they can find out anything?'

I shrugged. His colleagues were already investigating me. Why shouldn't they look for Tarik as well?

The months between Christmas and Easter passed like pages turning. No verdict had come from the Foreign Office yet, so it was in blind faith that I gave my notice at the library. Saul Hafler summoned me at once. His office was still full of oil paintings and shadows. Saul himself was less caustic than usual. 'I hope this man makes you happy,' he said. 'If I were you, I'd stick to books.' When I rose to leave, he said, 'Wait,' and handed me a page cut from a magazine. It was the foot of Botticelli's Venus, the toes curled like buds. 'A wedding gift,' was all he said.

I showed Adam this picture the next time I saw him. Laughing, he lifted up my foot and kissed the inner arch. Then he took my big toe in his mouth and bit it, and the Botticelli crumpled on the couch beneath us.

Later, as I was flattening out the creases, he said, 'I've got some good news.'

My heart lurched sideways. 'About my clearance?'

'No.' He frowned. 'I'll ask Dave what's going on,' he said. 'The vetting team are really taking their time. But I do think I've tracked down your brother. He's in Sarajevo.' Venus's foot slipped unheeded from my fingers to the floor. Adam had a colleague who knew of a Café Illyria in one of the cobbled alleys around Baščaršija. She had written out the address for me on a yellow post-it note. So Tarik had gone back to Sarajevo. That shocked me more than I can say. I had a flashing memory of him doing his chemistry homework, of all things, in the kitchen of our old house, while Mama rubbed up the Ottoman tiles to blue brilliance, and Tata buffed and scrubbed the old communist stove. But he would not be living there, because we'd heard from an old neighbour that the Serbs had pulverized Gnijezdo Street in '93.

For days I carried the yellow note around in my pocket. At last I posted a wedding invitation to the café – on thick, raw paper chosen by Naomi. The printed words dented this paper. They bled at the edges like ancient runes. *Come*, I wrote on the back. That was all.

April went by, then May. Adam said the vetting team was just dotting i's and crossing t's. He promised they wouldn't delay until the last minute. But according to his mother it *was* the last minute. A month before the wedding, she took me to a florist's in Cambridge. 'A day out for the girls,' she said. The shop was warm with the breath of potted and cut flowers. Porous, light-swallowing cactuses squatted on the floor, and on shelves near the ceiling were rows of white and mauve orchids, in all their dramatic, insect-like beauty. The florist put down a handful of spiny leaves and showed us her wares, talking in a quiet voice, as if in the musky dark someone was sleeping.

'The women in the bridal party must have corsages,' Naomi told me. 'Will your brother be bringing a girlfriend? A boyfriend, even,' she added magnanimously. 'Adam told me he's a chef.'

'No, he won't,' I said shortly. I had not yet received a reply from Tarik. I didn't want to admit, even to myself, that he might not come.

'Can I sit you next to Taro, assuming he turns up?' I asked Roisin, at the end of the flower shop afternoon. She had left me an answer-machine message – Did I have a quick hour? – and I had found her upstairs in Indigo, ignoring the customers she was meant to be serving, and drinking ginger tea.

'Taro?' she repeated.

'My brother, Tarik. If he starts any anti-government rants, I'll need someone to distract him.'

'What else is he into?'

'He used to like Aerosmith,' I said doubtfully.

Roisin grinned. 'Good choice. You know, a rant might shake things up. Getting married sounds like a pain in the bum. Florists and seating plans!'

'Tell it to Adam's mother. She's taking me cake tasting next weekend.'

'Okay, *that* could be fun.'

'Ye-es.' I spread my hands ruefully. 'Except the shop she's picked can't make a Bosnian wedding loaf, which is what my dad will expect. And the best man wants to give us wheels of cheese instead, to go with the champagne. But there won't *be* any champagne, because we're having an English sparkling wine from a vineyard she knows in Gloucestershire.'

Roisin laughed. 'Is the best man single?'

'The best man is Knuckles.' I glanced at her. 'Aren't you spoken for?'

'I got dumped.' She tried to smile, but her mouth twisted. 'He says he wants to enjoy his music. Drugs, he means. And other girls.'

Here I'd been worrying about cakes, cheese-wheels. 'Shit, Rosh. What can I do?'

'Don't get married yet,' she said, suddenly fierce. 'Let's go to Mexico. You be Thelma and I'll be Louise.'

I leant across the table, careful of the cups, and hugged her.

Then, one night in early June, while I was in the Pickerel Inn for a librarian's birthday party, Adam texted me. 'Can we talk? It's about your vetting.' I left the pub without saying a word to anyone and went out onto Magdalene Bridge. The cloying smell of the river rose up to meet me, and a rank odour from the college bins. They had found my hospital records: I was certain of it.

'Brace yourself, darling,' Adam said, when I phoned him. Then he laughed. 'You got a clean bill.'

I felt my heart's incredulous rising. 'It's over?'

'We can't visit the Balkans without permission. That's the only condition. Didn't I tell you not to worry?'

Worry didn't come close to it. Dread had filled my heart, squeezed my lungs. Feeling as if I had been released from a stranglehold, I pumped the air above the silk-black river with my fist.

'There's more good news,' Adam said. 'Dave's trip to Belgrade has been cancelled, so he's free for the wedding. You'll finally get to meet him.'

I stopped fist-pumping at once and grabbed the cold iron rail of the bridge. For months Adam's colleagues had been rooting through my past, cross-checking birth and death certificates, calling up old police records – just looking for a way to put him off marrying a foreigner, or so I guessed. And now, when my vetting had finally come through, it turned out that his boss was coming to my wedding, where he would meet every relative I possessed. My excitable, outspoken aunt, whose testimony had once got me committed to a psychiatric ward. Maybe even my unpredictable brother, who'd been in police cells, at least twice, for protesting the British government's indifference to the war. I couldn't imagine Tarik in a chapel full of suited bureaucrats. He had torched a suit once. Luckily not *on* anyone.

'Are you still there?' Adam said. 'Is something wrong?'

I let go of the rail, uncurling my fingers. I didn't want to spoil this moment, so I said, 'What could possibly be wrong?'

CHAPTER 9

The night before my wedding, I found myself back in the Pickerel Inn. Adam's parents were there, along with various Quin aunts and uncles and cousins, Knuckles and Tails, and Roisin. Tata and my aunt should have arrived by now, but their flight had been cancelled and rescheduled for the early morning. Of Tarik, still no news.

'Did you know the best man's real name is Steve?' said Roisin, as the people in front of us at the bar formed a very British queue.

'That's impossible. "Knuckles the Echidna" is written on his birth certificate.'

She laughed. 'Will Adam's mum expect me to dance with him all night?'

'Just the first dance,' I promised.

After a few drinks I slipped off to my bedsit on Chesterton Road. Adam and I had once eaten jabukovača here while rain poured down the windows, but I was not going to miss the squashed chips and kebab meat on the pavement outside, or the neon jitter of the shop sign. Everything was going to be better when I was married. Tonight, I felt sure of it.

I went down the corridor to run a bath, and as the taps spluttered, I could hardly stop smiling. So what happened next came as a shock. I hadn't listened to Dvořák's "Rusalka" since the day Mama died, but I swear I heard opera music over the sound of the taps. A water spirit sang of her love for a mortal man and her fateful bargain with a witch – to have her tail turned to feet in exchange for her beautiful voice. Sitting down on the toilet seat, sick and shaking, I pressed my hands over my ears. I also shut my eyes. I knew the bath was empty, but I also knew that if I looked at it, I would see Mama. Her face would be damp and clammy. Her blood would have stained the water a violent, unspooling red.

I got myself back to my room and crawled under the covers. It was just a few minutes later that Adam came up. 'I won't stay long,' he said. 'Are you okay?'

'I'm fine.'

He sat on the edge of my bed. 'You've got cold hands.'

'Yes.'

'But not cold feet?'

I did my best to smile at him. 'Toasty warm feet.'

'Good.' Running his thumb across my palm, he said, 'I wish I'd met your family. I'm nervous.'

You're nervous, I thought. Aloud I said, 'How could you have met them? Big Dave hasn't agreed to let us go to the Balkans yet, and Tata hates this country.' That was true. Tarik might be the one with the burning flag tattoo, but when Tata and I moved to Croatia he had renounced England with such intensity that I was no longer sure if he believed it existed. Nonetheless, six hours from now he was due to arrive at Gatwick airport with my aunt, then drive to Cambridge in a hire car. 'I still haven't heard from my brother,' I said.

'Do you think he'll come?'

When I shook my head, Adam lay down beside me, squeezing all his gangly kindness into that single bed. I should have told him everything then. Dvořák in the bathroom. Mama's laugh in the library. But nothing had actually happened to me. Saying it out loud would have made it too real.

I didn't deserve to sleep dreamlessly that night, but I did.

The next morning, Tata got to the college with only half an hour to spare. 'Beautiful!' he said, kissing his hand, when he saw me in my dress. He gave a conspiratorial wink. 'We baked you a proper wedding loaf. Your aunt is putting it in front of the ugly white cake.'

Soon we were in a room outside the chapel. It had the Sidney Sussex crest on the wall: a blue porcupine and a black bull chained beneath a crown. Tata pushed open a small wooden door and a piano began to play.

The chapel itself was long and narrow. Its high windows were covered in more crests, as well as fruits and Latin mottos: *Ave spes unica. O salutaris hostia.* The altar was at the far end from the door, and on the two remaining walls were double rows of pews made out of dark wood. Halfway down the aisle, Tata whispered, 'My soul, look who came.' I had been concentrating on my feet, on reaching the next sunbeam on the marble floor. But now I caught sight of Tarik, nine years older than I remembered him, leaning forwards to see me. I felt an ache in my chest. He had a short ponytail held back with a plain band, and a wary look that probably mirrored my own. Then we had passed him by.

Naomi was in the front row, unaware of the insult to her cake. Next to her Charles leant on a cane, his face composed and stately. And there at the altar was Adam, in his unfamiliar morning suit, with his familiar, embarrassed smile.

'If either of you know any reason in law why you may not marry each other, you are to declare it,' the chaplain said.

I don't, I reminded myself. Not a reason in law. Just something it got too late to tell him.

The words of the marriage service were like the walk to the altar, solemn and measured, patched with light and shade. Towards the end, the chaplain said, 'Who gives this woman to be married to this man?' Tata's fingers closed round mine – an ancient gesture.

After the ceremony we emerged into the sunlight of second court. Waiters circled with roasted carrots and sparkling wine. A dreadlocked photographer took pictures. When that was done, Tarik came up to us. He and Adam shook hands, then he kissed my cheek – stiffly, I thought. Though that could have been my imagination. He was taller than me, and darker; more like Mama, that's what everyone used to say. 'Thanks for inviting me,' he said. 'You're all grown up, little sister.' His voice was dry, with something in it that I couldn't identify. It might have been regret.

Adam's friend Katy appeared then, already mid-sentence, trailing her untidy husband behind her. 'Are those real pearls? My dress was lace too, but mine had a diamante motif.' Leaning towards me, she whispered, 'We flew in from Belgrade. I said to Martin, I never miss a wedding.' Over her shoulder I watched my brother walk away.

Other people came and went: Rupert and Mim, then Peter Rabbit, then some girls from the library. They said, 'What a lovely dress.' 'How lucky you've been with the weather.' The one who stands out in my memory is Big Dave. A quietly spoken man in a bulky grey suit, soft-footed and ponderous as a pigeon. 'Welcome to the family,' he said, bending forwards from his waist to peck my cheek. Somehow, he made it sound like a warning.

The wedding meal took place in hall. The long tables were covered with white cloths and blue napkins, and in the centre of each cloth was part of the present Tata had sent us before he left Dubrovnik: three cases of a smooth, dark Merlot that looked like oxblood. He had also given us four bottles of Krauthaker Graševina, a dessert wine made on the fossil-strewn slopes that used to be covered by the Pannonian Sea. He and Adam walked into the hall together, Tata speaking a mix of Bosnian and broken English – a language he had never fully mastered. I followed them nervously. What were they talking about? Then I saw Adam make the flat-handed gesture by which he had learnt the word *vila* on the day we met. I saw Tata laugh.

There was a shortage of women at high table. Roisin was there as a sort of honorary bridesmaid, and Naomi, cool and ceremonious, and my aunt, who held me fiercely to her and kissed me twice on each cheek. She smelt of olive oil and rose cologne.

'Tako mi je drago vidjeti te sretnu i da si mi bolje,' she said.

'Happy to see you in better health?' Adam queried, as we sat down.

'To see me looking great,' I said quickly. It was not a lie so much as a mistranslation. It was self-defence.

I was sitting between him and Tata, with my brother on the other side of the table, next to Roisin. Tarik was telling her that he'd learnt to cook in a dive joint in Budapest, from a drunk Slovakian who threw knives when she got angry. He added something I didn't catch and Roisin burst out laughing. I heard her say, 'Laura thought you'd burn the chapel down.'

'Laura knew me when I was eighteen,' he said, glancing in my direction. 'She has some excuse.'

It was equally hard for me to look at him or look away. Some excuse! We had nine years of silence to make up for. I wanted to ask him why he'd gone back to Sarajevo. What was it like? What was *he* like? But in a few hours, he was telling Roisin, he had to get back on a plane. Adam looked round at that moment. He'd been talking to Big Dave, over his shoulder, but when he saw the expression on my face, he put his arm round me. 'Don't frown, Mrs Quin. People will think you're having second thoughts.'

The starters arrived and Tata jumped up, ostensibly to help the women at our table to more wine, but really because he didn't approve of rectangles in dining rooms: he couldn't bear to be so far from all his guests. This charmed even Naomi, at whose side he lingered gallantly. 'The mussel –' he said to her, holding one up to illustrate his point – 'the mussel in the shell is the utensil perfect for its own – smrt?' That was Tata all over: a man who knew the English for *utensil* but refused to remember the word for *death*. He avoided hard things. He'd barely even spoken to Tarik. But he must have been listening to my brother with at least one ear, because when Naomi asked how long he and my aunt were staying, he said that they too must fly home tomorrow, to reopen the restaurant. 'I want Laura and Adam to visit,' he declared. 'For a moon of honey.'

I caught Adam's eye. 'We can't just now.' The Foreign Office hadn't signed off on a visit to Croatia yet.

'Both my children keep me at a distance,' said Tata, melodramatically, to the table at large. He helped himself to more oxblood wine.

'I think Laura is moving tomorrow,' Tarik pointed out.

And Naomi, always a pourer of oil on troubled waters, said, 'Oh yes! I'm afraid it's quite a state. Victorian plumbing! Rotten floorboards! Laura hasn't even seen it yet.'

66

"It" was her coup, her trompe l'oeil gift to us. In place of the dingy one-beds that were all we could afford to rent on Adam's starting salary, she and Charles had offered us the use of a tumbledown red brick house, empty since the death of her father, on the edge of Hampstead Heath. 'Yes, yes,' said Tata, gloomily. 'The house.' I understood how he felt. Who could compete with such generosity – such dreamlike largess? They had promised not to sell it for at least two years.

'We'll visit soon,' I said, leaning over to kiss his cheek. I really meant to go, if I could get Dave's permission. Maybe Tarik could join us. Seeing him today had made me realise how far apart we'd grown, and how much I regretted it.

His moustache trembling with disappointment, Tata pinched another mussel out of its shell. They were the opposite of camouflaged. They were open and unguarded, serving themselves up on a plate.

CHAPTER 10

While other civil servants rented flats in Vauxhall or Clapham, Adam and I found ourselves on a street just east of Golders Green. The house was two hundred years old and plagued by damp. There were long cracks in the walls where ivy had eaten into the brickwork, and the roots of an ancient wisteria writhed beneath the floorboards. But the leaves of the wisteria were pale green, and the wind brought the smell of grass and fir. 'What are those pink flowers on the bank?' I asked Adam, standing at an upstairs window and looking out at the garden.

'Corncockles.'

'And all this belongs to us?'

'Did you marry me for my garden?' he teased.

'Our garden. I didn't know about it. If I had I might have done.'

Through the open window I heard the whir of a bird's wings and caught a glimpse of yellow as it clawed onto a branch. What bird? Adam would know. He stood beside me, relishing my enjoyment.

'Have you seen the bath?' he said. 'The lion's paw feet used to terrify me.'

I hadn't looked. After what happened on the night before our wedding, I was avoiding baths. To change the subject, I said, 'What was your grandfather like?'

'Old,' he said. 'Old and angry. He flew a Spitfire in World War II. "Leaving already?" he used to say to us. "Well! You barely arrived."'

'Maybe that's how you feel when you're old.'

'Let's stay young, then.' He kissed me. 'Let's never say that to our children.'

Later that night we opened one of the bottles of Graševina we'd got from Tata. The wine was cold and fragrant. Elusive. It reminded me of stilettos, or alpine flowers. 'Something's come up at work,' Adam said.

'Something good?' We were sitting on his grandfather's sofa, the sag that tipped us together reflected in the boxy screen of an old-fashioned TV. Whitehall felt a long way away, a dull glitter of glass and marble on the north bank of the Thames.

'I think so. Dave wants me to add a new project to my portfolio.' I noticed that he straightened his shoulders, as if to support the weight of Dave's confidence in him. He said, 'I can't talk about the details, but it's of interest to both Serbia and Bosnia.'

There are moments that change our lives forever and we know at once. When Tata saw Mama in the Miljacka, he dropped to his knees on the bank, his hands clutching air. But at other times we miss a crucial twist of our fate. I listened to the tone of Adam's voice and I enjoyed the pride with which he spoke, and the way I fitted into the curve of his arm. I felt like I had got away with happiness. It didn't occur to me that this was the start of a reckoning.

At the front of our new house was a crab-apple tree, behind it a pond. Each morning fish rose to the surface of the water as if they were trying to breathe air. A skinny neighbourhood cat watched them with intent. For the first few weeks of our marriage, I wrote job inquiries in the kitchen, where I could keep an eye on this cat. During my breaks I shovelled dead leaves and rotten crab-apples up from the grass, making the house presentable to the street. The British Library wasn't hiring over the summer, nor was the London Library. 'Patience,' Adam told me. I felt a stab of jealousy. For him, patience was all it ever took.

In those early days of our marriage, my husband walked through walls all day, analysing secret conversations between people who had no idea they were overheard. The Bosnian mafia, I guessed, mindful of recent news stories on human trafficking, and what he himself had said – in Surrey, all that time ago – about a crackdown on organised crime. Katy Lyon had been right about one thing: Dave often kept him late. But for a while the house absorbed me. I framed *The Birth of Venus*, slightly creased, and hung it on the stairs. I liked to think about the goddess's first steps from shell to shore: the crunch of stones under unused feet, and the feet themselves – shapely, faintly disreputable, sexual. In the empty evenings I set up our internet connection. I replaced rotten floorboards and window frames, and plastered the holes in the walls. I enjoyed these jobs, for which I wore paint-spattered dungarees and tied my hair up in a knot. They made me feel I was at the start of a new life.

Our first weekends in Hampstead are bleached in my memory to the colour of an old photograph. The master bedroom had a deep gable window, and when I woke up Adam would be sitting on the window ledge with a mug of fresh coffee. He would already have shaved, a nick on his cheek from the terrible cut-throat razor his father had once given him. If it was Sunday, he'd be reading three separate newspapers – his face bright with sunlight, the tiredness gone from his eyes. Stay like that, I remember thinking. Don't move.

But movement was unavoidable. One evening, about a month after we got married, he came home early from work. The clothes line was between us, crowded with trousers and tights that kicked in the breeze like boneless dancers, and I was sieving green weed from the fishpond, so I didn't notice him at first. He pushed past the washing. 'I'm being sent abroad for a few days next week. Dave just let me know.'

I squinted at him. 'Another language course?'

Crouching down next to me, he detached a leaf that had got stuck in my hair. 'Not this time, no. It's to do with that new project I'm working on.'

'Adam!' I grabbed his hand to keep him there, and he rocked on his heels, nearly losing his balance. 'Should I be worried?'

'They just want me to talk to some people in Bosnia.' He spoke quietly, as if his voice might disturb something in the garden – the fish, the burdened clothes line – or something in me. The next thing he said was, 'Have you seen my diplomatic passport?'

'It's in your bedside drawer,' I told him reluctantly. He kissed me again and stood up. I was still holding the sieve, full of wet leaves.

There was a full moon the night he left. I said, 'It's werewolf weather.'

'Smugglers,' he corrected me. And then, smiling, 'Spies.' When his taxi arrived, he put his rucksack in the boot, then hugged me goodbye on the front step. I watched his tail lights disappear down the road. Then I went up to our bedroom, where I sat down on the floor. Something about his absence took me right back to the siege. I had the same feeling of fear that kept me awake when I was nine.

I ended up binge-watching a James Bond box set I found on Adam's shelf – Sean Connery and Roger Moore strutting across Europe all night long. What got my attention were the opening credits. Blood dripped from the top of the screen, slowly, like stalactites. Paper cut-out men ran about, and when they got shot, they burst into clouds of diamonds. The bullets left trails, like aeroplane smoke. I found these images disturbing in the same way that as a child in Sarajevo I'd been upset by cartoons. I'd hated how the characters were squished flat and then ballooned back into shape, how they got minced up by cleavers or pushed over cliffs or had their eyes popped out of their heads.

The next morning, shaky from lack of sleep, I decided to bake šape. I beat lard with sugar and vanilla, grated a lemon, then whisked an egg. This was the kind of violence that made sense to me – the kind that made things taste good. On the second batch of biscuits, I ran out of sugar and went to the corner shop for more. When I got home, there was an old woman in a blue headscarf standing by my kitchen sink, grinding coffee in a brass mill. At her elbow was a small copper jug. 'Dobro jutro,' she said. Her smile was animated but she was clearly dead. Corporeal, yes. Just pliant, somehow, in a way the sink and the table were not. I pressed my hands to my eyes, and by the time I took them away she had gone. It happened so fast I was not sure I had seen her at all. She might have been a trick of the light. I sat down in a chair. I felt at a loss, dismayed. When at last I stood up, I noticed a scorch-mark on the kitchen counter where her Bosnian coffee jug had been.

Adam got back two days later. He tried to smile as he came through the front door, but the hug he gave me was over almost as soon as it began. When he hung up his coat, I saw that the knuckles on his right hand were scabbed and bruised. 'It got complicated,' he said. 'Good god, Laura. I was caught up in a real mess.'

'What happened?'

He shook his head. 'I'm not allowed to say.' He put his rucksack down on the living room floor. 'I don't even want to think about it, to be honest. Do you have any news?'

When he walked in, I still hadn't decided what to do. But it was impossible to tell him about the old woman now. 'No news,' I said. 'I baked some biscuits.'

That was a quiet night. Adam took a shower, and I set out the plate of šape. Later he did say one thing about his trip. He was lying on his back in our bed, so still that I knew he was awake. I put my hand beside his bruised one, just touching it, and he said, 'At one point we were on a mined hillside, waiting for a helicopter.' He must have felt me wince, because he said, 'It wasn't all that dangerous. We had a map of the mines.' He took my hand and kissed it gently. 'We didn't even talk about anything important – I think we talked about how fast our toenails grow.'

The next morning, I picked up a paperback he had left by his side of the bed. A John Grisham. 'You don't read thrillers,' I said.

'Dave lent it to me for the plane.' He held out his hand for the book, which he shook, deliberately, by the spine. A crushed flower fell out of the pages. 'This is for you,' he said, with a wry smile. I took it in my hands – a husk-like smudge of yellow. 'What is it?'

'A winter aconite. I found it on that hillside. I thought—'

'—You were in a *minefield* and you thought you'd pick a flower?'

72

'A mapped minefield. I nearly stepped on it. I was thinking about you.'

I looked at the brittle flower that lay on my palm. I didn't know whether to laugh or cry. 'Don't die,' I said. 'I'm warning you, Adam. Don't you dare die.'

CHAPTER 11

As I went about the house in the week that followed, I sometimes thought I smelt ground coffee. I decided to ignore it. I had a more immediate concern. Adam had never fully retired his old Sega console, but since he got back he'd started playing it for hours on end. 'Just one more,' he said to me, as the blue hedgehog sped past mushrooms and palm trees. I remembered my days working in Tata's café, pouring drinks behind the bar. The harbourside drunks, those silver-tongued old men with the jittery hands, had always said the same thing: *Just one more.*

Twice in a row Adam fell asleep on the sofa in his clothes, his short hair sticking up as if in agitation. The first time I put a blanket over him, and at some point in the middle of the night, he crawled into bed next to me. But the second time I woke him. 'Tell me what's going on,' I said. He stood up from the sofa, rubbing his neck with one hand. 'The shrink at work says it's normal to want to escape sometimes.' He put his arm round me, clumsily, and his forehead bumped into mine. 'I'm not cracking up. I just wanted to talk some things through.'

Roisin phoned me that week. 'I've grand news,' she crowed. 'Can we meet at King's Cross?' The Northern line was running with severe delays, so I got out at Camden Town and walked the rest of the way. Roisin was in a café with her feet on two big pink suitcases. It turned out that her band, The Vagrant Revolution, had won a windfall travel grant; another group had pulled out at the very last minute, so she was off to tour Europe for six months, perhaps a year. 'We've got a new guitarist,' she said, winking at me.

I couldn't help laughing. 'Roisin Clery! Why is it always guitarists with you?'

Our coffee arrived, along with two enormous slices of red velvet cake. When the waitress had gone, Roisin leant across the table. 'What's wrong, love? You just got married – you're meant to be blooming.'

'Nothing's wrong,' I said. But then I asked her, 'Do you believe in ghosts?'

She sat back in her chair, looking at me with frank curiosity. 'Vengeful spirits and things that go bump in the night? No. Why?'

I shrugged. 'You've never seen anything you couldn't explain?'

'Well, once in Portugal Street I saw giant dandelions growing out of the cracks in the wall. But I was fried.' She crumbled the edge of her cake with her fork. 'Haven't you ever smoked? Even in school?'

'Tarik put me off. But I think I used to get contact highs.'

'Really? You saw things?'

'No giant dandelions,' I said.

She smiled. 'That was a crazy trip. Kind of beautiful.'

The day after Roisin left for Europe, Adam handed me an invitation to the Bosnian Embassy. 'Dave wants us all there,' he said. 'You'll need a posh frock – it's a big annual do.' The idea of this party thrilled me, but Adam left for work in an odd mood, and that evening he phoned to say he and Peter Rabbit were going to check out a new bar in Soho. Don't wait up, he told me. The next morning I woke to find him asleep on the sofa again, the Sega controller fallen slackly from his hand, yellow rings spinning across the screen. His face looked squeezed, and beads of sweat darkened his eyebrows to the colour of a wet sponge.

What could I do? I phoned Peter and asked if I could talk to him privately. He arrived by tube an hour later with a kite in his arms. The two of us walked to the top of Parliament Hill, Peter hunching his shoulders as if apologising for his height. The heath and the sky were grey, but the kite was vibrant – lime-green silk stretched over a bamboo skeleton. When he let go it surged upwards, tail lashing, as if to pull me into the air.

Peter came to stand beside me. Once the kite was stable, I said, 'Is Adam okay?'

'He had a rough trip. He'll be all right.'

I watched the kite soar. 'What he did while he was away, was it *good*?'

My thought was that Peter might open up to me if we were looking at the sky – that like the girls in English fairy tales who tell their troubles to caves and springs, he would believe no confidence was being broken. But all he said was, 'It will be good for Bosnia, I promise you that.' After a while he brought the kite down, lulling the wind out so it sank to the ground; then he rolled up the line, wrapping it round the handle. When the kite was back in his arms he said, 'Our job can be traumatic. We all find our own way of carrying that. Adam's doing okay.' He fidgeted with his bundle of sticks and silk. 'I'm not sure what else I can tell you.'

I said goodbye to him at the station. Afterwards, I couldn't stop thinking about the expression he had used. What does it mean to carry trauma? It's different from the Western concept of emotional baggage, which suggests suitcases, something handy and portable, also something that through choice or simple carelessness you might leave behind. *Trauma* is a heavy part of your own self. It's the weight you bear after an unbearable event.

CHAPTER 12

Adam could knot a bow tie without looking in the mirror. 'How do you do that?' I asked him, watching the loose ends form into a butterfly shape.

'Public school education.' He folded a square Union Jack into his jacket pocket. 'Laura, can I talk to you about something?'

'Make it quick? I still need to do my hair.'

'It will keep.' He smiled at me – a little effortfully, I thought. 'Do I look presentable?'

The only other handkerchief he owned was bright purple. He had worn it at our wedding. 'Very patriotic,' I said dryly.

We made our way down the Northern and Piccadilly lines to Lexham Gardens. The familiar blue-and-yellow flag hung from a balcony, and bearish men stood on the pavements, stubbing out cigarettes. We ticked our names off a list by the door and checked my coat. I felt excited, but Adam seemed to tense at once in this atmosphere of smoke and aftershave and growled Slavic greetings. He crushed my fingers in his, shouldering through the foyer. 'I could use a drink,' he said. 'Let's get out of this.' On the landing, a perspiring attaché told us the bar was downstairs. 'Fucksake,' Adam muttered. And to me, 'Red wine?'

I said, 'I'll come with you.' But he had already gone.

The attaché took my hand and kissed it moistly. The kiss evaporated, leaving a brief chill. 'Dobrodošli,' he said. 'It means welcome. I know your husband well.' I gave him a slight smile. Not very well, I thought, or you'd know I'm Bosnian. He showed me into a noisy room with its furniture pushed against the walls. 'What is your proverb about the Englishman and the fox?' he said. '"The unspeakable in pursuit of the uneatable?"' At the time I had no idea what he meant.

'Laura!' said a voice behind us. Big Dave was dewed with sweat, but he moved noiselessly, on velvet feet. The attaché slunk off into the crowd. 'He owes me a report,' Dave explained, wiping his chin with a handkerchief. 'How's married life treating you? Has Adam spilled all our secrets yet?' He spoke with humour, but he kept his eyes on my face.

'Your job would make me hungry,' I said carefully. 'Spilt secrets, and the Doughnut, and – honey traps.'

Dave laughed. He was not the fool that some people assumed, but perhaps it suited him to appear foolish, and he had discovered that the bigger he got the less visible he was – that people's eyes slid over him and they forgot to be cautious in his presence. When he stopped laughing, he said, 'Where *is* Adam?'

'At the bar.'

Together we contemplated the Adamless room. Sevdalinka began to play from a loudspeaker, the notes displacing little puffs of dust. That was a saz – I recognised its heart-plucking sound. Dave said, 'I'm making some changes to my team. I'll leave Adam to tell you the details, but I hope I can count on your support.' He met my eyes for just a second or two longer than people usually do. Was it a threat? If so, it was almost too subtle to see. But Dave was subtle. 'I'll just chase up that report, if you'll forgive me,' he said. Then he bumbled away in his tuxedo, ominous as a magpie. *One for sorrow.*

I sat down again, feeling shaken. What kind of changes? And was my husband draining the whole bar? Another attaché and a Foreign Office man I recognised from my wedding came to a stop in front of me, their shirt tails escaping their cummerbunds. 'February is the best month to step on a mine,' the attaché was saying. 'Under enough snow, it might not detonate.' Now I thought about it, Adam had seemed preoccupied all day. 'In Bosnia,' the attaché went on, 'the snow begins in December. By February it is several feet deep.' He put his gold-ringed hand on the shoulder of the Foreign Office man. 'My friend, I will tell you a thing not many people know. On Candlemas night in '94, a group of women fled Lisac village ahead of Mladić's tanks. At sunrise they arrived in Rastovci, where our Bosnian Army camped. They had crossed six miles of mined snowfields.'

I shuddered, caught up in the story in spite of myself. I could almost see those women. They did not speak, or they spoke only in whispers. They held the barbed wire apart for each other. But then did they run or crawl or dance, knowing that at any moment the solid ground might rear beneath their feet, the snow explode in flames? 'Excuse me,' I said, pushing past the two men. Mama was killed by a shell launched from just such a tank. I was not going to think about that now.

I moved away, trying not to stiletto anyone's toes. A chandelier hung from the ceiling, and under its electric candles a man in British military uniform bent over a woman in a limp pink dress. I quickened my pace. When I got out of the room, I found the stairs blocked by a secretive knot of attachés. In the middle of them was the man who had made the joke about Englishmen and foxes. Snippets of Bosnian floated up to me.

'...sweep-up operation...'

'...it was Adam Quin.'

I stopped to listen. The attachés glanced at me, then went on talking. They thought I only understood English.

'...interrogation. Their source confessed...'

'Yes, that the target gave him a jar of *honey*.'

'Honey!' the fox man repeated, looking right at me and laughing. To his friends he said, 'It won't come to anything. Bet you a night at the Platinum Lace Club.'

Heat and feral aftershave rose up the stairs in a sickening wave. Suddenly those attachés – their wet, hairy necks bulging over their collars – merged in my mind's eye with the women dancing on snow-covered mines as tanks flattened their village behind them. I retreated blindly into the room I had come from. Finding myself against a pair of French windows, I pushed one open and stumbled onto the balcony.

Out there I could see my own breath, fog-white in the lamplight. As my nausea subsided, I forced my mind back to Dave. The nicer he was to me, the more I felt he disliked me. I hope I can count on your support, he had said. My support for what?

'Hello,' a voice called out, and I spun round to see Peter Abbott by the flagpole, tugging at an elasticated bow tie. 'Tired of the party?' he asked me.

I went over to join him. 'It's all war stories in there. Tanks and strip clubs.'

Peter turned pink, with the unvoiced contempt that is the preserve of the wallflowers, the corner-dwellers and balcony men. 'I'm sorry,' he said. 'They show off when they get together.'

I shrugged and smiled at him. Girls with nipple-tassels were not my worry.

'Have you tried the šlivovica?' Peter went on. 'I think it's homemade. It actually tastes of plums.' He offered me his glass. 'This is a nice wind,' he said, as I took a sip. 'If I had my night kite, we could sneak off to the gardens up the road. I'm not really a party animal,' he ended ruefully.

I was only half listening, but that phrase – *party animal* – got my attention because in an odd way it did describe Adam. He wasn't someone who loved mountains or wildernesses, so when he coveted an empty space, he looked for it in groups of people. And in his current mood he was probably buying everyone shots. I did need to find him. Even as I decided this, the French windows opened and Katy came out onto the balcony, already talking. 'I'll never like sarma. Bosnians are so pushy. Oh, hello you two, have you run away?'

'Darling, I don't think we're meant to bring drinks out here,' said Martin, who was following her.

'Laura's got a drink. We had to come home for a pow-wow with Big Dave,' she told me, swaying a little and pronouncing her words with care. 'You're shivering – Rabbit, she's shivering. Give her your jacket.'

'I'm going in,' I said.

Katy didn't stop talking. 'You *are* like a rabbit, a very tall skinny one. You've got rabbity hair, like fur. Just a bit thin on top.' Peter put a hand up to his bald patch, as if to check on the hairs that were still there. 'Don't do that!' she said. 'You'll make it worse if you fiddle with it.'

I touched her arm to stop her pestering him. 'Have you seen Adam?'

'He was near the bar an hour ago. I waved at him to join us, but he mustn't have seen me. You know Rabbit, you *could* get a weave.'

Inside the French windows, the officer in uniform had lost the woman in the pink dress. I hurried downstairs to the bar, which was just a white-clothed table laid with bottles and glasses. It was surrounded by men whose drunkenness had taken the form of solemnity. 'We live in a wired world,' one of them was saying. I couldn't see Adam anywhere. A young waiter loitered in the hall with a tray of hors d'oeuvres – one of which he was eating delicately, his thumb and forefinger pincering its damp edges as if it was alive. He blushed when he saw me and thrust out his tray. 'Sarma?' he offered. 'Meat and rice in cabbage leaf, very traditional in my country.'

'No thank you,' I said. 'You haven't seen my husband, have you? Light brown hair, and a Union Jack handkerchief?'

'Jack?'

'Britanska zastava.'

'Oh! You are Bosnian!' With a relieved smile, he waggled his half-eaten sarma at the door. 'Britanska zastava, yes. I think this man leaves some few minutes ago.'

Outside the Embassy, Peter's kite-wind raised goose bumps on my skin. Too ill at ease to go back for my coat, I walked north on instinct, past the Park City Hotel and the entrance to Lexham Garden Mews; the houses locked up for the night, their owners unwoken by snatches of sevdalinka. Then I saw Adam. He was at the gate of the community gardens with his back to the Embassy, unmistakable to me even in the dark. A coke can crunched under my feet and he turned round at once. There was an empty bottle on the ground beside him, a full glass in his hand. 'Laura?' He walked quickly to me, pulled me close and kissed me. He tasted of bitter plums.

I took a step back. 'Why are you out here? It's freezing.'

Without answering, he took off his dinner jacket and fumbled it round my shoulders. Then he turned back to the gate, trying the lock with a key from his pocket. 'Fuck,' he said, when it jammed.

'Adam—'

'Found it in the lobby.' The gate groaned open. 'C'mon in.'

He was too drunk to hear reason, so after a moment's hesitation I followed him. The garden paths were gravelled, with trees hanging over them, and a wet fog crept up from a playground. Migrating geese flew above us, uttering their thin wild cry.

Adam took a gulp from his glass and sat down on a swing. 'Something happened,' he said. 'On that trip.'

My heart sped up. 'Tell me.'

He shook his head, but he didn't seem able to stop. Secrets poured out of him. Spilt. The Serbs, he said, had arrested a man in Belgrade. They had planted a stash of AK47s in his wife's wardrobe because he had information they wanted. The Foreign Office wanted it too. 'I can't tell you any more,' he said. 'Dave would crucify me.' He peered behind me, as if Dave might be concealed under the slide.

'I thought you were working on a Bosnian project.'

'Yes, but – oh, bollocks to it!' He drained the contents of his glass, clenching his free hand round the chain of the swing. 'I was talking to some people in Mostar. While I was there, I got an emergency call. Dave needed me in Serbia, right away. The Bosnians flew me over their border and I rode a Serb Army truck to a compound in the middle of nowhere. We drove off the map. Bojan –' he checked himself – 'the *source* was tied to a chair in a concrete room. Naked. Hadn't slept for three days. Guards ringing bells and flashing torches in his face.'

The geese had stopped calling out to each other, as if they had fallen from the sky.

'He had blue eyes,' Adam said. 'I can't stop seeing them.' He rubbed his hand over his face. 'The Serb interrogator kept asking, "Where is he? Where is he?"' He rubbed his face again. 'You know what I wrote in my incident report? "The source was uncooperative, so the Serb interrogator used physical force to persuade him."'

Very quietly, I asked, 'What did *you* do?'

His mouth got tight. 'That's the problem. I didn't do anything.'

'But I saw your hand. When you got back.'

'No – god, no. Nothing like that. I smacked it into a wall. I was – it was a fucking mess.' The glass he was holding cracked loudly and he lurched off the swing. 'Fuck,' he said. 'Fuck!'

'You're bleeding,' I gasped.

He cradled his cut hand, breathing convulsively. I could see deep gashes near his wrist. 'Come back to the Embassy,' I begged. 'They'll have first aid.'

He shook his head clumsily, pulling back from me. 'Dave doesn't drink. I don't want him to see me like this.'

'Adam, I can't patch you up!' My hand fluttered over his, afraid of touching it. Blood kept dripping and spilling from his wrist, horribly familiar.

He breathed in raggedly. 'Call a taxi. Ambulance is no good – they'd all come out. Just get me to A&E.'

Dear god. My fingers trembling with haste. I slid his jacket off my shoulders to find his phone. 'Five minutes,' a cool female voice told me. I started to pull the gory splinters out of his palm, my stomach turning.

'Gently,' he said, wincing away. I used his handkerchief for a bandage – ruining forever the neat lines of the Union Jack.

'Hold still,' I warned him, knotting the sodden silk.

'Thank you,' he said, repeating with drunken redundancy, 'Thank you.'

The taxi headlights came through the hedge as I was helping him put on his jacket, to hide his stained shirt. We hurried out of the garden and the gate shut behind us, its key lost in the grass. The streetlamps lit up my splotched dress. Adam said, 'Ah, Laura. I got you all bloody.'

'Hush,' I said, opening the taxi door. 'It doesn't matter.'

CHAPTER 13

I rose early, while Adam was still asleep. I didn't wake him. What he'd started to tell me last night had got mixed up with broken glass and blood. I desperately wanted to ask him more questions, but for the first time ever, I felt uneasy around him. I had married a man who bought the *Big Issue* and picked up lost gloves – someone who wouldn't hurt a spider. That's what I had always believed.

In the kitchen I made a pot of apple tea. It was cold by the time he came down. He shielded his eyes against the light, the bandage on his hand a shocking, crusty red. 'Do you need me to change that?' I asked him.

'Maybe later.' He came over to where I was standing. 'There's something I didn't tell you yesterday,' he said quietly. 'Dave is offering me a promotion. He wants us to move to Serbia for a year.'

Simply to occupy my hands, I picked up the teapot. So that's what Dave had been driving at. 'No,' I said. 'I'm from Bosnia, Adam.'

'I know it's a lot to ask.' His pulse was fast, I could see it in his throat. 'Martin is handling some big projects at the embassy in Belgrade. There's too much work for one person. Plus he's run into some problems with the Serbs.'

I thought of Martin last night, dishevelled and pernickety. Adam would be a better fit for Serbia, I saw that. But I didn't want to live there. 'Can you refuse?' I said.

He gave a reluctant nod. 'Dave says it's my choice.'

I fished the leaves out of the teapot with a long spoon and tipped them into the recycling bin. Then I swilled out the pot with cold water and put it upside-down on the draining rack. 'He's pushing you too hard,' I said. 'Yesterday—' I shrugged, feeling helpless. 'I feel like you're changing.'

'Would that be so bad?' His fair skin took on a high, dark colour.

'Look, an emergency came up last time I was away. It wasn't a normal situation. But the project Dave's asking me to take on in Belgrade is a desk job – an important one.' He ran one hand round the back of his neck. 'He's not pushing me into it. I think I ought to go.'

Dropping my gaze to my own hands, I saw them start to tremble. 'Could you come home at weekends?' I found myself asking. 'Have you thought about that? It's a short flight.'

'Ah,' he said. 'Ahh, Laura. It's not nine-to-five.'

I couldn't believe this was happening. Still without looking at him, I said, 'The Serbs attacked Sarajevo.'

'Believe it or not, their government wants to atone for that.' He leant his undamaged hand against the wall. 'We could get you a job teaching English at Belgrade University – maybe even a bit of translation. You keep saying you want to start earning again.'

'It's only been a few weeks.'

'I know that. I just mean … it's a cosmopolitan city. I don't think you'd hate it, if you gave it a go.'

I turned away. Why *not* give it a go? Teaching at a university would bring my dreams of becoming a translator closer. I said, 'Atone how?'

'I can't tell you the details. I'm sorry. This project is huge for Bosnia, that's all I can say.' His hand bumped gently against the wall. 'I'd be able to take a really decent holiday afterwards. We could go to Croatia, if you wanted. Spend some time with your dad.' He gave me his old, lopsided grin. 'I might even learn my way round a kitchen.'

'Pigs might sing.' I spoke sharply, but I felt myself softening at the thought of us visiting Dubrovnik together – of Adam trying to roast peppers and gut fish. I said, 'Do you promise it would only be for a year?'

He nodded. 'Twelve months. Scout's honour.' Colour flooded into his face. 'You won't regret it.'

'I'll think about it,' I said.

The following week I found myself at a meeting with Adam and Dave. I had hoped to get inside Whitehall, but Dave chose the Rose Pub instead – an outdoor table by the Thames, with splintery benches. When he saw me, he stood up and took my hands in both of his. 'Welcome,' he said, with an air of admitting me into his own private drawing room. 'You'll notice that I do let Adam see the sun sometimes.' He settled back onto the bench. 'Now, I have some conditions about Belgrade.'

'Conditions?' I said. 'I thought I was doing you a favour?'

Adam looked alarmed, but Dave said, 'Just listen.' He laced his hands over his belly. 'It doesn't need to be a secret that you're going, but I don't want you shouting it from the rooftops either. Family and close friends only.'

'What if people ask?'

'Find a story to tell them.'

I picked up my wineglass, feeling rebellious. 'I've got a condition too,' I told him. 'I want a job while I'm away.'

He blinked. 'This isn't a bargaining session.'

Adam said quickly, 'Martin has a friend at Belgrade University, the Vice-Dean of Philology.' He cleared his throat. 'He says Laura can teach some English conversation classes, and first year translation.'

'Well then, have Martin arrange it.' Dave turned back to me. 'I'm afraid you can't see the Bosnian members of your family while you're abroad. That's non-negotiable.' He splayed his hands on the table, one on either side of an empty ashtray. 'You don't go to them. They don't come to you. Am I making myself clear?'

I hesitated. I didn't like his tone. Also, I was worried about Tata's reaction. He wasn't a bigot, but he had problems with proportion, with scale. He remembered particular Serb soldiers and inferred a national psyche from them. When he heard I was moving to Belgrade, he would explode in historically charged horror – *No, no, no!* – striding about on his house phone, twirling the tight green cord. A cosmopolitan city, I reminded myself. But he wouldn't see

87

it like that. And if I didn't visit him all year? In the end, though, I closed my eyes and nodded. I felt Adam's relief at once: the way his breath huffed out, his shoulders fell.

'Good,' said Dave, ignoring my reluctance. 'Then we'll have you both there by the end of the month. I think my secretary can handle the other details.' As he heaved himself out of the space between bench and table, he stopped to make one final point. 'I said this to Katy Lyon, Laura, and now I'll say it to you – there are some Serb nationalists who are hostile to Adam's key project. We're encountering resistance from the government and the military, as well as the general public. You're in Belgrade at my discretion. If I tell you to come home, that's what you'll do.'

I got my approval for temporary residence in Serbia three days later, together with a working visa. And the day after that, a one-way plane ticket to Belgrade.

It happened so fast. If I'd had more time, would I have chosen differently? I don't think so. When I first moved to England, I had tried to keep Bosnia out of my mind. But then, slowly, I let things surface. Recipes. Memories. The old woman with her coffeepot. Staring down at my plane ticket, I found myself thinking of what Adam had told me about *Twelfth Night*. The Balkan peninsula of Shakespeare's imagination is home to dreamers, fighters and visionaries. I used to think I was done with that world. Now I was on my way back to it.

SERBIA

2010-2011

CHAPTER 14

Adam and I took an evening flight to Nikola Tesla airport on the last Sunday of August. As the screen showed us cutting across Croatia, the green plane on its arc of dots, I opened up one of my books. Adam said, 'What's that about?'

'The dangers of literal translation.'

He gave me a look. 'When you packed your hand luggage, you didn't think a romance might be easier going?'

'Romance is overrated,' I retorted. 'If I want a story with a happy ending, I'll read a cookbook.'

'Touché.' He tapped his chest, as if a fencing foil had struck him in the heart. 'So, am I in trouble?'

It took me a moment to realise that he wasn't talking about romance but about my book. And if the author was right, he was in trouble there, too. He had always been a very literal translator. I supposed it was his job, but it was also his nature. He wanted to make language unslippery – to pin it down. Whereas I liked meaning to be elusive, and also various.

Katy Lyon was at Arrivals to meet us, wearing a sky-blue hat and fawn chinos, as if Belgrade was half beach resort, half frontier town. While Adam wheeled our suitcase trolley towards the car park, she explained that most government staff were housed near each other. 'Martin and I live two doors down from you,' she said, waving her keys until a second-hand Fiat flashed and chirruped. If Adam had known this in advance, he hadn't said anything. Now he rolled his eyes at me – *Make the best of it!* – and set about stacking our cases in the Fiat's boot, which smelt faintly of tobacco and strongly of bleach. 'You'd better ride shotgun,' Katy told him. 'Your legs are longest. Just shove my shopping over in the back, Laura.'

She drove with a mix of timidity and bravado, nosing into busy traffic, swinging haphazardly across lanes. In the dark I could see little more of the city than its green road signs. As we crossed the immense Sava River, lights glinting on the water, Katy kept up a steady chatter. 'Zvezdanka Street is a bit shabby, but it's so convenient. Only ten minutes from the Embassy. Martin walks to work.' She turned left at a whitewashed church, coming to a stop outside a small, square house. The walls were a patchy concrete, the windows grimy with dust.

Leaving the Fiat parked skew-wiff on the curb, Katy led the way up a gravel drive. 'It's very spacious,' she assured me. 'Don't think about the plumbing.' She unlocked the front door to reveal a dingy hallway with a threadbare rug that ran its full length. Adam put down our cases, yawning frankly enough that she took the hint. 'I'll leave you to settle in.' She turned back to me. 'It's my half day tomorrow. I'm going shopping on Prince Michael Street, if you'd like to come?'

But I wanted to adjust to Serbia slowly, like walking into a cold sea. 'Maybe next time,' I told her.

Once we were alone, Adam switched off the hall light. 'Bear with me,' he said, dragging a chair out of another room and standing on it to unscrew the bulb. He did the same in the living room, which boasted a chintzy three-piece-suite and an old TV set, then in the homely kitchen, where battered saucepans hung over a communist-era stove, and finally in the bathroom and bedrooms upstairs. He also ran his hands under each item of furniture in turn. 'If Dave ever sacks me, I've got a future as an electrician,' he joked.

I said, 'You'd look good in cargo trousers.' But secretly I was unnerved. Who would bug our apartment? A nationalist faction of the Serb government, or of the military?

It was late by the time he finished and we were both tired. Yet sleep eluded me. Scooters puttered on the street below, more frequent and less throaty than the Hampstead motorbikes. At one point I heard a hoarse, startling scream. 'Fox,' Adam murmured. 'Nothing to worry about.' So I lay awake, worrying about nothing.

I woke up vaguely when he kissed me goodbye, then again to bright sunlight. The first thing I did was to take in the rest of the house: the bathroom scrubbed clean, but host to a sour whiff of mould; the kitchen old-fashioned, its plywood cupboards stocked with goat's cheese and sourdough and loose-leaf tea. I thought I recognised Katy's touch. Back upstairs, I put our clothes in a closet. Our books I left on the floor, since there were no shelves. I would have to fix that. But for now, I was still exploring. On the far wall of the bedroom was a Juliet balcony, little more than a dimpled grill. I opened the windows as far as I could, leaning into the rush of noise and brightness that was Zvezdanka Street.

Below me was a narrow road with parking for well-kempt, low-fendered cars. The buildings on the other side, faintly brutalist, went a long way up. There was a strong smell of exhaust fumes, and a sweet, yeasty odour from a café that had a hand-painted sign: КАФЕ ЊЕГОШЕВА. I grew up with Latin script – Cyrillic reminded me of the fake Serbian papers we'd once used to trick our way out of Sarajevo. But it was only an alphabet. Now that I lived here, I ought to learn it.

While I was thinking about this, a white-haired old man in a tweed suit came out of the café and tipped his hat to me. 'Dobar dan,' he called up, in what was unmistakeably a British accent. I raised my hand and smiled, warmed by the friendly greeting. He had a walrus moustache, and he carried a small parcel, wrapped in decorative paper, which made my stomach growl. But I shrank from exploring Belgrade by myself, even to get food. Adam's meetings at the Embassy were due to finish in the early afternoon. I would wait for him.

To blunt my appetite, I ate some of Katy's supplies. Afterwards I turned to our slim trove of books – a handful of novels, and two or three of Adam's old university texts. I picked up an anthology of Bosnian war poems. Until today I had always avoided it. Why change my mind now? But on the first page Hamdija Demirović had written, "I know the stars are sticky," and I was lost, surrendering

93

to the authority of his voice. From Sarajevo, the Pleiades used to look as bright and close as a newly painted ceiling. I could remember Mama boarding up my bedroom window with screws and plywood, singing in a low voice, as if to say goodbye to them.

A few loud noises broke through my concentration as I read – turbofolk playing on a radio in another building, a van with a loudspeaker that was broadcasting the slogans of the Serbian Radical Party. But when Adam got home, I looked up to find the light had turned to orange, and half an afternoon had slipped away.

'Sorry I'm late,' he said. 'Endless faff – Martin doesn't change.' He took off his tie. 'How was your day?'

'My day was fine.'

'You did some exploring?'

'Actually, I stayed in.'

A stitch of worry appeared between his eyes, but all he said was, 'Yesterday must have tired you out. Do you feel like going into town for dinner? Martin recommended a kafana.'

I put on my shoes reluctantly and waited for him to change the rest of his clothes. The hallway had a cracked stucco ceiling and a dank, loamy smell. WELCOME, said the doormat, in English. I hadn't noticed it last night. Now I decided to believe you could be welcomed out, as well as in.

We didn't have a car yet, so we took a tram to Knez Mihailova Street. The tram was exactly as I remembered it from my childhood: rattly, uncomfortable, governed by a clutch of overhead wires. 'Vintage,' Adam said, with casual appreciation. I leant my cheek against the window and watched a group of blue-jeaned men saunter along the pavement. They were Tata's age – old enough to have been soldiers, I realised. My heart rate quickened. Just for a moment, through the warped window glass, I saw their denim stiffen into uniforms and rifles sprout on their shoulders. They fell behind as the tram pulled off, but my heart continued its wild patter. For the rest of the journey, I set myself the sobering task of counting the militant Serbian eagles that dotted this city, fluttering on flags and carved in stone. My legs stuck to the sunbaked plastic seats, and when I stood up I felt like I was being peeled out of my skin.

The kafana turned out to be a pristine little place, with double rows of outdoor tables and jars of droopy flowers. As if we were on holiday, Adam pointed out everything I might find interesting: a guzla player, a street artist with wild black hair. But I made a distracted tourist. Behind us, a Serbian woman answered her phone and I sought out the moments of elision – *gde* for *gdje*, *lep* for *lijep* – that made her voice sound foreign to me.

We ordered beer from a busy waiter. Boys strolled by in leather jackets, girls in heels and little else. 'Meet you at the horse,' they told each other, peeling apart into garishly lit shops. Adam told me the horse was a statue, with Prince Mihailović riding on it. I said nothing. In my head I was making lists:

Familiar
The bakery smells.
The trams.
The high-heeled shoes.

Unfamiliar
The heat.
The Cyrillic street signs.
The absence of the call to prayer.

'Penny for them?' he said.

I shook my head. 'Tell me about your first day.'

'There's not much to say.' He glanced around us, but the tables were well-spaced and the noisy street masked our conversation. 'I share an office with Martin. Tomorrow, he'll introduce me to the Serb Action Team.'

'Can I ask a question?'

'Of course.'

'Dave said the Serb nationalists don't like your key project. But if organised crime in Bosnia has links to Belgrade, why wouldn't they want to tackle it?'

'Organised crime?' Adam repeated blankly. A beat too late, he said, 'The opposition we're facing is largely political. Some people don't want us involved.' And he nudged my foot, pointing at a tiny dog in a handbag, with impossibly big, whiskery ears. I smiled, but my mind was reeling. It was the first evasion I had ever caught him in. Now we were here, was this how things were going to be?

Our food arrived: a salad for me, a plate of grilled meat for Adam. He put out his hand to stop the waiter. 'Sorry, could I have a steak knife?' he asked, in fluent Serbian. 'Or just a sharp knife from the kitchen, that would be fine.' I found myself watching how he did it – the mix of friendliness and self-deprecation that made people want to help him. He didn't demand, he beguiled.

As the waiter went off for the knife, I said, 'Will we have your colleagues to dinner soon, like in London?' I wanted to hear about his project – the one that was not, after all, to do with organised crime – and I also wanted to know more about the Serb Action Team. Did they understand how brightly the stars shone above Sarajevo? Had they ever been forced to board up a window to stop a sniper killing a child?

Adam shrugged and picked up his beer. 'I don't think so. Except Martin, of course. And Peter, if he comes out. Look, it's better not to talk about my job too much in public. Is something wrong?'

'Nothing's wrong,' I said, gathering myself.

On the tram back to Zvezdanka Street, he said very little; he just hooked his arm over the back of my seat. 'In a year we'll be back to normal.' That was one thing he did say. But I was starting to realise we didn't have a normal. The labels were still on our wedding presents.

CHAPTER 15

Right from the start, Adam worked long hours at the Embassy. I began to go out just to escape the empty apartment. My first solo journey was to the public library – a large, pink, self-satisfied building with windows overlooking Kalemegdan Park. Having signed up as a borrower, I left with a Cyrillic alphabet and four detective novels. On other occasions, I visited the tall white temple of Saint Sava, and Kalenić market. In these places I found myself recalling Sarajevo so vividly that I almost seemed to be there. A pair of black swans used to swim on the Miljacka River, grave alter-egos of the white swans. My old street had smelt of viburnum flowers – a peculiar incense, like the hot sugared nuts that hawkers sold all over Belgrade, but sweeter.

Serbian voices rang up and down Zvezdanka Street every evening, and a smell of hair oil and cologne lingered on the air. Once, feeling lonely, I went to see Katy. I heard her raised voice inside as I rang the bell. Martin opened the door with blue paint spattered over his forehead, as if she'd just thrown a paintbrush at him. 'You've caught us at a bad time,' he apologised.

Adam laughed about this when he finally got home. 'Katy models herself on artists she admires,' he said. 'Right now, she's Jackson Pollock.'

That night I lay awake for hours, watching the alarm clock on his bedside table scroll through our time in Belgrade.

It was at the end of the second week that I made a friend of my own. We were on our way home from a hardware store on Saturday afternoon when we bumped into the old man with the moustache – the one who passed under our balcony most mornings carrying a cake. 'Oops-a-daisy,' he said, stooping carefully to pick up the bag I had dropped.

'Thank you,' I said.

He raised his hat. I think it was ingrained in him, that gesture of old-fashioned courtesy and louche charm. 'William Littleton,' he said. 'And you are the beautiful girl from the balcony.'

Adam laughed. 'Mr Littleton, meet my wife, Laura Quin.'

'Wife! You're both so young. What brings you to Belgrade?'

'I'm a civil servant, sir.'

William Littleton's eyes brightened and sharpened. 'I worked at the Embassy myself, once upon a time. In those days it covered a lot of interesting sins.' He touched the edge of his moustache. 'Quin, did you say? That rattles a bell. I believe an old colleague told me you were moving out here. David Focket?' Adam shifted the weight of the bag he was carrying to his other hand. 'I mustn't keep you,' our new acquaintance said gravely, 'but an idea has just slugged me. Since we're neighbours, why not pop round tonight for a drink?'

We spent that afternoon putting up our new bookshelves. 'Are you jealous that Mr Littleton called me the beautiful girl from the balcony?' I teased Adam.

'Mortally jealous. Look, be careful what you say tonight. Nothing about what I'm doing here.'

I sat back on my heels. 'Of course not. But he knows Big Dave, doesn't he?'

'Maybe. I'll phone Dave on Monday to check.'

The thought of that phone call made me twitchy. I had liked William Littleton, whose language made a self-ironising performance of itself, as if he got it wholesale from old pulp novels. I felt sure he was who he claimed to be. But I was frightened by Adam's distrust. 'The Serb Action Team are against what I'm doing,' I'd heard him complain to Martin only the night before. 'Given half a chance, they'd tie a brick to my feet and dump me in the Sava.' Martin had laughed, but there was real anxiety in Adam's voice. Since coming to Belgrade, he'd introduced habits of secrecy into our daily life. He locked the apartment each night, checking every window. That afternoon we had left one store because he thought someone might be following us. Who would care what shelves we bought? But his wraiths and shadows were starting to affect me. They got into my sleep, so that I woke with a start, my heart pounding.

William Littleton lived two streets away from us, in a jaunty, two-storey house with a yellowing marble facade. Instead of a doorbell he had a lion doorknocker, which brought him promptly to the threshold. He shook Adam's hand and raised mine to his lips. 'Waltz in,' he said, leading us through to a high-ceilinged room. The light was low wattage and the lamps had fringed shades, but I could make out a Turkish rug on the floor and a bar built into the wall. Liqueurs took the place of books for him. Most of them I had never heard of: Kulüp Rakısı, Shwe Lein Maw, a beautiful bottle of something called Kaoliang. This was the den of a world traveller. I liked it a lot.

'Park yourselves wherever looks comfortable,' he invited us, bending stiffly to pick up a newspaper from a dark green armchair. 'May I fix you some drinks? Gin and tonic? Gin martini?' His eyes twinkled at Adam. 'Any dram of scotch your heart desires?'

'Did you say you used to be a civil servant, Mr Littleton?' I asked, when he had made three gin and tonics, fetching a glass bowl of ice complete with tongs, and another of cut limes.

'*William*, my dear. You might say I was a civil servant for seventy years.'

'Seventy years?' Adam repeated, raising his eyebrows in polite incredulity.

William settled back in his chair, hitching the fabric at the knee of his trousers as he crossed his legs, revealing a maroon sock. 'Yes indeed. I was a child at Bletchley, you see, when they cracked the Enigma code during the war. Of course, I wasn't on the payroll then. My mother had been a servant at the house all through the thirties, and they used us children as messengers. We carried notes between the huts in return for chocolate.' He nodded. 'Yes. Those were good days. Gave me a taste for excitement, I suppose. That's why I joined the Service.'

I glanced at Adam, who sipped his drink, his eyes watchful. After a moment I asked, 'What was Bletchley like, Mr – William?'

'A very ugly house. Swarming with women! They started out with a chef from the Ritz. Indeed, they did! Lots of tennis. And love affairs under every bush,' he finished roguishly, winking at me.

It was impossible not to smile back. 'How about the code-breakers?'

'Oh, they were all musical and beautiful and terribly intelligent. A little off their rockers, or so my mother said, and I suppose it was true. Scarecrows, she used to call them, when they came off the night shift. Trousers held up by their neckties, setting fire to themselves with their pipes.' He laughed. 'They kept her busy making tea. Stewed until it was bright orange, with a splash of whisky in it.' Putting down his glass, he turned to Adam. 'Would you build me another drink, son? I'd do it myself, but my knees don't work so well as they once did.'

'With pleasure,' Adam replied. I noted in his voice the faintly mocking, public-school formality he sometimes used to hold people at a distance, but this did not seem misplaced in William's rococo house, nor out of keeping with his own prickly and intentful charm.

'Here's looking at you,' he quipped, when Adam had returned his glass. 'You know, you put me in mind of myself at your age. David Focket tells me you're a safe pair of hands.'

'I hope so, sir,' was all Adam could be drawn to say.

The conversation that night touched on many subjects. Our host described his reasons for retiring here, which came down to chance, he said: Belgrade had been his last posting, and he liked to keep an eye on what was happening at the Embassy. I asked him about the fox I had heard on our first night – there were a few in the city, apparently. And lastly we discussed the covert chauvinism of Serbia, where women did not go to football matches or into certain bars, and public office was overwhelmingly the realm of men. William's moustache was reminiscent of Lloyd George's, and so were his attitudes to equality: he was for it, in principle, but secretly nostalgic for his mother, a woman who wore aprons and was at home in her kitchen. After an hour or so, he said, 'Where did we start from?'

'Bletchley,' I reminded him. 'The code-breakers.'

'Ah yes. Mathematical geniuses, of course. But psychological geniuses too. Dreams and visions.'

Adam sat forwards, interested this time. 'I read that the German operators made lazy mistakes. That's how Enigma got broken.'

William nodded. 'They used swearwords or their girlfriends' names in test messages. Love or sleepiness, who knows which? Certainly not me.' He took another sip of gin. 'Love – ah, well. Love was not one of my success stories.'

'That's hard to believe,' I said gently.

He smiled. 'It's very easy to account for, my dear. Too egotistical. Too hard-working. Too charming to have substance, as my late wife used to tell me. Before she divorced me, I might add.' He glanced down at his hands. I noticed that he wore a wedding ring. 'Marie couldn't stand the embassy world,' he told me, his voice quiet. 'Overseas postings are tough on the wives. Find yourself something to do, that's my advice. And when you meet people you like, stick close to 'em.'

We left soon after that, as he seemed to intend it. He rose from his chair with stiff grace and saw us to the door. 'Goodnight,' he said. 'Tally-ho!'

CHAPTER 16

On the first day of term at Belgrade University, I got up in time to have an early breakfast with Adam. 'I might be a bit late home,' he said, smearing jam on a plain kifla. 'I've set up a ping pong tournament at the Embassy.' He laughed. 'The Serb Action Team is playing in it and so is the National Security Council. That lot have got me snared up in politics – I'm going to enjoy wiping them off the table.'

'I'm teaching this afternoon,' I reminded him, reaching for the jam.

He pantomimed smacking his forehead. 'Sorry, Laura. I've got so much on I forgot.'

The Vice-Dean of Philology had phoned me a fortnight ago to discuss my classes. Nine of his first-year students were taking a comparative paper on British and Serbian culture, with linked translation exercises: could I structure my weekly sessions around that? I didn't know much about Serbian culture, I had told him, alarmed. 'No problem,' he'd said. 'They talk, you correct their English.'

Now I looked at Adam nervously. 'What if I can't do it?'

'You'll be great.' He kissed my forehead, in mock benediction. 'Go forth and teach.'

He crossed a minefield, I told myself on the bus. You can survive nine students.

That afternoon I met them all in one group. I made them Earl Grey tea, which seemed suitably British. My classroom was on the first floor of the Philology building. There was a tiny kitchen opposite, to which I added an Embassy-issue teapot. Both rooms had warped glass in the windows, giving them a shipwrecked, watery feel. The classroom also contained twelve wooden desks and a painting of three men without faces, lifting a rock.

The students arrived in a pack, bringing with them a smell of peppery deodorant. Most of them wore T-shirts with words on in English: for the boys, SORRY, I ONLY DATE MODELS, or LOOK DOWN; for the girls, I MAKE THE RULES, and SUPERSTAR. They took the cups of tea cautiously, as if they might break. One of them also took four lumps of sugar.

'Good morning,' I began, more firmly than I felt. 'Today I want to get to know you. We'll split into smaller groups next week.'

A girl leant forwards – sharp blue eyes under a heavy fringe. 'I-am-Lana,' she told me, in phrasebook English. 'Please-to-meet-you.' She was the sugar taker.

'Are you from England?' asked a short, sallow boy, with black hair.

'I'm Bosnian', I said, a little too quickly. 'My family moved to England in the war.'

'Better for you.' He shrugged. 'Bosnia is dump.' The blue-eyed girl, Lana, elbowed him. 'What?' he demanded, with the self-absorption peculiar to teenagers. 'She is English now.'

Lana turned to me apologetically. 'He is in bad mood because of hangover. We are dancing late last night.'

'We like Beyoncé,' one of the other girls blurted out.

'Beyoncé is not English,' Lana objected. 'She is American. The Florence Machine is English – we like her too. They are playing her on the splavs.'

'The splavs?' I said.

'In Belgrade to dance you go on a splav, on the river. If you don't like its music you go to another. Midnight thirty is the best time. Before midnight there is no point.'

Now a second boy spoke up, a tall one, with bright curls that fell into his eyes. 'You can otherwise go to Sevdah café. They play on your ear – you order favourite song, they play just for you and your table.' While he was talking, I glanced surreptitiously at my sheet of photographs and names. He was Danilo; the shorter boy was Vuk. Then there was a muddle of brunettes, of both sexes.

Danilo broke off what he was saying as Lana popped a sugar lump into her mouth and crunched it. 'You are like horse!' he objected. 'That sugar is for tea, not to eat.'

'Sorry! Sorry!'

'No problem,' I told her, trying not to smile.

She wiped her lips self-consciously. 'When I was child I liked sweets. In the war with Kosovo my family could not afford black market, so if I saw sugar I ate it. Now it is my habit.'

'When I was child, I am wishing to be soldier,' Vuk chimed in. 'This type of stuff where you're drinking, fighting, having fun.'

Danilo gave me an uneasy glance. 'Man, you got all the wrong ideas. Do you even remember the wars? In Bosnia and Kosovo there wasn't drinking – there wasn't even water. Now we have to live with all that death, all that terrible thing.'

Vuk blew his nose. 'Only wrong thing with wars was how they ended. Every place that Serbs live should be part of Serbia.'

'*The* only wrong thing,' I corrected him. '*Those* wars.' I didn't trust myself to say more.

After that he sat silently through the rest of the lesson. At one point I said, 'Vuk, do you have anything else to contribute?'

'No,' he said.

Lana and Danilo looked at each other, and Danilo rolled his eyes.

I handed out a printed reading list from the Vice-Dean, along with a paragraph from a Serbian folk tale that I'd found in the library. It was about a young woman who expects to die in a wood full of wolves, but she meets a monster in a bearskin who turns out to be a prince. 'I'll teach you in threes,' I told them. 'You can decide on your own groups. Just make sure you email your translations to me at least a day before we next meet.' Then I let them go.

On their way out they passed under my open window. I overheard Lana say to one of the other girls, 'I like her.' I didn't hear the reply, but as they walked away their laughter floated up to me. So, that was teaching. I was smiling as I collected the silted cups.

After I left the Philology building, I wandered through Kalemegdan Park, across the sunbeaten grass. *Kalemegdan* means battlefield. The park had been one, off and on, for two thousand years. It still smelt of gunpowder. As my initial elation began to drain away, I found myself thinking about what Vuk had said. *Only wrong thing with wars was how they ended.* Who brings up a child to think like that?

I passed the fortress, which had a bulgy squareness – old bricks battered out of shape. Then I came to a collection of tanks, blunt and ugly and low to the ground, with long, deathful snouts. Sitting on a bench nearby were two old women, one of them wearing a blue headscarf. I knew almost no-one in Serbia. Even so, I was certain I recognised her. 'I'm worried for my grandson,' I heard her say to her friend, in Bosnian. And now, of course, I knew where I had seen her before – in Hampstead, as she boiled a pot of coffee in my kitchen. 'He's in a rock band with three older boys,' she went on. 'They call themselves Histerija. They worship some London noiseniks by name of Led Zip Pin.'

I laughed before I could help myself. 'Zeppelin,' I corrected her. She looked right at me. 'Zeppelin?'

'Young people just glue their eyes to the West,' said her friend, as if I hadn't spoken. 'It's always been that way.'

'Yes, but I don't like their music.' The coffee-pot woman frowned. 'All that banging and shouting. "We will conquer! We will conquer!" I asked my grandson, 'What is this conquer?' He said the Serbs will murder every imam and burn every mosque if we don't fight back. Such a quiet boy, he used to be. Now he thinks he'll grow up into arms.'

I walked quickly on, until I came to the place where the Danube meets the Sava. My heart was beating fit to burst. For a while I just stood there, breathing in the bitter, saltless smell of the two big rivers. What was the other thing Vuk had said? *She is English now.* But on that bank, with the words of the two old women echoing in my mind, I felt hostile to Serbia in ways that weren't English at all.

Back at the apartment, I started cooking kvrguša in an attempt to calm down. I seared chicken thighs. I mixed batter. I had almost finished when Adam phoned to say the table tennis players were going out for a beer. 'Why not drop in on Katy tonight?' he suggested. 'Martin's with me, so she'll be glad of the company.'

'Do you have to stay out?'

'For a few hours, yes.' He sounded hassled. 'This is part of my job, Laura.'

I didn't need to see him, I told myself, a little defiantly, as I hung up the phone. The shock of the coffee-pot woman's reappearance was already fading. The same thing had happened last time – absent, she seemed to drift from my mind. Even so, I didn't want to spend this evening alone. Nor did I want to see Katy. On impulse I took the kvrguša I had just made to William Littleton. 'It's a Bosnian chicken bake,' I explained, when he opened the door. All courteous surprise, he invited me in to help him eat it. Did I mind if he smoked? Not at all, I assured him. I laid the table while he lit a cigarette, which burnt with a musty smell, like seaweed.

As we ate, I told him about my students. He called Vuk *the brat*. 'How's Adam finding the Embassy?' he asked, with a mischievous twinkle. So he'd noticed my husband's reluctance to talk about his work. Feeling myself blush, I became wholly absorbed in mopping up a drop of sauce that had fallen onto the table. I was afraid that by dodging his question I would damage something that scarcely existed yet – some stirring of friendship. But William said kindly, 'Get him to look up my records. Until then we won't talk about it.' He dabbed his napkin to his lips. 'Whereabouts in Bosnia are you from?'

'Sarajevo,' I told him, grateful for the change of subject.

'Ah.' He lit another musty cigarette. 'A wonderful city. The jewel of the Balkans.'

'You've been?'

'I worked there in the eighties. I also flew into Butmir airport during the war.' He gave me a look that I couldn't interpret. 'I met

Ratko Mladić on the runway. A Reuters journalist was trying to get an interview. A very brave young man – American, I believe. Mladić close to throttled him. Bloodshot eyes. Stank of booze. He'd lost all sense of proportion by then – he held the power of death over so many people, he thought he was god.'

A chill went through me. 'It sounds like he stuck in your mind.'

'Well, he was my last job.' William tapped his cigarette over his plate. 'He dropped off the grid after Slobodan Milosević was arrested. I was here with the Foreign Office at the time, trying to persuade the Serbian Army to hand him over. That's how I came to wash up in Belgrade.'

I looked at him with respectful amazement – this man in his eighties, his shirt marked by spots of ash. 'You're not washed up,' I told him. He was lonely though. I could see that.

When I got back to Zvezdanka Street, Adam opened our front door before I found my key. 'Where *were* you?' he demanded. 'I was worried sick.'

'I had dinner with William Littleton.'

'For pity's sake, Laura.' A muscle beside his eye was jumping. 'Why didn't you answer your phone?'

I fished my mobile out of my handbag. Five missed calls. 'Sorry,' I mumbled. 'I wasn't expecting you home this early.' Slipping off my outdoor shoes, I went into the living room and sat down on the sofa. Adam leant stiffly against the wall. All this fuss seemed unreasonable to me. What was I meant to do on the evenings I didn't spend with him or Katy? Darn his socks and keep the home fire burning? 'William wants you to look up his records,' I told him.

'I did that this morning. I also talked to Dave.' Adam hunched his shoulders. 'The old man really is ex Civil Service. Apparently he's a bit of an oddball.'

I felt a rush of resentment against Dave. 'He's not odd!'

'Well, he's harmless.' Adam's voice softened. 'I was worried about you. Next time check with me first, okay?'

'Okay.' I moved my legs so he could join me on the sofa, slightly ashamed of myself now. I had promised to be on my guard in Belgrade, but instead I had opened myself up to unsanctioned encounters of various kinds, and I had only told Adam about one of them.

Even so, I felt a secret relief. Perhaps I could bend the rules enough to live inside them – enough to know and be known.

CHAPTER 17

Life everywhere tends towards patterns. The garbage men came to Zvezdanka Street on Mondays – I learnt to sleep through the sound of dragging bins, the Turbo-folk blaring from their radio. Katy went jogging every Wednesday after school, while trim Serbian ladies watched in astonishment from their windows. In Belgrade no one sweated in public. And on Thursdays, William Littleton and I ate cakes together in the café up the road.

At first I phoned Tata often, but I could hear a coolness in his voice, a hurt forming. During my wedding I had promised to visit Dubrovnik. Now I was out of excuses.

He said, 'Is it Adam who won't come? Does he not treat you well?'

'That's such an old-fashioned question, Tata.'

'I am old-fashioned.' He reverted to his original grievance. 'Family is important.'

'I know it is. Adam's very busy at work.'

'Come by yourself.'

'I can't,' I said.

'You just don't want to.'

After that we didn't speak to each other again. It was easier to let the silence between us swell.

At least I had my teaching. On the whole my students seemed to like me – because I made them Earl Grey tea, I suspect, rather than for any more scholarly reason. Also, because I digressed. They wanted to hear about England, so I talked about queues and crumpets, and I taught them *bloody hell* and *bollocks*. In spite of these detours, I felt pride in the fact that their translations were improving. 'Accuracy can take strange forms,' I kept reminding them. 'Look hard at what lies behind the words.'

The day before my birthday, I smuggled white wine and homemade Chelsea buns into the Philology building. 'Is it bread?' Lana guessed doubtfully.

'Not exactly,' I told her. 'It's an English treat.'

Everyone apart from Vuk had come. They stood in a semicircle and Danilo presented a birthday card to me. 'Thank you,' I said. I wanted to say, Bless you. Giving those words their widest scope. At home I put their card beside the others on my bedside table. Katy Lyon's was there, and Roisin's. For the first time, Tarik had also sent one.

On my birthday itself, Adam gave me a bracelet with a single charm on it – a tiny silver deer. 'Remember that day?' he asked me. Of course I did. I thought of our closeness back then with a pang of regret. Where had it gone? But I put the bracelet on at once, holding out my wrist so he could help me with the clasp.

I invited William Littleton to dinner that evening, in his role of adopted grandfather. When I asked him what he'd most like to eat, he proposed an old-fashioned English roast. All day I tried to fill the apartment with homely fragrances. I broke bread and blessed it, if that's not a blasphemous thing to say. And I didn't intend it blasphemously. I did hope some kind of blessing would come out of that meal.

'Heaven smells like this,' William said, when I opened the door to him. 'Bread sauce and chestnut stuffing. If I find I'm wrong, I will come back down to earth and haunt your kitchen.'

He prowled the room, a glass of vermouth in his hand. He'd brought the bottle from his house. 'These are a reproach to me,' he observed, pausing by a bookshelf. 'All my life people have been giving me books, but I never get round to reading them.'

Adam said, 'I think Laura's read everything we brought out here. Even the cookery books.'

William smiled at me. 'Especially the cookery books.'

I hid a tiny feeling of irritation. I loved him dearly, but he insisted on seeing me as a homemaker.

110

I had put a fresh cloth on the table, and candles in brass holders that I found in a cupboard. We ate at seven. The light was already gone, so the windows reflected our faces back at us. The chicken bulged under its amber skin, fragrant with nutmeg and herbs. I asked William if he would carve but he shook his head. 'It's a privilege to be waited on, my dear. I trust Adam to do a better job than I could.'

The pale slices fell away under Adam's knife. 'I did read a book last time I was in London,' William said. 'The first few pages of it, anyway. I found it on one of those tables they put in the middle of second-hand bookshops for old men to trip over. A history of the British Civil Service.' He took a last bird-sip of vermouth. 'I learnt a curious fact. When Vernon Kell set up MI5, he had his new recruits gallop across the country on horseback, making notes on their shirt-cuffs. Did you ever hear the like of that?'

I glanced uneasily at Adam. Exactly how much he'd unbent his guard to William was still not clear to me. But for now, he was dividing brown meat from breast meat as if that alone concerned him. I picked up a serving spoon. 'Was it Vernon Kell who wanted all the girls who worked for him to be well bred and have good legs?'

William laughed. 'I don't doubt it was! May I have three potatoes, dear heart?'

'Same for me, please,' Adam said. He moved the plattered chicken to the kitchen counter, careful of its remaining juices. As he sat down, he turned to William. 'I've read a few books on the origins of the Secret Services. Your rider was basically an early Signals Intelligence Officer – twenty-first century eavesdropping is just a bit more sophisticated.' His voice got quieter. 'Interrogation methods haven't changed at all.'

I watched him carefully, though I went on serving roast potatoes. I guessed he was thinking of what had happened in that army bunker.

'Interrogation is no Sunday school picnic,' William said comfortably. 'I saw some of it in my time. It requires a steady hand and a cool heart.'

'But you do think it's justified?' Adam leant forwards, his face troubled but intent. 'You remember the forties, and you worked for the government all through the Cold War. I want to hear your view.'

William shook his head. 'I think we're coming at this from different angles, son. Your generation insists the human body is sacred, but you've got nothing to enforce it except yourselves. So of course you worry that the damage you do is on your hands. It was simpler back then. We left the question of sacredness to god. And we fought bloodier and more absolute wars than you are ever likely to. If we were satisfied about the need for something, I don't believe we racked our souls too severely over the methods.'

'What if the war is over,' Adam asked, 'and it's a question of bringing someone to justice?'

'Civil servanthood is an old idea. I think that's the root of your trouble. I *am* old, so for me it's no trouble at all. I take the view that a servant of the state must do what the state perceives to be necessary. Reason not the need! Perhaps I'm wrong, perhaps in this day and age you must also bring your own reason to bear. That's something I can't tell you. I do suspect it makes things harder.'

Adam nodded – thoughtful, very distant. He was pursuing someone, I could tell. But I was tired of half hearing about it. If we weren't going to talk frankly, what was the point?

'Nobody's eating,' I protested. 'I got up early to stuff this chicken and now it's going cold before my eyes.'

William roused himself. 'I'm savouring every morsel on my plate. There's steam still coming off it. I'm sorry, dear heart. I've got a terrible lust for talking shop.'

And Adam gave me a rueful smile, acknowledging the gravy and stuffing and thinly cut meat, but preoccupied in spite of it. Hidden from view, I thought, though he was eating and drinking with us in plain sight.

Throughout the rest of that meal, William described the Foreign Office in the sixties, exaggerating himself deliberately for my enjoyment. 'It was a one hundred per cent rodeo!' In his stories the secretaries were all incomparably beautiful, with sultry eyes and plunging necklines. When he remembered to, he called them 'dames.'

'Tell me about your wife, William,' I said, handing him a slice of birthday cake, nut-thick, and a glass from the last bottle of the wine Tata had given us as a wedding present, the Graševina. It tasted different this time. Less sweet.

'Thank you, lass.' He sipped the wine slowly. 'Marie was a lovely woman, a real firecracker. She deserved a world of attention and I saw it too late. She had every right to divorce me.' He sighed. 'She died young. She'd just turned sixty.'

'You never thought of remarrying?'

'No. No, Marie was the woman for me.'

Later, after coffee, Adam and I saw him to the door. In the lamp-lit street he turned and waved to us. 'Night-night. It was a wonderful party.'

We watched him walk out of sight – stiffly gallant, a little unsteady on his feet. Then we went inside to do the washing up. I washed; Adam dried. The crusted pans. Gravy-thick plates.

'I've got some news,' he said. 'I'm going away with work again.'

I turned to him, holding a soapy knife. 'What?'

'It's only for a few days.'

'But—' I stopped. 'You told me you'd be working in Belgrade.'

He shrugged, though he reddened slightly, too. 'This project is important for Bosnia. I thought you'd be supportive.'

'Stop throwing Bosnia up to me! You just do whatever Dave wants of you. He says, "Jump!" and you say, "How far?"'

'It's my job,' he said brusquely. 'There are some people who need to talk to me.'

'Tell them to use the phone,' I snapped. I didn't want to look stupid. But if he went away again, I might not recognise him when he came back. Or he might not come back at all.

'You know it doesn't work like that.' His voice had hardened, but his mouth was twisted. I did know, that was the problem. *What*

113

should we do to bring justice to the Balkans? That was the question he'd been asking over dinner. And William had said we should do whatever is required of us. How could I, of all people, speak out against that?

'Just stay in one piece,' I said at last.

'Do you know I love you?'

'Careful—' I was crying now, trying for laughter. 'I'm still holding a knife.'

CHAPTER 18

Adam was gone for three days on that trip. I feel like my heart didn't beat the whole time – I'm sure I was holding my breath.

The night he was due home, I sat at the table and tried to prepare my teaching notes. What did you expect marriage to be like? I asked myself. There was no answer to that.

By nine o'clock I was on the sofa, marking one of Lana's translations. I had my charm bracelet on, which I wore almost constantly, and I kept rearranging myself into postures of grace. I was trying to look beautiful and desirable, but also unhaunted and serene.

When Adam came in, I jumped up, scattering paper everywhere. 'Sorry I'm late,' he said.

'How was it?' My eyes went instinctively to his hands. There were no new marks that I could see.

'It was fine.' He put his rucksack down and came over to give me a hug. He smelt of himself – of pine and resin. Even so, I felt shy of him. The lack of scars told me nothing. 'Is there any dinner?'

'I thought you'd have eaten.'

'Service station food. The less said the better.' He made himself a cheese sandwich, yawning once or twice. I poured us both a glass of red wine. When he'd finished eating, he pushed back his chair and yawned again. 'I might turn in.'

He used the bathroom first, shaving with the cut-throat razor that never travelled with him, but lay like an instrument of torture on his shelf. I went in and out, quickly, then switched off all the lights before getting into bed. I'd missed him every night he'd been gone, but he didn't reach for me, and I was too proud to move towards him. I could feel his warmth across the mattress. Hear his breathing. 'Goodnight,' I whispered.

'Goodnight.'

I lay awake long after he fell asleep. When we were in Cambridge, he once told me I had a blue-stockinged mind. Now I wished that I could prowl through his head in stockinged feet and trip the switches on the right memories. Our first kiss on the bridge over the river, scarce and gentle. The Portugal Street mornings when he would pick me up and spin me round the kitchen. As the red digits on our alarm clock twitched past midnight, my mind turned to the party at the Bosnian Embassy and the secret he had started to tell me. And then, all at once, I knew what I wanted.

For ages I didn't move. I scarcely breathed. What I was thinking was indefensible: it broke every silent treaty of our marriage. But I told myself that Adam would let my heart go through a thousand contortions simply by saying nothing. He was becoming a stranger on the far side of the bed. At one o'clock, I slid out from under the duvet and crept on bare feet across the creaky boards to the living room, where he had left his rucksack on the floor.

I knelt to open it, my heart in my throat. On top was a layer of dirty socks and shirts; beneath them, his wallet and passport. At the very bottom was a thin manila envelope. It was unsealed. I took it to the moonlit window, and when I turned it upside down a note in pencilled Cyrillic slipped out. Listening for any sound of movement from the bedroom, I began to decipher the alphabet I had learnt, laboriously, from Serbian novels.

Adam,

Very nice to see you in Banjaluka yesterday. Here's the transcript of the Feb '06 audio surveillance you wanted, when we mic'd our friend B. It's good he is cooperating now! The photo of M was taken just before B drove him to the New Belgrade safe house, that we raided too late. It's the last time anyone had eyes on him. No mention of his inner circle, though.

Aleksandar

116

As soon as I finished reading, I turned to the envelope's other contents: a stapled transcript on yellow sheets of paper; and a poor-quality photograph of two men greeting each other in the Balkan fashion, cheek against cheek. In a detached part of my mind, I identified the one on the right as the driver, "your friend B" – B for Bojan, that must be, the man Adam had seen in the bunker. He had a pouchy body, but I could not make out his face because it was hidden behind the face of the other man; nor did I care about his face very much because that other man was General Ratko Mladić, who was wanted on charges of torture and terror and murder that included Mama's death. He looked frailer than he had on the news fifteen years ago. But there was the hated profile: the small eye, the slab of jaw.

My hands shook so badly as I opened the transcript that I became afraid of tearing it. The text was in Cyrillic again, but it was typed, making it easier to read than the note had been. Turning the thin yellow pages, I felt like I was hearing the voice of that war criminal crackling over the microphone, at once formidable and sulky, while Bojan's car rattled through backstreet Belgrade. I imagined the concrete buildings, the linden trees in flower. Outside the safe house there would have been cigarette stubs lying around; on the walls the usual spray-paint vampires and signatures like coils of barbed wire. Bojan would have pretended to check it for recording devices, or other spyware – unscrewing the lightbulbs, running his hands beneath tables and the undersides of shelves. He must have thought he had picked the winning side in the nick of time, that an arrest would happen in just a few days. That was four years ago, and Mladić was still free.

A hollow groan in a water pipe recalled me to the danger of my situation. I took a photograph of the transcript with my phone. Then I put everything back in the manila envelope and returned it to the bottom of the rucksack, covering it with the passport and wallet and the dirty clothes. That done, I went very quietly back to bed, sliding in beside Adam, who stirred and mumbled in his sleep before rolling over to put his arm round me.

When I woke up the next morning, he had already gone to work. The socks and shirts from his rucksack were in the washing machine, and there was a half-dried rosebud beside my place at the breakfast table. For a moment I felt guilty, remembering the aconite he had picked in the minefield. But the feeling went through me, leaving barely a trace. Reaching for my phone, I opened the photographs of the transcript. I read it through from start to finish, twice over. Then I fetched a small black notebook I'd bought in Kalenić market for a diary, but had never used, and I pasted the frail rosebud onto the first page. In my neatest handwriting, I wrote: *October 24th, 2010. Republika Srpska. Adam is looking for Mladić.*

Nothing was different, but everything had changed.

Serb Action Team
Official Audio Transcript
22/2/2006

[Microphone static. A click like an opening car door.]

M: Give me your arm!

B: General, I'm afraid I must ask you to keep your head down.

[Footsteps, and another door opening. Then engine noises.]

B: I hope I am not jolting you, General.

M: Who are you?

B: Colonel Ðogo sent me.

M: Yes, yes. Your name.

B: Bojan Lepović, sir. Your cousin Goran's son.

M: You're very young.

B: Yes, sir. I'm taking you through the back streets. It might be bumpy.

M: After the war I came here in an armoured truck. [Coughs.] They cordoned off roads for me. I sat in the Hotel Moskva and girls drank rosé at my table. Rosé! [Coughs.] The waiter spilt it on the cloth.

B: Please, General. Keep your head down.

[Half an hour of silence. Then the sound of a goods train passing the road. This indicates they are at Brankov Bridge.]

M: I want a coffee.

B: They say coffee is bad for the heart, sir. When we arrive, let me make you a cup of tea.

M: Peacekeepers and journalists drink tea! What is bad for my heart is to crouch in a car. I crossed this river at the head of the Bosnian Serb Army!

B: Times have changed, sir. Keep your head down. Please.

[After about an hour of silence, the engine noise stops.]

M: Where are we?

B: Close to the Chinese market, sir. [The sound of a car door opening, and footsteps. Presumably he is assisting Mladić to get out.] They made a Dutch horror film here.

M: That is unsurprising.

B: Colonel Đogo chose it carefully. It is a tall building. No security guards, no cameras. The apartment is not at the bottom or the top. All this makes it safer. Come inside, please, General.
     [The unoiled whine of a door opening and closing. Feet on stairs.]

M: Don't go so fast! I'm not so fit as you are.

B: Take my arm, sir.

M: I don't want to be helped as if I am a blind man! [A few seconds pass.] I'm ready now.
     [The footsteps continue, stopping often. There is the sound of a key in a lock. Prolonged and muffled movement.]

M: I feel as if I have left Belgrade. The architecture is very ugly on this side of the river. Like in Budapest.

B: Yes, sir.

M: Even the food is different. They eat catfish here.

B: General, why do you not grow a beard? With a beard you would be less easy to recognise.

M: I am a soldier. Soldiers are clean-shaven.

B: But I am responsible for your safety, sir.

M: Let the Europeans think on my safety! I did not take part in any crimes, I only defended my country.
     [Pause.] I am General Ratko Mladić! [Pause.] The whole world knows who I am!

CHAPTER 19

Adam did several more short trips that autumn. He always told me it was routine work, which might have been true, whatever *routine* meant here. But I noticed that he slept restlessly, and he had dark marks, like bruises, under his eyes.

No more ghosts appeared on Zvezdanka Street in his absence – no smell of coffee, no signs of a blue headscarf. I might have welcomed a splash of colour. The Košava wind was blowing down from the Carpathian Mountains, making the city unseasonably cold. One night we wrapped the water pipes in foam rubber; on another we put cling film over the draughty windows, which gave them a whorled, blurry look. 'Like fingerprints,' Adam said, smiling at me. I tried to smile back, but he was due to leave the next day and things between us felt brittle.

He had got into the habit of bringing home flowers – as husbands do. He picked them on his travels, carrying them in his pocket like a blessing or a prayer. A red Kosovan poppy. A white gentian he found in Slovenia. From Montenegro, a blue iris. I pressed the frail petals carefully into my notebook, but charms and tokens were no longer enough for me. We were on the same side: that's what I told myself. I wanted Mladić brought to justice. So did he. I had my excuses ready. It didn't matter if none of them were good enough, because after reading that transcript, I was hooked.

The first thing I did was to visit William Littleton. 'Does Adam know you're questioning me about Mladić?' he asked, tipping my homemade honey biscuits onto a china plate.

'No,' I admitted. 'I found out what he's doing by accident.' I rearranged the biscuits in a neat circle. 'Mladić killed my mother.' I had never put it so starkly before. But I saw the sympathy on William's face and I knew it was the right thing to say.

121

As the day's light slipped from his living room, he told me what he knew about Mladić's early days on the run. Back then, the old general still used to turn up at horse races and famous restaurants. He had friends in the government and the army, so he was always one step ahead of his pursuers. But the last of his military support fell away when he was almost caught in 2006. Now his protectors were civilians – or so went the theory – using tactics passed on to them by the Serbian Secret Services.

William tugged fastidiously at a crease in his trouser leg. 'Most of this is ancient history. It's beside the point now.'

'If you were looking for him again, what would you do?'

'Well, I'd start by talking to the relatives. All those second cousins scattered across the Balkans. They were scared ten years ago, but one of them might come forwards.' He stroked his moustache, smoothing the bushy white tips. 'It's a question of getting into his mind. The man's an egomaniac, but he's almost as old as I am. He must be tired of running.'

'Have you told this to anyone?'

'Oh, it's all on my file.' His hands dropped to his knees, as if the effort of memory had exhausted him. 'Laura, my lamb, you have to stop this now. The Serbs will track Mladić down.'

I said, 'You're the one who told me to find something to do.'

He gave me a wry smile. 'I had in mind cross-stitch.'

My research developed a momentum of its own. Adam kept his diplomatic passport in his bedside drawer. That's how I traced the flowers he gave me. Poppy: *October 8th – Kosovo*. Gentian: *October 17th – Slovenia*. Iris: *November 2nd – Montenegro*. His next trip went unrecorded, and I guessed that sometimes he became transparent. He slid through borders and no one saw him, though perhaps they sensed his presence; the hair on the backs of their necks rose up, their skin goose pimpled. So, the day after his return – Cosmos: *October 20th* – I went through his pockets while he was out for a run.

I found his wallet first: a brown leather flap-over, scuffed to tan. The display pocket held a folded cash register receipt. Behind it was a photo of us from our Portugal Street days. I felt my heart clench. If I put the receipt away now, still folded, could I become that girl in the photo again – smiling at the camera, blinking from the flash? But I barely recognised myself in her. I'd come too far to turn round.

```
SLASTIĆARNA SARAJEVO
9.11.2010
3 X KAFA
3 X ČOKOLADNA TORTA
        10 BAM
```

Sarajevo. Two days ago, he had been in the city of my childhood. He'd sat in a café – at one of those tables that looked out on Baščaršija, probably, where stray dogs lay on their sides by the water fountain and pigeons flocked. Squatting on my heels beside our bed, I smoothed the receipt between my fingers. According to William, Adam would be visiting all the places where Mladić had once been; he'd be speaking to people who might provide information by way of bribery or coercion. This trip didn't seem as military as his first one, in spite of his unstamped passport. His conversation had taken place in public, with men who drank coffee, who ate chocolate cake.

At that moment I heard the door handle turn. From behind me, Adam said, 'What are you doing?'

I scrambled to my feet as if I'd been bitten. 'Clothes wash,' I lied. 'I'm about to put on a load.'

He came right into the room, so I toed his open wallet swiftly under a hanging fold of sheet and closed my fist over the receipt. But all he did was reach for a towel. 'Wait for my gym kit. I'm going to do half an hour of weights.'

When he left I lay down on the bed, my heart exploding with

guilt. What I was doing could destroy our marriage – fragile as it now was, tenuous as it had awfully become. I needed to stop. This time I almost meant it.

The Košava blew itself out in mid-November. Adam came back from Albania during a murky storm that signalled the tail end of it. I was making us a pot of apple tea when Roisin phoned. She had a last-minute gig in Belgrade, she told me, her voice crackling down the bad line. Would she see us both there?

By now we had a car, a low-slung silver Fiat. The traffic was bad all the way to Brankov Bridge, and Adam drove with unusual aggression. He was high from his trip, that's how I thought of it – like acid, which I had never taken. 'I was in a military plane yesterday,' he said. 'It's as if can still hear the noise.' I guessed he also had doubts about seeing Roisin. There had been no time to speak to Martin or Dave.

'I promise not to sell her any state secrets,' I said, bracing my feet on the floor as he cut up a Ford Fiesta.

'That's not funny.'

But it was a bit funny. When had he stopped laughing at himself?

He parked outside an auto shop and we walked quickly through Spomen Park. Most of the floating nightclubs – the splavs – had shut down for winter, but one billboard announced The Vagrant Revolution. The girl on the door sold us two tickets, tutting at our lateness. Inside, disco balls cast glittering shadows along the glass walls. Roisin was singing on a platform stage. Behind her was the river, and rope lights that cast a wet glow. She sang "Use Me" and "Ain't No Sunshine," then finally "Time is a Healer," her voice echoing over the dark water. The hundred or so people in that tiny space swayed and clapped.

When the set was over, we waited for her by the bar. Adam bought us each a bottle of beer. 'Those American songs – so sad, bre,' said a girl in a pink miniskirt, ending untranslatably on a very Serbian emphasis.

124

Her boyfriend wore a blazer and a leather string tie. He said, 'That woman had a great voice.' He looked up at a poster. 'Roisin Clery.'

And then there she was. She pushed through the crowd towards us, the bouncer behind her pulling her two big pink suitcases. 'You're an angel out of heaven,' she told him. 'Here –' with a kohl eye pencil, on the back of his hand – 'Call me.' She ran the last few steps. Hugged me; hugged Adam. 'It's grand to see you both! Buy us a drink, Adam love? I'm parched.' When he was back at the bar, she gave me another, longer hug. 'Are you all right?' she demanded. 'You look pale.' Before I could answer, Adam returned with two more bottles. Roisin said, 'Cheers so,' but she kept an arm round my waist. 'I've booked us a table at a bar on Strahinjića Bana Street. Is it true it's full of gangsters? This is my last night in Serbia – I want to go somewhere with serious scandal and great cocktails!'

I should have known Roisin would like the sound of Strahinjića Bana Street. Adam and I had driven down it once or twice – past the men with gold teeth and huge watches, and the sleek, bronze girls with impossible breasts. Embassy staff were meant to stay away from that part of town. But Roisin was adamant, impossible to argue with. In the end, Adam shrugged his shoulders and drained his beer. It was as if he were still up in that military plane, shedding his caution like ballast.

The gangster bar had a French Riviera glamour and sweeping windows. Dim streetlamps and a crescent moon cast their light over our table. Adam ordered a Jameson whisky – a 'double no, a treble.' I saw Roisin glance at him, glance away.

The tables were so crowded that we had to shout to make ourselves heard. Four men in tight red trousers were getting drunk on champagne to our right. 'A Mer-*ce*-des!' said the woman behind us, in ringing tones.

'How different is Belgrade from Sarajevo?' Roisin asked me, pushing back her hair.

'Some things are really similar,' I admitted. 'It makes me miss the mosques – I keep expecting to hear the call to prayer.'

Adam finished his whisky fast and pointed to Roisin's martini glass. I had barely touched mine. 'Another?'

'Jesus, not yet.' As he went up to the bar, she called after him, 'If it's drowning you're after, don't torment yourself with shallow water.'

I said, 'He's under a lot of stress.'

'He's bolloxed, my love.' She spread her hands flat on the table. 'Why not come to Croatia with me and the band? I mean it! You look tired. And we could drop in on your dad and your aunt.'

I smiled in spite of myself. It wasn't possible. *You don't go to them, they don't come to you.* Those were Dave's conditions. To Roisin, I said, 'It's the middle of term.'

'Bunk off for a week. A holiday would do you good. Am I not right?' she appealed to Adam as he returned with a fresh glass of whisky.

'Always. Right about what?'

'Nothing,' I said quickly.

The night tilted on. Roisin and I had another martini each. I don't know what Adam had, exactly. He ordered several more whiskies. They weren't small ones. He was at the bar when the loudest of the red-trousered men climbed onto a table and executed a wobbly kolo step, then fell over his own feet and landed in a heap at mine, along with some glasses and bottles of which, remarkably, only one smashed. Adam got back to find Red Trousers on the floor of the hushed room. He held out a hand. 'You're a big unit,' he said, grunting as he pulled him to his feet.

In Serbian this sounded much more like an insult than a joke. A few people sniggered, and Red Trousers turned red in the face, too. He looked round for his friends, who put down their beers and moved forwards in a flying V, as if they were migrating ducks. Emboldened by this, he lurched at Adam in what looked like a wrestling move. Adam rocked back his upper body and drove the top of his head into the man's face. There was a horrible crunching noise, and his opponent staggered backwards into a wall and slithered down it. I was dimly aware of Roisin leaping off her chair, then another man got an arm round Adam's neck, and his elbow smacked into the arm-owner's chest, and I was on my feet too, shouting 'Hey!' and 'Stop!' and then, thank god, a bouncer with a coil in one ear was making his way swiftly between the tables, saying, 'What's going on? What's the problem here?'

Adam's fists unballed slowly, as if cramped. 'No problem,' he told the bouncer, with the heavy dignity of the very drunk. He had lost his glazed, embattled look. He'd come back to himself.

'Sir,' said the bouncer, in a tone of intimate regret. 'I'm going to have to call the police.'

'No!' I was appalled. If Adam was arrested, I didn't know what would happen – all I knew was that it would be my fault, because I had insisted on seeing Roisin. I turned pleadingly to Red Trousers, who sat collapsed against the wall, bleeding from his nose. 'We don't need the police, do we?'

The bouncer turned, too, and the man gave a mute shrug. Adam hefted Roisin's suitcases, one in each hand. He didn't say another word; he just walked out. The bouncer inclined his head. 'Ladies?' It was an invitation to leave, and under the avid eyes of Friday-night Belgrade we made for the door. Only then, when it was all over, did I feel myself start to shake. I'd never seen that blind violence in Adam before.

We caught up with him at the end of the street, the suitcase wheels sparking on the cobbles. 'Thank you,' he told me. The threat of arrest had sobered him. He'd come back to himself.

Roisin touched my shoulder. 'Are you okay?'

A cold rain was starting to fall. 'Yes,' I said. 'Let's get indoors.'

'I can't miss my train. Are you sure you're okay?'

'I'm fine.'

But when we left her at the station, I felt bereft.

Adam and I were both quiet as I drove home. He unlocked the front door of our apartment, then locked it behind us, while I filled two beer glasses with tap water from the kitchen sink. In the bedroom he kissed me, tasting of whisky, all slurred love and clumsy hands. That was a bittersweet night. The moon through the window bow-shaped and gleaming. Adam swearing when he hit his elbow on the open drawer at the edge of the bed. His breathing; my own.

CHAPTER 20

After Roisin's visit, November settled into a period of quiet. We had now been in Belgrade for three months, and Adam's short trips seemed to have stopped. 'Let's go home for Christmas,' he said. 'I ought to take some leave.' He had got himself under control again.

For my part, I taught three faultless lessons on the folk tale my students would have to translate in their January exam. Katy dropped in to tell me a rumour that Peter Rabbit was coming to visit Belgrade. I took William some baklava, but I made it a point of honour not to bring up politics. Everything held to a precious normality, until the morning I went to put on the charm bracelet that Adam had given me as a birthday present. I couldn't find it in my jewellery box. Nor was it under the bed, behind the chest of drawers, in the bathroom or the kitchen or trapped, impossibly, down the back of the bookshelf. I went outside. The driveway? No. The front step? Nothing. Slipping through the broken gate that led to the back garden, I scoured the grass around the rotten shed; I even looked in the fishpond, where bulbous eyes stared back at me, half hidden in the weeds. Last of all I checked the earthen pots and broken bits of slate beneath the kitchen window.

Just as I was getting up, a banging door inside the house made me drop instinctively back to the ground. There were people coming into my kitchen, their footsteps quick and heavy. 'It's okay, Captain,' said Adam's voice. 'She's gone out.'

'Why didn't we know this strike was coming?' A man, speaking Serbian with a thick English accent. 'We've got a static team outside Novak's house. Audio in every room. Christ, Bojan, we even had his cell phone tapped.'

There were three of them, then: my husband, an English captain and Bojan – who must surely be Bojan Lepović, the man I had once

129

seen with Ratko Mladić in a photo. I knelt under the window, hardly breathing, like a fish under weed.

'They don't use their phones,' said Bojan. 'I've told you that.' To keep myself from panic I focused on his gruff voice, the whine needling through it. What had he looked like? I remembered a slabbed belly, and sparse, quill-like hair. 'It's all done through handwritten messages,' he insisted. 'They only turn their phones on after driving ninety minutes from where they live, and they switch them off—'

'Bullshit,' interrupted the captain. 'We had a mobile tailing Novak home from a meeting with the whole fucking inner circle, and a Land Rover jumped two red lights and promoted him to glory. His brains were all over the floor. Now you're telling me he didn't get made?'

'Not before the meeting,' Bojan said. 'Your man got made tailing Novak home.'

There was a thud right over my head, as if someone had driven a fist into the kitchen wall. 'Our man!' the captain shouted. 'You're in this up to your neck, Bojan, because *our* man is being flown back to his family right now in a closed casket, and *our* static team is still outside Novak's house. So, I'm asking you again, does he know about them?'

'I already told you. No.' There was a long pause. Someone ran a tap in the kitchen, and water gushed instantly through a drain by my foot, frightening me almost beyond what was bearable. And then Bojan said, '*He* got a message to me,' in a mocking echo of the captain's earlier emphasis.

I felt the jolt to Adam's attention, viscerally, in my own flesh. 'Mladić?' he said.

'My birthday was last week, that's all. Novak's daughter brought round a jar of honey from him. Same as I told you my wife got last year.'

'Was there a note?' Adam persisted. 'Any hint of where he is?'

'Somewhere in Serbia, that's all I know.' The whine rose again in

Bojan's voice. 'This is getting too dangerous. I have my family to think about.'

'No harm will come to your kids,' the captain said firmly. 'Look, if you hear anything about the static team – you pick up a rumour, even – use the drop box. Otherwise, I'll see you in three weeks, back in the usual place.'

I lay under the window, hardly daring to breathe, as their footsteps retreated. At last there came the sound of the front door opening and closing. Relief spread through me like a fever. I was shaking, my teeth chattering. And now that it was safe to move, I saw my bracelet. Most of the silver chain had slithered down a deep, snake-like crack between the wall and the paving – just the deer charm had caught, precariously, on the leaves at the edge. Beech leaves, I think. Slimed by rain. Brown as honey.

Adam did not come back to Zvezdanka Street until late that night. He said nothing about the dead man, so I held my knowledge to myself, hugging it tight to keep it from escaping.

There followed two days when he left the house before I woke up and returned after midnight. On the second day, Katy knocked on my door. Had I heard? Did I know? 'A car crash,' she whispered, puffed up with tragedy. What more could you expect, given the insane way Belgraders drove, smashing through red lights, bouncing off curbs? And she folded her arms across her belly, as if to protect herself.

I confronted Adam the moment he got home. 'Why didn't you tell me?' I demanded, three days of frustration balled up into the question.

'I didn't want you to worry.' He put his rucksack down on the floor. 'It was an accident.' At once I felt much more afraid. Secrets were a bad habit of ours. The more we kept from each other, the more they felt like lies.

I folded my arms across my chest. 'What kind of accident?'

'I don't want to talk about it. I saw some pictures—' A look of

131

disgusted horror passed over his face. 'We'll be fine,' he said. 'Just carry on as before.'

Until that moment, I hadn't even thought about *us*. Now I imagined a Land Rover pulling up outside the apartment. Armed men. Brains all over the floor.

On the Friday of that week, Adam got in from work exhausted, his eyes bloodshot. Before the death he had invited the newly arrived Peter Rabbit to dinner, together with the Lyons. But when he saw the table laid for guests, he said urgently, 'Can you tell them to cancel?'

'Peter will be halfway here!' All afternoon I had cleaned and cooked, placing the meal between myself and my unspeakable knowledge; the idea of losing this obstacle filled me with panic. To avoid debate, I went down the street to buy some late roses, and by the time I got back Adam had gone into the bedroom to change. I arranged the flowers on the table, in an Art Deco vase I had found in a cupboard. It had probably been put there by Katy.

Peter arrived first, ducking his head under the concrete lintel. He hugged me shyly, all ribs and elbows. As he went into the main room, he caught his foot in the rug and steadied himself on the table. He seemed more awkward than usual, more ill-at-ease in his own skin. 'Laura?' he said.

'Yes?'

'Nothing.' Then, after a moment, 'Did you know there's a dead-head among the roses?'

Adam came in with three open beers. 'Cheers!' He gave Peter a bottle. 'Better to be drunk than old!'

I said, 'Where's that from?'

'It's a song,' Peter started pulling petals off the dead-head. 'It's by Plavi Orkestar.'

Katy and Martin were half an hour late, in spite of living two doors down. 'Last minute phone call,' he apologised, as she stopped in the doorway to kiss me. Englishwomen kiss from a distance, so their bottoms stick out. Also, they lack a firm understanding of the rules. Is it left cheek to left cheek, or right to right? One kiss or two? I'm a continental when it comes to kissing. The English should stick to shaking hands.

In our living room Katy planted herself on the sofa next to Martin, her hand on his knee. 'Beer?' Adam asked her.

'Martin will. Water for me, please.'

'How about some wine?'

'I wish I could. It's been a dreadful week, hasn't it? That poor man.' She smoothed her skirt. 'The truth is, we're trying for a baby.'

I looked up, startled. 'Here?'

Adam laughed. 'Laura isn't a fan of Belgrade.' He still seemed exhausted, but there was a resolute cheerfulness about him now. Only for some reason it excluded me.

'I don't like it much either,' Katy told me. 'Did you hear our cleaners got deported? They were Kurdish or something.' She pulled a face. 'It's such bad timing, because school is wearing me ragged. And we're, you know, all the time.' Peter made a choking noise into his beer and she said, 'Really, Rabbit. It's just nature. Maternity leave can't come quickly enough,' she went on. 'The headmaster of my school is a monster – he sleeps with all the secretaries. Once there's a baby I want to stay in London for good.'

'Don't get pregnant,' Adam told me. He meant it as a joke, but it landed badly. To tell the truth, I no longer found it easy to imagine him as a father. His love barely stretched around me.

Afraid that my feelings would show on my face, I went to the kitchen, where I opened a cupboard and three or four packets of nuts fell on me. 'Damn!' I said.

Peter came in. 'Are you snorting ground almonds? Is there anything I can do?'

Tears rose to my eyes, but I dashed them away with the heel of my hand. 'Yes. Take that casserole through.'

I had him put it in the centre of the table, and then lay a mat for the potatoes I was carrying. 'It's a Bosnian stew,' I explained. Leaving

Adam to serve, I went back to the kitchen one last time to fetch the salt.

'Katy was asking why the meat is so dark,' he said, when I returned.

'It's meant to be like that. It's blood sausage.'

Katy laid her fork down, looking horrified.

'It won't hurt you,' I said. 'It's cooked.'

From then on she ate only potatoes, picking them off the edge of her plate.

I turned to Peter. 'Would you pour me another glass of wine?'

At least no one could fault the dessert, which was tufahije – poached apples stuffed with cream and walnuts and brown sugar. I'd nearly added a splash of white wine. That would have truly fixed Katy. 'I'm thirty,' she informed us, as I served up. 'I've got a ticking clock. Imagine if we had to adopt! We want our children to be like us.'

'Doesn't everyone want that?' Peter wondered, picking up his spoon.

Adam tucked in too. 'I want my children to be smarter than me.'

'I want mine to be happy.' I put my hand low on my stomach, just for a moment, the way I'd seen pregnant women do. I did want children, some day. But I didn't want to bring them into all this.

By the time I rejoined the conversation, Martin had changed the subject to the ping pong tournament at the Embassy. 'Remember the game last Thursday?' he asked Adam. 'The one when you beat the Deputy Director of the National Security Council, and everyone went crazy?'

Each week, they played members of the Serbian police or Civil Service as a way of fostering international cooperation – or refining international hostility, sometimes it was hard to tell which. Adam had come home from that match in a state of martial triumph. 'They couldn't resist me,' he joked now. 'My blond good looks.'

'Blond!' Katy said.

'In the Balkans he's a blond,' Peter explained to her.

Martin said, 'Blond or not, he got us thrown out of the Paradise.'

'What did he do?' Katy shot back at him. 'Eat an apple?' I laughed with surprise. 'I looked it up online,' she told me. 'They call it a strip club, but it's all fishnets and feather fans. No big deal.' For once, her attitude made sense to me. There were clubs like that in Dubrovnik too. They had a low-key sordidness, lacking glamour – seedy old men pretending to be young, and young men, eager to fit in, pretending to be older and seedier than they were. 'I've always wanted to take my clothes off on a swing,' Katy went on. 'I was at a burlesque night once. It looked complicated.' I saw Adam trying not to laugh and caught his eye. For a moment things felt good between us.

Then Martin leant back in his chair. 'I guess I'll have to take over the ping pong rota for a while.'

I said, 'What do you mean?'

Everyone except Katy went very still. The silence in the room took on a sudden, strained quality. Adam cleared his throat. 'The British military forces in Serbia need a Polad – sorry, a Political Advisor. The brigadier asked Dave for me specifically.'

'Is it because that man died?' Both Martin and Peter shifted in their seats, so I knew I was right. 'When does Dave expect you to start?'

Adam cleared his throat. 'In three days.'

I ought to have trodden cautiously, as if on ice. But I was subject to forces beyond my control. I was like the tide, sucked in and then sucked out. 'I need to speak to you alone,' I told him. 'Right now.'

I sat rigidly at the table while our guests found their coats. They looked at me from under their eyelashes, the way people look at a traffic accident. Adam saw them out. As he came back, I couldn't stop myself from saying, 'When were you going to tell me?'

'I asked you to cancel dinner, remember.' He rubbed his hand through his short hair, so that it stuck up in spikes. 'I've got twenty-four hours to decide. I have to let Dave know by close of play tomorrow.'

'The army wants you because someone else *died*.'

'It was a car crash. Just bad luck.'

I bit my lip. I knew he was lying, but I couldn't say so. 'You're telling me this is a desk job?'

'I'm telling you not to worry about me.' He rubbed his hand through his hair again. 'If I don't step up, there'll be no one mediating between us and the Serbs. Dave doesn't trust them. They've let people slip through the net before.'

That stopped me, for a moment. The dead man had been following someone – Novak – who was part of Mladić's inner circle. What had William said about the old general? *He thought he was god.* If he was allowed to avoid justice, it sent the message that some lives were not precious. It condoned torture, massacre, ethnic cleansing. It invited people to commit those crimes again.

'I can do this job,' Adam said, into my silence. 'I know I can.' A note of pride had crept into his voice. A brigadier of the British Army was asking for him by name. Even his father could hardly fail to be impressed. 'No one else knows the project like I do. And Dave thinks the work itself won't be all that different, only the locations.'

'How long would you be gone?'

'I have to agree to six months.'

'Adam!'

'I know.' He wouldn't meet my eyes. 'It's a civilian post, but they treat Polads like the army.' With the air of someone determined to get everything unpleasant off his chest at once, he added, 'There's one other thing. I probably won't be able to contact you.'

'At all?'

'Hardly at all. We're being very careful, because – well, we're being careful. Look, you don't have to stay in Belgrade. You can go home to London.'

He took a step towards me, but I got to my feet, knocking the flower vase off the table. Glass and water and bruised roses spilt over the floor. Adam said, 'Laura!' I felt like the room was full of beaks and talons all rushing against me. My feet crunching on shattered glass, I stumbled through the front door and let myself out into the night air.

On wintry, moonlit Zvezdanka Street, I felt the raging presence of black vilas – Slavic bitch-goddesses with ragged wings. I walked quickly past the café, and an old man with a cane who was tottering out of it. Then I stopped, because the old man was William.

'Is that you, Laura?' He seemed weary, and thinner than I remembered. Did I notice that then? Some part of me must have done. 'What's up?'

I looked at his lined face and coarse moustache and burst into tears. William put his arms round me and patted my back. 'Come on. Spill the beans.' For some reason that struck me as funny. Why beans? Because they go everywhere, they roll over the floor and then it's hard to find them, to pick them all back up. Crying and laughing, both at once, I told him a man was dead, and Adam had been asked to advise the army. 'This is what you sign on for,' William reminded me, fishing in his pocket for a handkerchief. 'It's not a vicarage tea party.'

'I didn't sign on.' I accepted the crisp square of linen he held out. Blotted my eyes with it, blew my nose. 'What should I do, William?'

'If he wants to go, let him.' He bent down to retrieve his cane, which had fallen to the ground. 'Let him go, and pray he comes back safely.' When I began to speak he cut across me. 'Don't tell me it's not fair.'

'It's *not* fair, though.'

He took my chin between his fingers, tilting it. 'You look just like Marie did when she was angry. I'm sorry, my love.' He winced, putting his hand to his chest. 'I have to get home.'

I watched him to the street corner, into the orange afterglow of a long burnt-out sunset. He had recommended only the old-fashioned virtue of patience. But at least I'd felt that he cared for me – he, William. I'd never seen him with a cane before.

When he was gone, I went back to the apartment. Adam was

already in bed. I took off my clothes and got under the covers and he put his arms round me. We didn't say anything. It felt like a peculiar and precious calm, a state of grace or truce. But it wasn't – not really. Really it was mutual exhaustion.

He left three days later, in the sleep-ridden hours before dawn. I barely woke up when the bedside alarm went off. 'I'm going to make kifle,' I said.

He kissed me on the forehead. 'I like them with jam.' Then I think he said, 'Goodnight,' although it was less night than day, at least for him. And maybe, 'I love you.'

In my dreams it was not him who was leaving, but me. He stood in an open doorway watching as I walked away, and if he made a sound the air held on to it, if he called me back the words did not reach me.

CHAPTER 21

I didn't sleep well on Zvezdanka Street on my own. Outside my window, late at night, the foxes started their unearthly howling. They sounded like a woman dying horribly, like a child asleep in the grip of demons. The chimney made a falling noise at times, as if soot was coming down it – or something worse. The coal-black body of a pigeon. An inept thief. A noisy ghost.

On some mornings there was frost on the pavement, and once I saw a stray dog, all gangly legs and striated ribs. I went out to escape the empty house. A few doors down was the café where William Littleton bought his cakes. The waitress wore a black apron with DONT ASK written on it in wobbly white Velcro letters, or sometimes ASK ME L8ER. Her English came from American films, and now also from me. She began to keep a corner table free so I could plug in my laptop. 'Don't buy the strudel,' she would whisper. 'There's hot doughnuts in the kitchen.' This was often the closest I got to a conversation all day.

The café was busiest in the afternoons. The women who drank coffee then were rich and thin, with loud, mink coat voices. 'I'm gaining weight,' they complained. At other tables were teenage girls who had discovered make-up but not how to put it on. They wore lipstick in a cherry-black mouth around their real mouths, and their eyebrows shrank to grâve accents, as if gauged out with a knife. For them, the waitress spelt out a new Velcro motif: YOLO.

I began to read about Ratko Mladić when I should have been planning lessons. On the café Wi-fi, I googled the places he hid after the war, jotting down my findings in my notebook – the one stuffed with dried flowers. *In Han Pijesak*, I wrote, *he hunted deer. In Crna Rijeka, he kept goats. In Lazarevo, bees.* I was surprised, because bee-keeping is such a mild pastime. You have

139

to move slowly, speak softly. It's hard to imagine a murderer tending a hive.

I also read up on the siege of Sarajevo – its long and bloody evolution. I skimmed twenty-year-old news articles. I looked at photos. A small boy hung off a tank instead of a climbing frame, grinning at the camera; a woman lay neatly in the street, her head shot open by a sniper, her daughter squatting beside her, clutching a high-heeled shoe. That one got to me – that little living girl. 'Look!' I wanted to say to the teenagers and the mink coat women, and to the Vice-Dean, who was still waiting for my mid-term reports. 'Right here! Isn't this important to you?'

At the end of November, I had two phone calls.

The first was from Big Dave. He sounded surprised when I picked up, as if he had hoped for an answer-machine. I heard the beep of a pinger, the clink of cutlery. Imagined microwave curry for one.

'How are you?' he asked.

'I'm fine.' As always with Dave, I was guarded, remote. I kept my emotions out of my voice – the lash of grief and rage.

'There's no need to worry about Adam,' he told me, chewing softly. 'He's safe as houses.'

I said nothing. It was a poor choice of simile: houses in the Balkans were riddled with bullet holes.

Dave tried again. 'Did he explain that he's working closely with the army?'

'Of course he did,' I snapped.

'He won't be in Belgrade for a while, I'm afraid. I've been wondering if you might be more comfortable at home?'

'Do I have to come back?'

'It's your choice, for now.'

I could tell he wanted me to choose London. That alone made me determined to stay.

'I'll leave you in peace,' Dave said, through a mouthful of food. 'No news is good news. That's all I wanted to say.'

The second phone call was from the Vice-Dean. I let it go to voicemail and listened to it the next day. He wanted to know where the following were: my reports, my sorry self, my explanation. He had expected me in his office yesterday and I hadn't showed up. He wondered if there was a good reason why?

As it got colder, I sat in the café reading about old ladies at the end of the siege who froze to death in tenement flats. They ate dog food and pigeon eggs, garden snails with macaroni. My own appetite suffered in sympathy. The waitress said I looked tired. 'I'm fine,' I told her. After that I stopped going there so often; instead I took long walks. Veliko Ratno Island was home to kingfishers, but I never saw a flash of orange – though once a robin landed on the ground in front of me, a small act of grace. I passed the lido where men were swimming, breaking the ice with their bodies, and a lake with moorhens skating on it like novice dancers. The sun softened the cold but did not dispel it.

On these walks I sometimes allowed myself to think about Adam. I did this cautiously, small bits at a time. His hands, the blurred edge of his jaw. Never whole. In Cambridge he used to turn up at the library with gifts of chocolate. Once he brought a hot red chili plant. He enjoyed surprising me. Soon after we got married, I told him I felt out of place in Hampstead and he said, 'Call a name that sounds like a labrador.' When I was cold, he put my bare hands between his and held them there.

I was afraid of using up these stories if I told them to myself too often. The light would show through, as it does with old cloth. They would shred and tear like chiffon.

Once I walked from the bare top of Kalemegdan Park all the way to the British Embassy, that pale yellow fortress of a building on the south bank of the Sava. I stood below the spiked fence and looked up, twisting my wedding rings on my finger. There was probably an office inside where Adam's face appeared each day, pixelated, on a plasma screen. 'Good morning, Belgrade,' he would say. 'See and hear you fine.' After he made his report, he would vanish, replaced by a different face.

I imagined dropping my rings into the Sava. I imagined them sinking to the bottom of the river, among the weeds and bottle-caps, and I imagined the peace that might come from such a relinquishing.

I was so caught up in my own worries that for a while I didn't miss William Littleton. I failed to notice how many days had passed since he last walked under my balcony, returning from the café with his morning cake. Then the note came.

> Sweetheart, if you had time to visit one day soon, you would make an old man very happy. Dear Laura, don't take this too seriously. W.

It was in his own elegant handwriting, familiar from the birthday card he had given to me. Not noticeably shakier. But I went at once.

His house seemed drawn back from the street. A dark-leafed aspidistra pressed against one window like a face. When I rapped on the brass knocker, the door was opened by a nurse. There was no way of telling this from her dress, but I could tell anyway, because of her scraped-back hair and the rubbing alcohol smell that filled the hall and lingered on her particularly. And because why else would she be here?

She greeted me in fluent English. 'Are you Laura? William will be pleased to see you. He's talked about you a lot.'

'What's wrong?'

'It's best you come in.'

I followed her upstairs, a part of the house I had never seen. Heavy maroon curtains. A bronze globe. She opened a door. 'We've got a visitor.' Then she moved aside so I could go in.

William was in bed, propped up by pillows. His hand rested on an oxygen mask that hung round his neck. The paraphernalia of extreme sickness cluttered the room.

'Ah, Laura.' He winked at me. 'Come in.'

142

I sat down in a chair next to the bed. His breathing was laboured, and he lifted the mask to his face. The bones fanned through his fingers. 'My ticker's given up,' he told me, when the mask lay on his chest again. 'The doctors say I'm dying. Don't look so sad, beloved.'

'You *can't* die,' I said.

He took my hand and held it between his. 'You're thinner. Are you eating properly?'

I tried to smile. 'I'm fine.'

'Good girl. Don't skip breakfast. Porridge, with lots of sugar.' His laugh turned into a cough that shook his frail shoulders. He was wearing a nightshirt with thin crimson and navy stripes, unbuttoned at the neck in a way that made it look like a hospital gown. He pulled himself up in bed with thwarted restlessness. 'I believe there are some cigarettes in the drawer to your left. Would you turn off my oxygen for a moment, please?

I don't think you should smoke.'

'Poppycock. I have it on good authority that I'm not going to die of lung cancer.'

I glanced round for the nurse. She had left us alone, so I did as he asked. He took the cigarette and put it in his mouth, but the lighter trembled in his hand, and he gave them both back to me.

'This reminds me of a story they tell about the examinations at Sandhurst,' he said. 'One of the questions is, How do you dig a trench? And the right answer is, You turn round and say, "Private, dig me a trench."'

Smiling slightly, I put the lit cigarette between his lips. Smoke trickled from his nostrils, a tired dragon. He coughed again, and I took it quickly back. 'That's not good for you.'

'Mother's milk to me,' he wheezed. 'Shall I blow you a smoke ring? A smoke heart?' But he let me stub the cigarette out in the pot of a geranium on the windowsill. I buried it under the soil, feeling furtive. There wasn't much I could do about the smell. When I sat down by the bed again, he took hold of my wrist. 'Promise me something?'

'Anything.'

'Ah Laura, always too trusting.' He paused, mustering himself. 'I want this to be goodbye. Don't come to my funeral, sweetheart. I've never liked them. I wish I didn't have to go myself.'

I remember that afternoon as made up largely of silences. William didn't want me to leave, but he didn't have the energy for much speech. Occasionally he twisted and winced, as if he had run out of comfortable ways to lie.

I thought he might mention Adam, or Mladić, but he never did. At one point he asked me to fetch him a photograph from above the chest of drawers on the other side of the room. A dark-haired woman laughed out of the frame, holding her arms above her head as if she had just finished dancing. I put it into his hands, carefully, and he looked at it for a long time.

'This is Marie,' he said.

'She looks happy.'

'She couldn't resist me.' He smiled wryly. 'You seem dubious. I'm not such a paralysingly beautiful sight as I used to be, dear heart.'

Then he went back to looking at the photograph. When it slipped from his hands onto the bed he didn't seem to notice. His eyes were hooded, his fingers twitching slightly. There was a knock at the door.

'Come in,' I said, since William did not respond.

The nurse was holding a syringe. 'Time for our morphine,' she told him. Once she had administered the drug he sank into a more distant quietness, and I stood up to leave. He caught at my hand.

'Fix me a drink, Marie. Have one yourself.'

'I can't,' I said softly, bending down to kiss his cheek. 'I've got to go.'

On my way out, I gave my phone number to the nurse. 'Please let me know at once if he gets worse,' I said. 'I don't want him to be alone.'

She phoned two days later. 'He's fading,' she told me. 'He won't know you, I'm afraid.'

I held his hand all that afternoon. When it was over, the nurse said, 'He went very peacefully. He didn't feel any pain.'

CHAPTER 22

After William died, I didn't know where to turn. In obedience to my promise, I stayed away from his funeral, though I received a black-edged invitation from his solicitors. On the day it took place I ate porridge and sugar, in his honour. Then I walked past his house, which already had a FOR SALE sign outside. I missed him. His courtesy and humour, his seedy charm. I missed Adam too, in spite of everything. And Tata, who was no longer talking to me. I felt hollow and dizzy with so many absences.

When I got home, the old woman with the blue headscarf was in my living room, holding a wedding photo that I kept on top of the bookshelf. 'What a nice-looking man,' she said in Bosnian, putting the photo back. She stuck out her hand with a crack-toothed smile. 'I am Ana. Pleased to meet you.'

'Pleased to meet you too,' I told her. That was the first time I shook hands with a ghost.

'It's getting late.' She moved towards the door. 'Next time I'll bring the others, shall I? We'll meet here, nearer your Christmas?'

I did hesitate, then, just for a moment. I had no idea where all this might lead. How could I? I knew nothing about her. But I was lonely, and curious. 'I'd like that,' I said.

I rang Dave an hour later. I told him I needed to speak to Adam. He asked if it was an emergency and I said I didn't know. What would count as an emergency? He said he'd see what he could do.

That evening Adam phoned. The line was full of static but he started talking straightaway. 'What's wrong? Are you okay?'

It was the first time I'd heard his voice since he left: for a moment that was all I could think about. 'William died,' I told him.

'What? I can't hear you properly.'

'*William,*' I said. 'William Littleton's dead.'

There was a silence. The line crackled. He said, 'I thought something awful had happened to you.'

'His heart failed.'

'I'm sorry.' Another crackly silence. 'Is anything else the matter?'

Yes, I thought: I saw a dead woman and I invited her to haunt me. I wanted to say it but I lost courage. So I said, 'Isn't that enough?' mustering a little anger by way of self-defence.

Adam took a deep breath, or it might have been the line. 'Things aren't going well out here. We're all a bit on edge.'

'I didn't know.'

'Of course not. Anyway, what have you been up to since I left?'

'Nothing much.' I gave a shrug he couldn't see. 'Reading, mainly.'

At that moment Adam said urgently, 'Bloody hell, I've got to go – I'm sorry. Yes, okay,' he said, to someone he was with. 'Don't be sad, Laura. Stay warm. Eat lots. Oh, for fuck's sake!' There was a short click, followed by the dialling tone.

The last day of term fell on December 10th. When I left the Philology building, I already felt homesick for its reassuring rhythms. Six empty weeks lay ahead of me. Although I had new students coming in January, I would miss Danilo and Lana, especially. Ten years from now I would be a story to them, a pleasant one they told when they met up for a drink. Do you remember the Bosnian woman – what was her name? – who taught us English. The cups of tea. The Chelsea buns. I would have faded in their memory; I'd be glowing with sepia light. That was how I wanted it to be.

The following afternoon, Katy came into the café on Zvezdanka Street with a pert bump and Martin in tow. 'Laura!' she crowed. 'What a coincidence! I didn't know you were here.' That was transparently a lie. She had come to show off.

'Congratulations,' I said, as she lowered herself into a chair. I couldn't deny that pregnancy suited her. She looked glowing, rosy.

'Ask if they've got soy milk,' she instructed Martin. While he did so, she turned to me. 'I was longing to tell everyone at your dinner, but the first trimester is quite risky. It's the size of a peapod now. It's got fingers and toes.' She folded her hands over her womb. 'Sorry – this is probably boring for you.'

A waitress brought two cups of decaf tea, and Martin quietly poured a sweetener into his. He looked characteristically rumpled in a bobbled wool waistcoat, his shirtsleeves trailing threads. 'We're moving back to London next week,' Katy told me. 'Dave needs Martin in Whitehall, and I want to be close to my mum.' When the waitress was gone she lowered her voice. 'Has Adam been in touch?'

'Once.' Tears filled my eyes, and I brushed them away. I didn't even know what I was crying about. Him. Us. Everything.

Martin frowned. 'He's probably just trying to prove himself. You have to do a bit of that when you're working alongside the military.' He stirred his tea. 'Look, why not come back to London? There's no need for you to stay in Belgrade.'

Katy said, 'Can he really not visit you at all?'

I stared at her, over the top of my coffee. I imagined describing this conversation to Adam on the phone. Katy doesn't know what she's talking about, he would say. He would be appalled.

At last they stood up to leave. Martin held his jacket in his arms, jiggling it up and down as if practising for fatherhood. 'We're shopping for baby clothes,' Katy said. 'There's a little boutique on Prince Michael Street.' She kissed me on both cheeks. She was heavy now, tethered. Her voice had taken on a creamy fullness, like butter forming in a churn. Whereas I was the opposite of full: I was empty.

CHAPTER 23

The middle of December was very cold. Five months, I had been in Belgrade now. Nearly half a year. With no teaching to structure my days, I felt restless; I went to bed early and didn't sleep, or I woke with a start, as if I had fallen. One morning I opened the curtains to see tiny yellow icicles hanging from the roof. The beech tree was bare, and the fishpond was covered over with ice. The fish would be sluggish down there, barely moving. Breathing slowly, in and out.

I had my laptop out on the kitchen table, planning my classes for next term, when Ana came back. 'You want some Bosansk kaf?' she asked me. She had walked through the wall with two of her friends. I felt a rush of nervous pleasure.

'Don't tell her it's Bosnian coffee,' said a woman I'd not seen before, adjusting a purple headscarf that had been knocked akilter by its passage through brick and plaster. 'It's made the Turkish way.'

'Yes, yes,' Ana agreed. 'Turkish. But also, it's Bosnian. You have some,' she pressed me, pouring from her long-handled pot into four cups she had taken from a cupboard. My coffee packet lay open by the stove, spilling grains. 'It's very good for you. Good for work, good for the brain.'

'Thank you,' I said. The ghosts broke my sugar lumps into the coffee and stirred it. My eyes were drawn to the one in the purple headscarf. Under her coat she was wearing an old, sequined cocktail dress that shimmered when she moved, as if a scraggly and antique bird of paradise had found its way into the kitchen. She said nothing more that morning, and in fact I never saw her again, but the other two couldn't talk fast enough: they swallowed their last syllables in a way that reminded me of Tata, saying *Bosansk* for *Bosanska*, *kaf* for *kafa*, breaking off each word as if they were in a hurry to start the next. Full of life, though I realise that's a strange thing to say of the dead.

'She's a Muslim,' Ana told me, nodding at her quiet friend. 'That's why she says it's Turkish coffee. I am also a Muslim, but I'm from Sarajevo.' She eased herself into a chair. 'Excuse me if I sit. My sciatica is playing up. My doctor says my bones are pressing down on each other. He means I'm shrinking.' But the aches and pains of the afterlife did not seem to worry her unduly. 'You know Sarajevo well?' she asked me.

I shook my head, embarrassed. 'Not anymore.'

'Oh, you should. Best city in the world! All over Bosnia it was war between Serbs, Croats and Muslims. But in Sarajevo, for us to say I am Muslim was more of a cultural thing, more like a custom. My husband and I went to church sometimes, because Serbs and Croats were our friends, our work colleagues – we went to their family saint-days, they celebrated Bajram with us.'

'I'm Marija,' the third woman interrupted, leaning across the table to kiss me on both cheeks. She was a bit younger than the other two. She had red high-heeled shoes and dyed orange hair, and her eyebrows had been plucked into surprise. In one hand she held a rosary. 'Before the war, Sarajevo was a cosmopolis. On its skyline it had steeples and also many minarets.'

'Everyone walked together in the street,' Ana agreed. 'There was the call to prayer and there was the cathedral bell.'

'Bells,' Marija corrected her.

'Yes, bells. Actually, my husband bought our first radio so I could listen to Nada Mamula. You know of Nada? She was a singer who moved from Belgrade to Sarajevo – she was Serbian, but she felt our traditional Bosnian songs.' Ana frowned. 'In Sarajevo we were happy living with each other. When the war started, a boy came to the central post office in the night and wrote on the wall, "This is Serbia." The next night my grandson wrote underneath, "You idiot, this is the post office."'

Marija burst out laughing – a smoky, throaty sound. 'That's true. I saw it.' She turned to me. 'We don't want the world to think we are barbarians.'

149

Just then my screensaver turned on. It was a photo of me and Adam, squinting in the sunlight of our Hampstead garden. I shut my laptop quietly so as not to interrupt their stories. The cathedral they had mentioned was the one I used to attend, every Christmas and Easter. The post office was fifteen minutes from my old house.

'"Shell them until they're on the edge of madness,"' Ana was saying. 'That's what General Mladić told the army above Sarajevo.' His name made me look up sharply, but all Ana said was, 'They reported it like that, right on my radio.'

'Mladić wanted to kill the spirit of the people.' Marija shook her head. 'In fact, it was very beautiful. The tracer fire lit up the hills at night. The forest was burning.'

Ana poured herself more coffee. 'Sarajevo was burning. Every morning of my life I woke up to the tram bells, but the day the siege started they didn't ring again for three years. It seemed like everything stopped, even gravity. Snipers were killing people in the streets, and by the time anyone dared to move the bodies they were stiff. I'll never forget how the arms stuck out and the heads twisted sideways instead of flopping.' She took a sip from her cup. 'Our men fought, and we made jokes.'

Marija nodded. 'We told them, "There's enough tobacco from the old factory to make cigarettes for four years. When that's gone, you'll surrender."'

Seeing me recoil, Anna put her hand on my arm. 'The siege lasted four years. No electricity, no heat. Shells day and night. We developed a very black sense of humour.'

'I only remember the beginning of it,' I admitted. Flames like frantic flowers, dust and rubble falling.

'It got worse,' Ana said. 'To sit in a basement, people go crazy. So we decided no. You can surround us but we want to live.'

'Take my husband,' Marija agreed. 'He walked five kilometres to work each day, across Sniper Alley. I tried to argue but he said the Virgin Mary told him he'd die in his bed. The funny thing is, she was right. A howitzer shell came through the roof of our apartment

150

when we were sleeping. Pouf! Our whole bed was destroyed.' She leant over to check how much coffee was in the pot, as if violent and untimely death was just a fact of life. For her, of course, that's exactly what it was.

Anna nodded. 'There were feathers in Gataćka Street next morning. I'd never seen a block of flats ripped inside-out like that.' She turned to me. 'I shouldn't have stopped moving. That's why they called it the Sarajevo shuffle. Two sniper bullets hit me –' she touched her shoulder and her chest – 'here, and here. The last thing I remember seeing was some graffiti on the wall: *Fejzo loves Mina forever.*'

A shudder went through me and Marija put her hand on my forehead. 'Good Lord! You're burning up!'

'I'm fine,' I protested, but they were already gathering their coats. I said urgently, 'You will come back?'

'Oh now—' Ana looked concerned. 'We don't want to impose.'

'Stay for as long as you like,' I insisted. 'Make yourselves at home.' She smiled at me.

As they left I heard Marija say, 'Fejzo and Mina were walking down my street when a mortar got them. Their ribcages just splintered into each other. You could see clear through his sweater to her heart.'

CHAPTER 24

In the run-up to Christmas, I slept for fifteen or sixteen hours at a time. Every morning I woke aching and feverish. I was 'under the weather' – that English saying, as if I lay prostrate beneath the cold wet sky.

On Christmas Day I felt a bit better. I made porridge for breakfast. While the oats were cooking, I sorted my post: six cards, three bills and two letters – one from Roisin, one from Tata. His hurt came flaring off the page because this year, again, I hadn't visited him. Her van kept breaking down in dusty Spanish towns. The last card I opened was from the Lyons, who were going to have a boy. Katy's message said he was the size of a grapefruit now. He had toenails.

Adam hadn't sent anything.

Who spends Christmas alone? After breakfast, I set every place at the table. Then I went outside and picked a head of hellebore, which was the only flower in bloom. It should have been a marigold – my aunt filled her house with them on All Souls' Day, to guide lost spirits back home. She also lit candles, so I put some tea lights on the table. If the Bosnians were busy, I hoped William might come. But perhaps you can't pick and choose among the dead.

I caught myself there, tending a crumpled and smouldery shrine. Had I really—? Did I honestly—? I sat down at the table, my head on my arms. When I got up, I blew out the tea lights and threw the hellebore in the bin. Then I fetched a blanket and curled up on the sofa in front of the TV, with its safely everyday visions. *It's a Wonderful Life*, subtitled in Cyrillic. *The Snowman*. And then Adam phoned.

'Happy Christmas,' he said. He sounded far away.

I said, 'Happy Christmas!'

'How are you?'

'I'm fine.'

'It's snowing here. I wasn't sure if you'd be free.'

'I'm having a quiet day.'

'Not on your own?'

I didn't want him to picture anything so deliberately sad. I said, 'I've been ill.'

'Laura! Call a doctor.'

'I'm over the worst part.'

'You're sure? Have you talked to people today, at least? Your father? Your brother?'

Tarik. I'd had post from him, too. A Christmas card with an address inside for the place where he was working, CAFÉ ILLYRIA, RIBA ULICA, SARAJEVO 71000.

Come, he had written on the back. But I had buried that card in a drawer. I couldn't do anything about it right now.

'I'm fine,' I repeated.

We talked for a stilted quarter of an hour. Then Adam said, 'Be safe.' He added, 'Listen, we may be onto something here. I can't explain on the phone. It might mean I'm home sooner than I thought.'

'I hope so,' I said.

'Goodbye, then. Happy Christmas.'

'Happy Christmas.'

When I put the receiver down, I thought I would feel happy. Instead I felt more sad. Adam didn't know that leaving someone could not be put right simply by coming back. He had strong hands, but that meant his forté was lifting heavy objects. Small things slipped through his fingers. Fragile things cracked in his grip.

Just before New Year's, I had another phone call. I was in the attic, for the simple reason that I hadn't seen it yet. I'd opened both windows to air the room, though there wasn't much up there: a broken chair by a water tank, some empty cardboard boxes, a wooden sledge. I felt as if I had climbed above someone else's life, or at least into the most trivial remnants of it.

'I am calling,' Big Dave said, 'to tell you it's time to come home.'

I held the phone tightly. 'Why?'

'The Embassy is knocking down its properties on Zvezdanka Street. A block of fancy apartments is going up in February.'

I pressed the phone closer to my ear. 'I've got classes at the university.'

'Then I suggest you let the Vice-Dean know. Your flight is on January 20th – you'll get an e-ticket from my secretary. I did warn you that you were in Serbia at my discretion.'

Dave rang off. One of the windows in the attic banged shut, and I sat down by the broken chair.

CHAPTER 25

I must have spent too long in the damp attic because the next day my fever spiked. I went back to bed. I felt cold and hot at once; slippery with temperature. Three or four days passed like that.

The night I was sickest, the Bosnians returned. I remember Ana stooping over my bed. I think the orange-haired woman, Marija, said a prayer for healing. They seemed insubstantial, but so did the walls of my room. My own feet.

When I crept downstairs the next morning, Ana was in the kitchen with a man I didn't know. He had his head in his hands. Over the days that followed, unaccommodated ghosts filled the house. The oldest arrived first, shapeless, clutching suitcases. They came from Sarajevo, Mostar, Banjaluka, from sixteen years ago. They had walked past engines blown out of vehicles and the half-cremated remains of other human beings; they had fallen over cliffs, stepped on mines, and been shot with guns – in the eye neatly once or in the back many times. They had borne most, without a doubt, so it was not up to me to question where they chose to put it down.

There were often three or four pensioners round my living room table now, and sometimes as many as ten. They straggled through the wallpaper, which blistered with their passages. They told me where they came from but not why they here. If I did ask, they had a habit of disappearing. An answer of sorts: they were not. But also, they were. They were restless and grouchy, or sorrowing and bewildered. 'Have you seen my husband?' they asked me. 'My daughter?' All I could do was make them cups of tea. I found the teabags in an old tin caddy. The tea was a little stale, a little dusty, but that didn't matter because they never drank it; they flittered their hands, got up and down, peered out the window or cracked open the door.

Only a few of them actually stayed. At first they settled shyly, then with more confidence. They needed clean towels. They needed kajmak – cream cheese. Whenever I popped out to the local shop, one of them would press a list of ingredients into my hand. Soon it felt like I was running a guest house, or ghost house: a bed and breakfast for Bosnian spooks.

January 2011 was a difficult month for me. A placard at the bottom of Zvezdanka Street gave notice of the scheduled demolition, and the Lyons' old house was already empty, awaiting the wrecking ball. I knew I should make plans for my return to London, but I still felt weak from the flu. I spent a lot of time wrapped in a blanket on the sofa, the clock on the wall ticking away the hours. It was nice to have company, and mostly the ghosts were good house guests, though sometimes they moved things and it took me a while to find them. Small things, usually: the tea strainer, a dishcloth. When I walked past, they reached out to touch me. They brushed lint from my jumpers, unsnagged my hair. I thought of these attentions as friendly.

While I was eating breakfast one morning, Ana and Marija turned up with a map of the Balkans. They spread it on the kitchen table next to me, weighting down the corners with coffee spoons. 'Don't mind us,' they said. 'You're not in our way.'

'We'll use sunflower seeds in places he's definitely been, and soybeans for unconfirmed sightings,' said Ana.

'Laura bought those beans for grah,' Marija warned her.

'Grah is nicer with pintos.'

They fancied themselves as detectives, that much was clear. Or was it spies? I suspected that Ana enjoyed a good John Le Carré.

'What's a soybean doing in Sarajevo?' asked Marija. Her mouth was full of bobby pins to curl her orange hair.

'It rolled there from Han Pijesak,' Ana said, licking the bean and popping it back.

Marija shook with her familiar laughter. 'That's fitting, anyway. Each day in Sarajevo was like playing roulette.'

'Roulette?' I repeated, intrigued.

'Russian roulette! You could be killed in an argument, or a kiss, or during a chess game, or doing the laundry.' She punctuated each remark with a hairpin. 'When we ran out of cigarettes, my husband smoked camomile tea in chocolate wrappers. In soap paper. I used to say to him, "Don't smoke, it will kill you." "I should be so lucky," he said. "That I should live so long."'

'He was a character,' Ana said. 'Tell Laura about his shirts.'

Marija laughed again. 'Those shirts! I'd hung them to dry on the line between our buildings, and a sniper on the hill used them for target practice. He shot a hole through each breast pocket! I was so mad. But my husband wore one every day – for protection, he said.' She picked up a striped sunflower seed, turning it between her fingers like a rosary bead. 'That shell got him, so it's true he wasn't shot.'

In the silence that followed her words, I looked again at the map. Beans marked each country Adam had visited last year. There were seeds in Belgrade and the Serbian part of Bosnia. I said slowly, 'Are you trying to find Ratko Mladić?'

Ana and Marija swapped glances. Then Ana said, 'Yes, dear. Like your husband.' As if that should have been perfectly clear. Of course it was, now I thought about it. These women had aimed to sit on porch swings through summer evenings, but then Mladić had blundered into their modest lives, burning their houses and bombing their vegetable patches. They were his dead. Ana said, 'Do you know anything that might help?'

I knew Mladić was somewhere in Serbia, but that was a secret. 'I'm so sorry,' I told her. 'I can't talk about Adam's work.' I felt awful even as I said it. Where else could they expect answers, if not here?

Just then, a hand on my shoulder made me turn round. It was a young woman in jeans, with a silk scarf at her throat. 'Are you hungry?' she asked. 'There was beef in the fridge, so we made ćevapčići.'

My kitchen, I realised, was full of the rich, oily smell of fried mince. People I hadn't seen before bustled about, fetching crockery from the cupboards. One of them passed me a plate of hot flatbread, slit open and stuffed with thin sausages.

'Thank you,' I said.

They watched as I ate the ćevapčići with both hands, wrapping the bread round the meat and scooping up chopped raw onion, brushing my lips free of oil and crumbs. The young woman with the silk scarf smiled at me. 'You want some more hleb?'

'Kruh,' Marija corrected her at once.

I turned uncertainly to Ana. Kruh was the word I had always used. 'Hleb is the Serbian word for bread,' she explained. 'But in fact,' she scolded her friends, 'this flatbread that you eat with ćevapčići has its own name – we all call it lepinja.'

At that moment a tune started up from the other end of the room. In the doorway stood a thin man with flakes of pastry in his beard, singing softly, and accompanying himself on an accordion. 'That's Timor,' Ana told me, in the piercing whisper of the slightly deaf. 'He's an artist, or some such thing. He's a good singer but he's always drunk.'

Timor winked at me. His eyes were a surprisingly bright blue.

CHAPTER 26

The next morning I stayed in my bedroom, trying to respond to an email from Dave's secretary. My visitors kept twisting through the seams of my concentration. They were a strange kind of company, though perhaps that's always true of the dead.

At lunchtime I went downstairs to make a salad. On my way I heard a loud knock. I opened the front door to find a man on the step, with a bucket in one hand and a business card in the other. I was so surprised to see a living person that I nearly slammed the door.

'Cleaning windows in the area, miss,' he said. 'Could yours do with a rub?' When I shook my head, mutely, he held out the business card. 'Call me if you change your mind.' Then he added, 'Everything all right? You look like you've seen a ghost.'

The kitchen was empty at first. I began to cut up a lettuce. Soon Ana appeared, coffee-pot in hand. 'Salad isn't enough,' she scolded me. 'You ought to eat more.'

Next the young woman I had met yesterday came in from the garden. 'Hasan!' she called. 'Lunch!' A small boy crawled out from under the table, clutching a scrawny ginger kitten. He looked at me with solemn eyes before going to stand by his mother. I noticed that she still had a scarf round her throat.

'Will you have some dolma with us?' she invited me, fetching three bowls down from a cupboard. My guests were sometimes solid and sometimes not in relation to my walls, but they seemed to be consistently solid in relation to my crockery. She opened the oven door, releasing a savoury smell of hot oil and roasted peppers. 'I made plenty.'

'Thank you,' I said. 'I'd like to.'

159

The boy climbed onto a chair at the opposite end of the table from the map, his elbows sticking out like chicken wings, and the kitten clung to him, digging its claws into his woolly jumper. I looked away from the neat piles of beans and seeds, so many of them in places I knew Mladić was not.

'Hasan,' his mother said. 'Where does an animal belong when we're eating?'

Slowly, Hasan got off the chair to put the kitten down. It sat bolt upright, tail curling round its two front paws. It had a piquant brown face with dark marks above its eyes, like frown lines. Thin white whiskers and coarse hair. It was just a waif of a cat.

Ana dropped a piece of stuffed pepper to the floor, and the kitten pounced on it at once. 'Look at you,' she laughed. 'Little skin-and-bones. One scrap of mince and I'm your best friend in the world.'

Hasan watched this intently. His mother sighed. 'When the shelling got bad,' she told me, 'he used to sit on the floor under our table, promising that kitten it would be all right. He had a toy gun he held onto as well. I hated that.'

'You let his father give it to him,' Ana said disapprovingly. 'I told you not to, Sara.' She turned to me. 'Ivo was a pacifist, but all the children wanted to play soldiers. He never did have the heart to refuse Hasan. He thought the world of that boy.'

'Our prayer for our son was that if he got shot, he'd die fast,' said Sara. I looked again at the scarf round her throat. Most tales are parabolas: they dip then rise. But the ghosts' stories were straight lines. Plumb down.

She put a plate of dolma in front of me, and I sopped bread in the warm and salty juices. 'This is lovely,' I said.

'You like it?' Her eyes brightened. 'It's a recipe from before the war.'

Ana smiled. 'In the war, dolma was just a nettle-leaf filled with rice. Or soya,' she remembered. 'That tasted worse than tree bark! No one was fat in Sarajevo.'

'You could get food on the black market sometimes.' Sara

spooned yoghurt over Hasan's plate. 'It was a long walk from Gatačka Street – always snipers, and once a shell exploded.'

The kitten chose that moment to spring up the wall and bat at the second hand of the kitchen clock. Hasan laughed, breaking the sadness that had fallen between the two women. 'You can't catch it, silly! It's under glass. And if you do catch it, you can't eat it.' He twisted in his chair. 'Mama, is there any bean cake for pudding?'

She touched his head gently. 'Hasan remembers the kitten doing that same thing at New Year,' she explained to me. ''93, it would have been. How we still had batteries in a clock, I don't know. I think we must have saved them for the midnight countdown.'

Ana chipped in. 'All day there had been more shelling than usual, and Ivo said, "The chetniks are getting drunk up on Igman." But by the time the other guests came the shelling had stopped, so I told him, "Now the chetniks have passed out."'

'We laughed a lot that night,' Sara recalled. 'We always did when Ana was there.' She poked her friend's arm. 'Between us we made a cake, of Viennese wafers mashed together with navy beans, and a pinch of sugar. "That your year may be peaceful", we said to each other. "And the previous one, let it not be repeated ever."'

Ana smiled. 'Nedžad Salković, the famous Sevdalinka singer, used to tell his friends, "I wish you golden palaces." In Sarajevo that winter we had smaller wishes. Bread. Water. Another day of life.'

Sara said, 'We got three more weeks of life. After New Year, Ivo was made to join the Bosnian Army. They pulled men off the streets. He was a bad shot, my husband. A kind and clumsy man. I don't suppose he ever hit anyone. While he was gone, I took Hasan sledding up in Alipašino Polje, near our house. I thought it would be good for him to get some fresh air. A shell fell and hit six children.' She bowed her head. 'He died softly. That's what I had prayed for him. They laid them in rows, on stretchers. He still had red cheeks from the exercise.'

I was sick at heart for her. To watch your child die. To blame yourself.

Ana took her hand. 'He had svjetlost,' she said.

'It's a beautiful word. I can't translate it. It means something like brightness, or something like light.'

'I saw them put his body in the car,' Sara went on, 'and I kissed his forehead. Then I went home and cut my throat. I don't know what happened to the kitten. It must have starved or frozen to death. Poor mite.' She turned to look at Hasan, who sat quietly in front of his half-empty plate.

I said, 'Mladić is somewhere in Serbia.' It felt like a betrayal of Adam, but it was all I had to give them.

Ana touched my arm. 'Thank you.'

'Finish your dolma,' Sara told Hasan. 'I made you some baklava for pudding. It's better than bean cake.' Her son looked up at her, his face full of trust.

A voice from the doorway said, 'You know what is nice also?' It was the singer from last night. At the unexpected sound the kitten fled to Hasan's lap and squeezed into the smallest possible size, as if to annihilate itself. 'Hurmašica,' the singer said to the boy. 'It's a good word, isn't it? It sounds a bit like a sneeze.' He smiled at me. 'Or like a woman's sigh in sleep.'

'Good morning, Timor,' Ana greeted him, caught between disapproval and indulgence.

Sara said, 'You can have some lunch if you want.'

Timor shook his head. 'Keep your vegetables. I have a love affair with sugar. A sticky love.' He turned to me again. 'Hurmašica. Cherry brandy.' Taking a small bottle out of his pocket, he raised it to his lips. Hasan watched.

'He was in the Bosnian Army with my husband,' Sara told me. There was a sorrow, like sediment, at the bottom of her voice. 'Ivo was a lecturer when I met him – he taught modern poetry, and Timor was an artist. Then the war made everyone soldiers. They were great friends, though Ivo was much younger. But he survived, God be praised, so now he is older.'

162

Timor laughed. 'Death! The price of eternal youth.' He took another sip from his bottle.

'Timor,' Ana warned him, 'you are drinking too much brandy again. Be quiet or you will frighten Hasan.'

He bowed. 'Come,' he told me, touching my arm. 'We will talk outside.'

Although Ana pursed her lips and shook her head at me, I followed him without hesitation through the kitchen door. He had a boy's slim-muscled shoulders, but the face of an older man – the wearied skin and knowing eyes. A fox lay asleep on the roof of the shed. We sat by the fishpond, on its stone ledge.

'Cheers.' Raising his little bottle to me, he took a slow sip and sucked his teeth, which were blackened and crooked: siege teeth, without benefit of dentistry. 'Timor is a Hebrew name. It means secret. It's good to keep them. But you told Sara one about your husband –' I started, guiltily – 'so I will tell you mine.' He bent closer. 'My secret is that I am Bosnian. Only then am I Jewish. I carry my country like that other Jew carried his cross.'

Ana appeared beside me with a curt pop. 'He always was a dreamer. He wasn't crucified – he was killed by the chetniks near Vrelo Bosne. What you did was good. Don't listen to him.' With that, she vanished again.

Timor watched her go. Then he asked me, 'Do you know why we're here?'

'You're all victims of Mladić,' I said quietly. 'You're here because my husband is looking for him.'

'You could tell us to leave. Have you thought of that?'

I was silent for a moment. When I spoke I did so slowly, testing the words to make sure they could hold what I felt. 'I don't know where Vrelo Bosne is, or how you got from there to here. I do know that a hundred thousand people died in the war, and my mother was one of them. If I can help you find Mladić, I will.'

Timor dipped his fingers in the pond, spreading tiny ripples. A red fin under a lily leaf twitched and vanished. When he looked up again, he smiled at me. 'Vrelo Bosne is a spring. It's the source of the River Bosna. Before the war all Sarajevo went there at weekends.' He took a sip from the bottle of cherry brandy.

I remembered something. 'People used to drink the water.'

'Yes. We wanted to drink from the well-head of our country. When you are unhappy, everything is symbolic. Also, when you are alone.' He took another sip of brandy. His shaking hands had a frail elegance. 'Once I saw a girl sitting with her feet in the spring, as if she were its vila. A Bosnian water spirit, you know.' I looked up, startled, but Timor didn't seem to notice. 'She made my heart explode. I kissed my hand to her, but I didn't speak. Now I carry her memory –' he touched his chest and his forehead – 'here, and here.'

'Fine.' I shrugged. 'Lucky her. Why are you telling me this?'

He took my hand between his, and I felt an unexpected warmth flood through me. 'I'm trying to warn you, little vila. I don't believe you can help us. You may hurt yourself.'

CHAPTER 27

The day of my flight came round faster than I could believe. 'London!' Ana kept saying, as if it were the other side of the moon. 'Aren't you happy here with us?'

All morning I tried to pretend it wasn't happening. I packed my suitcases in the afternoon, hastily, and piled them by the front door. Then I went into the living room to say goodbye. 'Wear your red coat,' Timor had said at lunch, sounding sad. 'It's good luck to be colourful on a plane.' He wasn't here now; only Hasan lay on his stomach in a patch of sunlight, teasing the kitten with a bit of string. Then Ana walked through the wall beside me, coffee-pot in hand. 'You want a little Bosansk kaf?' she asked me. 'Yes, you have time. Sit here next to me.' She held out her hands, palms down. 'Tchk! Look at this. My doctor calls them liver spots. I said to him, "Doctor, it seems to me I'm going mouldy." He gives me cream for them, but I don't like to use it. Allah never meant for us to cure old age.'

I checked my watch. 'Ana—'

'Now Ivo,' she mused, 'he's a Muslim but you wouldn't know it. I've seen him drinking brandy, he even eats sausage rolls. "Never at the same time," he said to me once. He had such wicked eyes. Dark, like motor oil. Could you pass that cushion, dear?' she interrupted herself. 'Ouf, that's better! At my age a body has too many bones, and they all get closer to the surface. Of course,' she went on, 'in the siege, pork wasn't the question – what worried Ivo was how to keep Hasan fed. The poor child looked worse than the dead, and no wonder. He'd eaten bread made of oats, then of the stalks of hazel bushes, then of ground apple skins. Not that he ever complained, mind you. I'd pop in to visit – with a bit of salt, maybe, or a handful of winter greens – and I'd see shadows from the candles jumping on the wall, Hasan with his hands making birds fly or deer shake their antlers. Ivo, though, he'd be out in the street, just shooting the Serbs off the hills with his eyes. You could hear him from inside the house. "Give me a rifle," he'd say. "Give me a gun and I'll show them."'

Here she paused for breath, and I glanced at my watch again. I was already cutting it fine. But I said, 'I thought Ivo was a pacifist?' He was starting to feel like someone I knew.

Ana shook her head. 'Could you watch your child starve? My husband, Allah rest him, was just as bad. Those two used to talk the whole night long. Politics, they called it. Grief is what it was. They said the West had forgotten us. It's my belief the West never knew we existed.'

I put down my coffee cup. 'I have to go. I'm so sorry.'

I left the room quickly, threading my arms through the sleeves of my coat. My taxi turned up as I was carrying the last of my cases down the drive. The driver made short work of the journey to Nikola Tesla airport, but when he pulled up in Departures I just sat there. I didn't move. He squinted at me in his rear view mirror. 'Need a hand with those cases?'

'No thank you.' I bit my lip. 'Please take me back to Zvezdanka Street.'

Okay, I know. But it was the right choice, because as soon as I made it I felt lighter.

I stayed in Belgrade to help my guests look for Mladić. But there were so many other things to do. Just keeping on top of the housework took most of my time. The wallpaper had started yellowing scabrously where they kept pushing through it; whatever I did, damp spots, like mildew, curdled and spread. Every week there was a new problem. The washing machine began to stop mid cycle, then to tear up sheets and towels, so I washed them myself in a bucket in the garden. I remembered photos I had seen online of women bent over tubs of linen in Sarajevo, once the generators were dead. Sometimes I saw a curtain moving in the house next door, the outline of a wedge-like bosom. But my nosy neighbour didn't come any closer, and despite my chapped hands and sore back, I was happy. I hung the washing on the line when the weather was dry, and once I surprised the fox by the pond. It hurried away at a stiff trot. *Foxtrot*, I thought, making myself laugh.

The greatest difficulty of my new life was money. My bank card had passed its expiry date, and by the time I found out, the replacement had already been sent to Hampstead. I tried to change my address by phone but apparently I needed a password. It was Adam who had set up our joint account. I explained that to the woman in the call centre, and she tried a different security check. The street he was born on? His first pet? Weren't these things I should know about the man I had married? 'It doesn't matter,' I said, hanging up the phone. But it did matter, terribly. I counted up my cash on the kitchen table. Including British money, and the euros and Bosnian coins from Adam's bedside drawer, I had just over four thousand dinar – the equivalent of three hundred pounds. I could get by for several months, so long as I bought cheap sacks of rice and flour, and vegetables that would keep. Onions, potatoes. I put the money in a jam jar above the oven and resolved to live frugally from now on.

As January turned into February, more ghosts arrived. Mostly men. The unsavoury elements of Sarajevo, Ana called them. War profiteers. Black marketeers. Mafiosi. 'How did Mladić get away last time?' they asked each other. 'Corruption!' they jeered. 'The Serbs dragged their toes and they lost him. This time it better be a big raid, like Saddam Hussein.' To make the wait easier, they opened the suitcase containing Adam's single malt whisky. They also smoked constantly, dropping the butts on the carpet. I don't mean to be rude, but it wouldn't have killed them to use an ashtray.

It was the living room that attracted the greatest number of these new arrivals. The fumes from home-grown Bosnian tobacco mixed with the earthy smell of American cigarettes accepted as bribes or bought on the black market: Smokin Joes and Camel Reds were passed across the coffee table by card-playing soldiers whose fingers were stained pollen-yellow with nicotine. 'You arsehole,' they muttered. 'I hope a bug eats your balls.'

'Wash your mouth out with soap,' I said once. That just made them laugh.

When they were winning, they switched to battle tunes. 'The scent of lilies fills the meadow,' they sang under their breath. On the other side of the room, a dead Serb glared. His head was shaved so closely that the skin looked blue, and on the back of one hand he had a tattoo of a cross, with a C in each corner. Ana stuck her head round the living room door and beckoned me over. 'It's a chetnik slogan,' she whispered. She had a shopping list in her hand, and on the bottom of it, to explain what she meant, she wrote, Само слога Србина спасава – *only unity can save the Serbs*. Sniffing, she crossed this out again. 'He's one of Mladić's. Looking for trouble, you mark my words.' Then she said, 'We're very low on groceries, dear.'

Going out into Belgrade was getting harder. People jostled me, and I flinched at so much warm and solid contact. It took me a long time to get my bearings in the too-bright light, the too-sharp air. I must have missed the post while I was at the shops, because a neighbour turned up at the front door around noon, waving a long cardboard tube. Flowery coat, ledge-like bosom: this was the curtain-twitcher from next door. 'Did you hear the demolition has been pushed back to June?' she asked.

I could feel myself smiling as I took the cardboard tube. 'That's good news.'

'Seen you in your garden, doing your laundry.' She peered at me through her bifocals. 'You keep to yourself, don't you?'

'I've had flu.'

'It's plain you've been ill – you're as white as a fish. How about a cup of tea?'

But at that moment I heard footsteps on the stairs, and a feeling of sheer panic overcame me. Ana in one ear, this other old lady in the other? It was not a social situation I could tolerate. 'I'm sorry,' I told my neighbour. 'Now's not a good time.' She stared at me. 'I don't feel well,' I said. I more or less shut the door in her face.

Afterwards, I slumped against the coat rack. Would the ghosts have been visible to her? Would she have been visible to them? I looked down at my hands, which trembled slightly. Did it matter? There are things only some of us can see.

Later, in the kitchen, I spread out the map of Serbia that had come in the cardboard tube and opened a pack of sunflower seeds. 'Mladić will be in New Belgrade,' Marija said, chewing on a zebra-striped handful.

'Don't you believe it,' Ana told her. 'He'll have gone to the north.'

He was the needle; Serbia was the haystack. I said, 'He hates New Belgrade. I saw a copy of something he said in 2006. He doesn't like the buildings. He finds the food indigestible.' I scraped up the pile of seeds Marija had left there, remembering William Littleton's advice. 'If we're going to find him, we have to work out how he thinks.'

'He thinks like a jumped-up peasant,' Ana said promptly. 'He comes from the mountains – his family is mud poor. Other generals lived it up in the war, but he was more at home in an army tent.'

I pushed the seeds north, spreading them loosely over fields and forests. People trust what they know. Mladić was not a city type; he had never put much faith in the rich and powerful. When things got tough for him, my guess was that he turned to his scattered family, the farmers and villagers who'd known him from childhood.

'Would a little something to eat help?' Sara asked, looking up from the counter by the kitchen window, where she was tossing fresh Turkish delight in sugar that rose in puffs and sweetened the air.

By the end of February, a month after the ghosts moved in, my forays out of the house had got rarer. The lights were too bright, the streets too noisy; sounds like cars backfiring made me jump. What if I ran into the Vice-Dean, or one of Adam's old colleagues from the Embassy? I preferred to devote myself to my guests – their

169

hunches and leads, and their stories. I had stockpiled enough food to get by for a while.

It was Sara who did most of the cooking. She filled the kitchen with the smell of garlic frying in paprika; then she got distracted by an argument about politics or ingredients, and burnt the bottoms of the pans. 'What are you making?' I asked her, one morning when I had come in to search for a bin liner. I wanted to tape it over a cracked window that Timor had fallen against, drunk. Glass confused the ghosts at the best of times.

'Burek,' Ana told me, from the other side of the kitchen. She and Marija were sticking photos from an old newspaper onto the wall, in imitation of a police investigation board. A grainy picture of Mladić was at the centre, wearing a military cap. 'He's wonky,' Ana said. 'Come up on your right – your *right*, dear. It might help if you stood on a chair.'

'At my age,' Marija joked, 'it's hard enough to stand on the floor.'

'At your age,' said Ana severely, 'you ought to buy sensible shoes.'

Sara was opening a tin of corned beef. 'The frozen mince is almost finished,' she explained to me. 'I thought I'd try a wartime recipe.' The beef slid out of its tin in a clump, spongy and gelatinous, and she mashed it into the pan.

'Should I go to the shop?'

'We can make do.' She began to roll out pastry. She had maternal hands, red and chafed, marked by cuts from kitchen knives and scalds from boiling water. As I watched her coil the burek into a round cake tin, Ana and Marija resumed their conversation.

'Just his face makes me angry,' Ana began.

'It's those ears. And his chin.'

'The butchering peasant!'

'I wonder what occupies him these days.'

'He used to keep bees. No doubt he still jeers at his goats.'

'The ones he named Major and Mitterand and Kohl?'

'Yes, after those Western politicians he despised.'

'His health too must be much on his mind.'

'He's old by now.'

'So would I be, but for him.'

'So would we all be.'

A memory almost came to me – something I'd read about Mladić a long time ago. Bees, bees. Surely that rang a bell? Timor appeared in the doorway and the memory vanished. He tapped one finger on the side of his head, in the universal gesture for doolally. 'Them, not you,' he said, with his war-ruined smile. I frowned at him. Still, they *were* a little ridiculous. A pair of posthumous Miss Marples, playing at a manhunt.

Turning away from the photo of Mladić, I followed Timor to the living room, which was full of arguing card players. It smelt of old sweat and smoke. A soldier with moles sticking out all over his face like flies was sitting on the coffee table, wearing army trousers and a wife-beater shirt, and pulling the cap off a beer bottle with his teeth. 'Beautiful arse!' he said to me. 'Have a drink?'

I felt myself flush, but all I said was, 'I'm fine.'

'I did not ask if you were fine, I asked you to have a drink.'

Timor said, 'She told you no.' His hand touched my back, lightly, between my shoulder blades.

The soldier spat out the beer cap. 'We're just talking, man. What's it to you?' He rose laboriously to his feet. Under his shirt, he had a paunch like a skinful of rocks – the thick, slipped slabs of old olive groves. He put his face near Timor's face, but Timor did not flinch, and finally the soldier walked away.

Once he was gone, I tore the black plastic into ragged pieces that would cover the broken window. Then I climbed onto a stepladder. Timor steadied the base. 'Don't let go,' I warned him, making my voice sharp, to hide the lightness that always filled me in his presence.

'Don't worry,' he said. 'You'd fall right into my arms.'

'That's what I'm afraid of.'

Timor laughed. He shook the ladder gently.

CHAPTER 28

By March, the beech tree was in flower. Sparrows sang in the garden, which began to explode in a slow-motion firework display. Snowdrops gave way to daffodils and tulips, and the old fox limped through the flowerbeds, cocking a grizzled leg. But we were no closer at all to identifying Mladić's hiding place. And neither was anyone else, so far as I knew.

Indoors, the house inched towards chaos. Wallpaper browned and sagged. Plaster dust fell from the ceiling. The bin liner that blacked out the living room window made little sucking, rasping noises when there was a breeze. Sometimes it blew back and I felt surprised to see Belgrade behind it. Though what did I expect to see?

I spent most of my time in the kitchen now, helping Sara to cook. We peeled old potatoes; we rubbed flour and oil together for pastry. There was no butter left. Sometimes Ana joined us by the warm stove, clutching her eternal coffee-pot, or Timor helped himself to a piece of halva made with the last of the white flour. In the dust left on the table, he drew planes and helicopters for Hasan.

'You were a painter,' I said to him, as he added a pair of wings to a fighter jet. I felt myself blush; the ghosts occupied a confusing tense. 'I mean, you are one.'

He smiled. 'I quit. Instead, I took up brandy.' He raised his bottle to me with the listing charm of a drunk. 'Because we were conscripts, Ivo and I were sent to the front line. There was a sign saying, "Welcome to Sarajevo." Underneath it, in whitewash, we wrote, "Welcome to Hell." That was the last thing I painted.'

'Hasan,' said Sara softly. 'Go and play in the garden now.'

Timor watched the little boy leave. Then he turned back to me. 'You know the history of our country? It starts with iron stirrups six thousand years old. You can dig them up from the banks of the Bosna.' Leaning against the kitchen counter, rolling a cigarette, he spoke of the men who had forced their feet through those misshapen stirrups and ridden to rape and conquest: the Illyrians falling to the long swords of the Celts; the slouching Japodes engraved in stone on horses with long legs and hooves like wheels, a prey to Roman cavalry with metal armour; and the mountain tribes who routed those Romans with beautiful and deadly clubs that shattered bone, then succumbed to the Ottoman Sipahis – their arrows and scimitars.

'And after the Ottomans, the Austrians, and after the Austrians, I, Timor, with my Russian-made rifle and my German-made bullets and my – let us speak honestly – not so very steady aim.' He shrugged his thin, beautiful hands, that shook unceasingly. 'In Bosnia there are no solutions, only patterns.'

Why hadn't I thought to ask Timor how he died? I said, 'Tell me what happened to you.'

'The chetniks took us to a school field,' he said quietly. 'They made us sit on the ground with our hands behind our heads. Over six hours, they killed all the Bosnian conscripts they'd caught. They sang while they did this. They shot at the backs of our heads.' He looked down. 'In our stomachs.'

They *sang*, I thought.

I guess they got tired, murdering all those men. I guess their backs ached and their palms grew raw, and the blood was an irritation to them.

'Motherfucking Chetnik!' we heard, through the kitchen door.

'Sisterfucking Turk!'

In the living room, the coffee table had been overturned and playing cards swooped through the air like startled birds. The Bosnian soldier with moles on his face and the Serb with the shaved head were circling each other, fists up and glaring. 'What does it matter why he's here?' Marija was scolding the soldier, a blazing sight with her red high heels and newly dyed orange hair. 'So what if he's a chetnik? What can he do?' I thought she'd get herself squashed, but two of the Bosnian soldiers grabbed the Serb by the shoulders and he allowed himself to be shunted towards the door, grumbling loudly and cracking his knuckle tattoos into his palms.

I was very quiet for the rest of that evening. Mladić had to be found soon, that was clear. Or else where would all of this end?

For dinner we ate a thin soup, with dried macaroni and the last of the beans. Sara called it Begova čorba, but that was optimism talking: it was nothing like the rich celebratory soup that got its name from the Ottoman chieftains. Afterwards, when I tried to wash up, no hot water came out of the taps. I went to the attic to check on the tank. I didn't expect I'd be able to do much. But the attic was peaceful, and the broken chair by the water tank was a good place to think.

In the early days of our marriage, Adam had sometimes come home to find me sitting in the dark. 'Hello,' he used to say, and it was a caress, not a word. I realised with a shock of guilt that I hadn't thought about him for days.

Timor came up the ladder with a torch. 'Do you need any help?' he asked me. He reached out to brush a lock of hair behind my ear.

'Timor,' I said, 'I'm a married woman.'

'I'm dead,' he said. 'You can't let the little things stop you.' But he moved away from me. His torch beam quavered over the water, lighting up the swollen body of a dead mouse. 'If it becomes a ghost, Hasan's kitten can chase it.' He rubbed his neck. 'We're a rough crowd. I do wonder why you put up with us.'

'You're my guests. I want justice for you.'

'Yes. But you've got someone at stake who's still alive. We don't.'

I was silent. I hadn't seen it like that before. 'Adam's just a Political Advisor,' I pointed out at last. 'If they find Mladić, the army will take care of it – he won't be involved. Anyway, he knows how to take care of himself.'

'It's good one of you does.' Timor shook his head. 'Look in a mirror, Laura. You haven't eaten properly in weeks. It's making you ill. You should ask us to leave.'

I laughed, a little bitterly. 'None of you will leave until something happens. You know that.'

'Go back to England, then.'

That, too, was a new thought for me – that I might just walk out of the house. The street would be warm with spring. I would not turn round; I would keep right on walking. 'I can't.'

'Can't? Or won't?'

I thought of Hasan's hungry eyes. His mother with her scarf across her throat. Timor himself, in that field, his hands tied savagely behind him. Once I had wished to be made of stone, and my guests, whatever else they might be, were the unexpected answer to that wish. Instead of hardening, I'd become porous to histories. I had absorbed epitaphs – the kind that would be written above graves if any chisel could keep pace with love, if any mausoleum could rise high enough.

'Both,' I said. I stood up, and so, with a shrug, did he.

In the weeks leading up to Easter, morale among the ghosts grew low. Formerly the old ladies would sit for hours over cups of coffee, to gossip and plot, and even the soldiers had exchanged theories and brandy as often as blows. Now they squatted against the living room wall and chain-smoked cigarettes. 'What if he left the continent?' they asked each other. 'What if we never catch him?'

'Fuck this shit,' the soldier with moles on his face complained, tilting a bag of tobacco to the light. 'When is the army giving out marijuana again?'

'Why did they give you marijuana?' I asked him, intrigued. I'd come in to check on the state of the room. Burn marks were multiplying on the furniture, and splintered glass fell on windy days from another broken window to the floor.

The soldier rolled his head sideways against the wall to look at me. 'It helped us live with all the killing.' He laughed. 'No, but I miss it. I'd give a lot to have a rifle under my chin again.'

Timor tossed a cigarette butt at his feet. 'It's the war, man. No one wants to hear about it.' The carpet blackened under the glowing stub, with a smell like singed moth.

'Pick that up,' said Marija, wobbling on her heels as she collected dirty plates. 'Shame on your mother.' So, in my house, Bosnian Muslims, Jews, Orthodox Christians and Catholics bickered and fought like family.

On Easter Friday I was in the garden, hanging sheets out to dry, when Hasan slipped his hand into mine. We were by this time shy friends. He led me across the lawn into the shed and squeezed a path to the workbench at the back. There were cobwebs in this corner and a rusted set of gardening tools. But what Hasan had found was a treasure-trove of old seed packets, with pictures showing bell peppers, tomatoes, and waxy bunches of spring onions. I kissed the top of his head, brushing off the lacy prayer cap of a web. 'Are there any baklava seeds?' I asked him. 'Or a beef stew plant would be nice.'

'Burek plant!' he said, giggling. 'Sausage grah! Ćevapčići and chips!' His eyes got rounder and wider as he spoke, until I had to look away.

Back in the kitchen, we planted all those seeds in plastic pots, along with some potatoes. The soil got under my nails and at one point I touched my dirty finger to my tongue. It tasted of iron, like blood. We put the pots on the windowsill, Hasan standing on a chair and pulling fish-faces at the old fox on the lawn. And then I heard the sound of the front door opening.

'Listen,' I whispered. Hasan unsquashed his lips from the window glass. Sara and Ana stopped peeling old potatoes.

'Boiler's bloody ancient,' a voice grumbled in the hall. 'It's off all right. Gas company must have got it wrong.' Dear god, the man worked at the Embassy. I recognised his voice from when Adam used to play table tennis with him. He could not be more than eight feet away from me.

'Send the bill back to them,' another voice advised. 'Always knew it was a wild goose chase.'

'They'll send us out on another job if we go back now. How about a cup of tea?'

'No point without milk. Although – d'you think there might be some honey?'

I stood as if frozen. My eyes flicked to the back door, but there was no point trying to slip out. If they came into the kitchen, it was over. The map was on the table, the photo of Mladić on the wall, and every room in the house was riddled with my possessions.

'Worth a look.'

Footsteps shuffled closer. I couldn't move or breathe.

'You know what, leave it,' said the goose-chase man. 'This place gives me the creeps.'

'Right you are. We can stop for a coffee on the way back.'

The voice of an angel.

And the footsteps of angels, receding now towards the front door.

Ana put her hand to her heart, all wet with potato juice as it was. 'Praise be to Allah,' she whispered.

As the door banged shut, I sat down on a chair. My legs felt like water. *D'you think there might be some honey?* And, just like that, a memory stirred. I'd heard something about honey in this house before. Elbows on the table now, I pressed my fingers to my eyes as if blindness might help me remember. I could sense the attention of the other women. And then my eyes popped open and I said aloud, 'Bojan!'

Hasan wobbled on his chair. Sara put out her hand to steady him. A confused glance passed between her and Ana.

'The British Army has a local contact,' I told them urgently. 'Bojan Lepović, the son of Mladić's cousin.' I thought back to the transcript I had read on Zvezdanka Street, in secret, by moonlight. 'Mladić trusted Bojan to take him to a new hiding place in 2006. He should have been caught because Bojan was working secretly for the British government, but they didn't move fast enough.' I took a deep breath. 'I think Mladić still trusts him. He gave Bojan a present last year, a pot of honey.'

Sara adjusted the scarf round her throat. 'Mladić trusts his cousin's son. So what?' She shrugged. 'This Bojan hasn't revealed the new hiding place to your husband. Maybe he's loyal now. Or maybe he doesn't know where Mladić is. I'm telling you the truth, no one will ever find him.'

'Adam dismissed what Bojan told him as useless. What if he missed the point?' I clenched my hands together, willing my thoughts to come clear. 'He didn't pay attention to the gift,' I said. 'Honey. It's a funny present. Like chutney, or dandelion wine. It's the sort of thing you'd only give to someone if you made it yourself.' The silence in the room seemed to change its nature. They were all listening now. 'Didn't Mladić own some beehives once? Somewhere in Serbia – I'm sure I read that. Do you see what this means?'

'He might be where the bees are!' Hasan shouted, clapping his muddy hands together. 'Be where the bees,' he repeated in English, laughing.

His mother picked up a seed potato and rubbed it on the sleeve of her blouse. 'Where were those hives?' she asked softly.

'Ljuba?' Ana said.

'No.' She shook her head. 'It's on the tip of my tongue. He had lots of relatives there.' She rubbed the potato on her sleeve again.

There was a long pause. Then she and Ana, almost in the same instant, said, 'Lazarevo!'

We looked at each other with tentative amazement. It really did seem to fit. Mladić had stayed close to his family during his early years in hiding, that was a well-known fact. There were internet videos of him dancing the kolo at a wedding, stamping in time to tambourines, stiffly hopping. I had wondered before if one of his countless relatives might be hiding him. Lazarevo was the perfect place for a fugitive, Ana told me now, her voice crackly with excitement. She bent over the map to find it, sweeping the dusty sunflower seeds aside. A dot of Cyrillic in the flat farming region of north Serbia. Tiny and isolated. Right off the grid.

The news of our breakthrough spread quickly. Marija twisted her rosary and patted her curls in her excitement. Timor leant against the door, watching me with hooded eyes. Most of the people who flocked to the kitchen wanted me to tell Whitehall. 'What harm can it do?' they asked. 'If we're wrong – *bof*! – we're wrong.' There was another problem, though. Who would believe us? They talked round and round that. In the end, Marija suggested an anonymous phone call. 'Don't do it from here,' she warned me. 'Better you go into town, so they can't trace it back to you.'

There was a violent disagreement about this. Marija said a sparrow in the hand is better than one on a branch, but Ana said every bird has a hawk above it. She meant I was being foolhardy. In the end, I said we didn't have a choice.

And that was how I found myself, perhaps half an hour later, leaving the house for the first time in weeks. Sara had picked out a baggy jumper to hide how thin I was, and Hasan had watched as I coloured my cheeks with powder and brushed my tangled hair. The evening was bright and dry, but as I went down Zvezdanka Street a wind rose up. On the pavement I saw paper espresso cups and cigarette ash like bird droppings. When I moved too quickly, these things trembled as if they had lost their substance and been remade of air, as if I was holding together a falling-apart world. The responsibility of this frightened me.

By the time I reached the main road, I was walking carefully, hunched forwards as if into a wind. A group of schoolboys laughed at my unsteady progress. When I bought a phonecard, the shopkeeper looked at me as if I might steal something. Even so, I didn't use the first public phone I saw. Marija's cloak-and-dagger warnings rang in my ears, and as I hesitated a woman with a toddler barged into it. I went on to one of Belgrade's iconic red booths. It had a smell of piss and mould. By now my hands were shaking, and

I dropped my phonecard twice before I managed to get it in the slot.

After I dialled, there was a delay so long that I almost hung up. Then the connection kicked in and a smooth female voice came through the receiver. I had reached the switchboard of the Foreign Office, it told me. Did I know what extension number, person or department I wanted?

'I have information about where Ratko Mladić may be hiding,' I said, loudly enough to be heard over the night sounds of Belgrade.

The voice on the other end of the line wanted to know my name.

'I don't have much time,' I said. 'I've got reason to believe General Ratko Mladić is in Lazarevo. I think he's staying with a relative, someone who owns beehives.'

Who was I? the voice asked. Where was I calling from?

'He's in Lazarevo,' I repeated. 'It's a village in North Serbia. Have you got that?'

In the middle of being told to please hold the line, I hung up the phone. I felt like I was in an airport thriller. I had never felt like that before.

CHAPTER 29

I thought everything would change after that phone call but instead life carried on exactly as usual. The fox sunned itself at the bottom of my garden. In the pots on my windowsill, shoots pricked through the soil, obedient to light and their own mysterious timing. Had anyone acted on my tip-off? There was no way of knowing.

Hasan and I began to pick the bell peppers at the end of April, a week after I had spoken to Whitehall. We did it hungrily, while they were still small and green, though they were not so sweet as if we'd left them to mature. In the middle of this harvest, Timor appeared with my phone, holding it directly to my ear. My muddy hands flew to my heart at the sound of Martin Lyon's voice. 'What's wrong?' I said. 'Has something happened to Adam?'

'He's fine,' Martin assured me. I let my hands fall away from my heart, hunching my shoulder so Timor could let go of the phone. It was a while before my breath evened out again. 'How are you enjoying being back in Hampstead?' Martin went on. 'We haven't heard much from you.'

'I've had flu.' My old excuse.

'I'm sorry to hear that.' I pictured him holding the receiver cautiously away from his ear, as if I might infect him even from a distance. 'Katy had a scan this morning,' he went on. 'Everything's fine. I've got some nice new snaps –' as if, I thought, he had taken them himself, with a Kodak – 'How would it be if we popped round to show you?'

I felt my pulse speed up. Thinking quickly, I told him I was planning a long trip with a friend. A walking holiday, I invented. Otherwise, I would have loved to see them. When he rang off, I slid the phone shut at once, ignoring all the other messages and missed calls. What if I hadn't picked up? What if Martin and Katy had just set out, unannounced, for Hampstead, where dead crab apples would be lying all over the garden and post stacking up on the doormat? I rested my head in my hands, black spots jittering on the edge of my vision.

'Don't crowd her!' the ghosts said, crowding me.

'Let her breathe!'

'Do you feel faint?'

'Put your head between your knees.'

'Shall I get her some water?'

'Brandy is good for dizziness.'

'Someone find Timor!'

Ana brought me a cup of chicory coffee. 'Something must be happening,' she said. 'Why else would he phone you up out of the blue?'

I said, 'Excuse me—' and made for the kitchen door.

Alone in the hall, I sat down opposite a fly-specked mirror. My reflection looked like a typhoid victim – all hair and eye and bone. Had Martin called me because Adam was in Lazarevo? Mladić was much older now than in the photo on my kitchen wall. Perhaps he was no longer a threat. Or perhaps he was only so shaky as to be dangerously erratic, the bluster that was once for show now hardwired in. How many men had he killed during his life?

Timor came out of the kitchen. 'Mind if I join you?'

I glanced up at him. 'Have you come to tell me what to do?'

'Run away with me,' he said. 'What, not a smile, even? Crouching down against the wall, he took my wrist and turned it over, examining the sharp tendons and hollows. 'Ah, Laura. You could get him out of it, you know. Tell the Foreign Office you're ill.'

'It's too late. They'll raid Lazarevo right away. They could be doing it now.'

Timor shook his head. 'It will snarl up in politics. The Serbian government has to agree his arrest, and they've been turning a blind eye to him for fifteen years. You still have time.' Then he said, 'Mladić used to take two pistols everywhere he went.' He reached in his pocket for the brandy bottle. 'Russian Makarovs. Eight rounds. The old fox doesn't miss.'

Hasan poked his head out of the kitchen, looking curiously from me to Timor. 'Mama is laying the table.'

I said, 'Give us a minute, sweetheart?'

Very softly, he closed the door. For the first time, I made myself think about the way Saddam Hussein had been brought down – brutally, because an attack squad is always vulnerable: if there is an armed defence, any number of men can die. But Adam knew what risks he was taking. He'd made his decision. Now I was making mine.

I got up, and so did Timor. 'Hey, little vila,' he said. 'I want you to think this through.'

I said, 'I've thought it through.'

'Laura—'

Turning away from him, I opened the kitchen door.

April became May. We ate only two meals a day now, eking out lentils and rice. The light bulb in the living room went, then the one in the kitchen, but I found a stash of candles, which gave the house a shimmering appearance. I hung around the places they were lit. I didn't trust my guests with naked flames. In any case I was reluctant to sleep, because in my dreams Adam was dying. These days I found it hard to recall the precise details of his face, but I felt a frightened tenderness for him. So, I sat up night after night, with the windows blacked out and the candles burning low.

In daytime I played endless games of cards with Ana and Marija, while Timor lounged in the doorway, not meaning to stay but never quite going, and the soldiers dropped in and out like disreputable uncles. Whenever I was alone, one of them sidled through the walls of the room. I did wish they wouldn't do that: it left marks.

By the middle of the month, four weeks after we realised Mladić was in Lazarevo, we were down to a single meal a day. Sara would send Hasan to pick wild garlic from the bank in the garden; she'd stew up nettles like spinach. Once Timor said to me, 'You're as thin as a wishbone.' I didn't mind, in a way. I felt lighter – as if I might fly up into the air, trailing strings like an escaped kite. It's true that I also felt constantly dizzy and tired. I took to avoiding mirrors, knowing what I would see: the sharp notch of clavicle, the bitten-out dip beside my shoulder blade. I didn't know how much longer I'd be able to go on.

One afternoon, Timor came into the kitchen through the garden door, his cupped hands blue with cold. 'What are you up to?' Sara asked him.

'I've been pond dipping.' He made me stretch my own hand out, fingertips towards him. 'Close your eyes,' he said. So I felt the goldfish before I saw it, its whole body gulping and gasping in my palm. As I looked down, its eye filmed over, wide open, and a shudder passed through it like a sigh.

'It's dead.' To my surprise, I found I was crying.

Timor said, 'Ah, Laura. Too fragile for an army wife.'

Sara took the dulling corpse from my hand. 'What do you want?' she scolded him. 'She can't marry you.'

I didn't look at Timor. We both knew it was true. If everything had been different – places, timings? If the world had spun otherwise? But it hadn't.

He brought her the rest of the fish in a sieve and she gutted them over the sink. The tiny viscera fell away between her fingers, pulpy and glistening. She fried the bodies in a trickle of oil, then laid them out on beds of rice, their popping eyes turned up to meet ours. We ate the black and crinkly skins, so fine we couldn't peel them off, and the white, tasteless meat, and the tiny bones. At the end of the meal, only the tails remained on our plates. 'The Sarajevo diet,' Timor joked. 'You count the calories you need to stay alive.'

I chiefly remember the troubled sweetness of those final days. More and more Bosnians came to the house. They lined the walls like the figures in an old fresco, jostling each other but making no noise about it. Timor retreated outdoors. He sat in the garden with a glass in his hand and Hasan's kitten beside him, twitching its tail. He was a gentle drunk – a chain-smoker of rolled cigarettes, a singer of songs. "Žute Dunje," he sang. Yellow Quinces. "Oj Mjesece Bekrijo." Oh Drunken Moon.

'Sara is baking green tomatoes,' I went out to tell him. Steadying myself on the fencepost, I saw the fox limp across my neighbour's garden, its hind leg dragging. 'They'll be ready in half an hour.'

'You eat mine,' he said. 'I need only brandy.'

'It's not good for you.' I sat beside him on the edge of the pond.

'Brandy is very healthful,' he disagreed. 'If you have a cough or a heartache, you drink brandy. If you have a temperature, you rub it on your skin. Today I have a cup so you can try.' He looked about him and frowned. 'Actually, I have lost that cup.'

Ana, appearing beside us with her arms full of early roses, said acidly, 'He'd lose his head if it wasn't screwed on.'

Those two were always bickering. 'You were on the same side,' I pointed out to her. 'Timor fought in the Bosnian Army.'

'He didn't fight well.'

'That's true,' Timor admitted. He winked at me. 'I was a dead loss.'

Ana ignored that. 'You were drunk.'

'I drink spirits,' he told me, after she left. 'At least I choose something appropriate.'

'That's another bad joke.'

'Yes. It's a joke though.'

I kissed his forehead, and he caught my chin between his fingers. 'You missed.'

The last time I sat outside with him was a Thursday, towards the end of May. A number of unfamiliar ghosts hurried up the garden path into the house, moving furtively, as if they didn't want to be seen.

Ana came out to join us, with a tray and a jug in addition to her usual coffee-pot. She put the tray on the garden table and poured

185

two glasses, one for me and one, surprisingly, for Timor. The liquid was a beautiful pallid pink.

'What is it?' I asked her.

'A rose drink.'

Timor put his brandy bottle down. 'Rose for a rose,' he said, touching his glass to mine.

'Just the smell from that jug reminds me of home,' said Ana, pulling up a garden chair. She poured herself a cup of chicory coffee, the movement causing a swirl of displeasure among the sugar-hungry wasps. 'Of course, a Sarajevo rose means something different now. When a shell killed a person outright, they filled the hole in the pavement with red resin.' She batted a wasp away from her cup. 'The shapes they made looked like petals.'

Mama might be one. How had I never thought of that before? On the bank of the Miljacka, a red resin rose. As we sat in the sun-filled garden, I found myself describing her death to Ana and Timor. The wound-coloured water. Her hands blown clean off. Ana poured herself another cup of coffee and I was moved to see that her own hand was shaking, rattling the long handle of the copper pot. 'Allah forgive us,' she said. 'How can people do these things to people?'

That was the moment Marija opened the kitchen door. 'Come quickly!' she called. 'It's Mladić at last!'

CHAPTER 30

Everything slowed down and at the same time sped up. Ana dropped the coffee-pot. She began to run towards the house. I ran after her – my heart clattering in my chest, my mind full of violent images.

Mama a scar of red resin.

Timor holding his stomach as blood soaked through his shirt.

And now Adam – Adam creeping through Lazarevo, his sandy hair marking him out for Mladić's pistols.

In the living room, everyone was crowded round the old television, jostling each other for the best view. Timor swung kitten-clutching Hassan up to his shoulders. I fought through the fray to a spot by the screen.

'Months of careful planning lay behind the dawn raid,' said an autocued Serbian woman at a newsroom desk. The ghosts inhaled a collective gasp. I couldn't breathe. 'We are able to reveal this exclusive surveillance footage, which we have just now received in the studio.' On the television, a quick fizz of pixels gave way to a technicolour shot of sky. My eyes darted to the date. 25 APR 11. One month ago. Only two days after I had made that phone call.

The camera came wobbling down, panning over fields where sunflowers were growing, then over an old barn and a thick-legged woman picking early greens. 'We've got eyes and ears on them,' said a voice that I recognised instantly as Adam's. It felt like he was leaning over my shoulder, close enough that I could breathe the pine-needle smell of his skin. 'The farm belongs to one of the target's second cousins,' Adam went on. 'They've got a few goats and some strawberry beds. Peppers and beans. The target rarely leaves the house except before dawn and after dusk.' The camera lens, less wobbly now, had climbed up a yellow wall, found a dusty window. 'Hang on, I'll refocus,' Adam said. And then the camera picked out Mladić, sitting at a kitchen table. It was definitely him: he had the same jug ears. Behind me the ghosts shifted and hissed. Adam said, 'Visual confirmation positive. Let's get some audio.'

On the screen, Mladić pulled the end off a knobbled white loaf and basted it with honey. Speakers fizzed and spat. 'You must open the hive today,' he said, in Serbian. 'Check there are eggs,' he went on, munching bread and honey. 'Muslims are like bees, but a single male and lots of females. In the war they wanted to put all Christian women in harems. I'm telling god's truth, if you make way for one he'll bring six wives, and before you know it there's a village.'

Another man came into view. He had a lumpy bald head and broken veins. The farmer-cousin? He picked up the pot of honey. 'I've got bad news from Belgrade,' he said.

'Open the hive at a time with no wind,' Mladić went on, stubborn or deaf. 'You mustn't risk the eggs.'

'Your wife has been questioned again, Ratko.'

The old war general looked up, roused from apiarian concerns to personal grievance. 'I've not even spoken to Bosiljka these many years!'

'They took her to the police station.'

'Is she hurt?'

'No. Bosiljka – hard to frighten. But Bojan Lepović, he is pissing himself.'

'Bojan!' Mladić made a dismissive flick with his fingers. 'He was interrogated only once. It was routine.'

The cousin frowned. 'Police, yes, that is routine.' He took out a handkerchief and wiped his face with it. 'Bojan though, he was taken by Special Forces. Also an Englez. A thin blond man.' My heart missed a beat.

'Special forces?' said Mladić. 'Why did you not tell me this before? Am I a child that you keep things from me?' The words flew from his mouth in a burst of spittle, clearly visible on the screen. 'Visit Bojan's home,' he spat. 'Remind him we are relatives. Family is sacred. Blood is blood.'

'You don't trust him?'

'I trust only my wife and my son.'

The cousin put the pot of honey down. 'What if Bojan told the Englez of this house, Ratko? Maybe it's time you should go.'

'Bojan knows nothing,' Mladić said. 'Where should I go? Tell me that.' He reached under the table and brought up two pistols – clumsy looking, with old-fashioned, heavy barrels, but slick and gleaming. His practised fingers undid the safety catches. Flick. Flick. 'Let the Englishman come here.'

At this point the news programme cut back to the brightly lit studio, and the reporter at her virtual desk. 'We'll be discussing this extraordinary footage in a moment. But first, let's look in more detail at what happened next.'

In the top right-hand corner of the screen, a photograph appeared of three Serbian policemen and an old man in a baseball cap, walking away through a door. The ghosts in the living room erupted at once; they whistled and shrieked. 'We got the bastard!' they rejoiced.

'The prisoner was getting ready for a pre-dawn stroll—'

'Shh!' they hushed each other.

I dug my nails into my palms.

'When four armed men burst into the farmhouse. Mladić was thought to be planning a kamikaze last stand –' dear god in heaven – 'Yet police say he accepted his arrest politely. "Checkmate", he apparently conceded. "Which one of you is the foreigner?"'

'Adam's safe,' said Timor. He reached for my hand, but I pulled away from him, snatching up the TV remote from where it lay on the shelf. The four armed men were ten plain-clothed police or twenty commandos, depending which channel you picked. Mladić was handcuffed or he was not handcuffed; he was made to sit in the yard or he was taken into the house; he offered his captors homemade brandy or bread with cheese or fresh honey. But no one got hurt: they all agreed on that. Adam was alive. He was fine.

The soldier with moles on his face took the remote from me and flicked back to the female reporter and her desk. 'High-tech surveillance and tracking techniques were behind this operation,' she was saying. 'The American and British Armed Forces have been formally thanked for their support in following up an anonymous tip.'

Hasan asked, 'Was that Laura?'

'Yes, dear,' Ana told him. 'That was her.'

I felt ready to burst with happiness and pride.

All day long my guests were jubilant. They wanted a banquet, a celebration – they wanted, when it came down to it, a wake. Most of them also wanted to keep watching the news, so although I would dearly have liked to see the story unfold, I offered to help in the kitchen.

The first thing we made was Bosanski lonac, as this would take five hours to cook. Ordinarily, it's a potato and lamb stew. The potatoes I dug out of Hasan's window pots, feeling for them under the soil. They came up small and hard, with black spots that had to be cut out. I thought meat would be impossible, but Sara opened the bottom drawer of the freezer and produced a bag of chicken thighs. 'Always save something for the future,' she said triumphantly.

We defrosted the thighs in warm water. Then we layered chunks of chicken and potato with vegetables – mostly tomatoes and peppers – and poured a horded bottle of red wine over the top. Sara stopped often to check on Hasan, so I was the one who turned on the gas and put the stew in the oven.

While it was cooking, we made sarma, rolling blanched nettle leaves around tiny portions of rice and onion. Timor appeared in the kitchen now and then, smoking a festive cigarette, to ask how long it would be. Sara shooed him out. After about an hour, she began to improvise a kind of halva, mixing wetted flour with oil and honey, tossing little balls of it in icing sugar. The air filled with a back-of-the-throat sweetness, and another smell I couldn't identify, which made me uneasy.

I went into the living room to get away from this smell, and also to see what was happening on the news.

The Serbian president was talking to a collective of reporters with flashing cameras and Dictaphones. 'Today we close one chapter of our recent history,' he said.

Right after that there was an almighty bang. I was knocked violently off my feet and thrown backwards over the top of the sofa on a wave of broken bricks. A vase on the sideboard, leaping into the hot air, seemed to hang like a lantern for an instant before exploding outwards in a rainbow of ceramic shards. I hit the floor, and Ana and Timor began to run towards me, reaching out their hands. There was another bang – a crack like a gunshot. As I lost consciousness, Timor's blue eyes were the last thing I saw. They were always remarkably clear.

CHAPTER 31

I woke to a ringing in my ears. The sensation of lifting. Faces loomed over me, then receded, and yellow paramedic jackets glowed at the edges of my vision. The memory of an ambulance came back to me. A siren scream. Flashing blue lights.

'She's been slipping in and out of consciousness,' said one of the paramedics, answering a question I hadn't heard because the voices were fading from loud to soft to loud again. 'Says she's got health insurance through the British Civil Service. It's hard to tell if she's fluent in Serbian – lots of slurring. Is that Englez still here on his elective?'

After a short pause, a doctor bent over me. He looked very young, but I knew he was a doctor by his stethoscope. He said, in English, 'Can you tell me your name?'

'Laura,' I said. My lips felt clumsy. 'Laura Quin.'

'Just lie still for me, Laura.'

He listened through the stethoscope to both sides of my chest. I flinched as his hands moved to my skull. 'No indentations or bleeding,' he murmured. He turned to the paramedic who had spoken before, switching to excellent Serbian. 'You said an explosion. Do we know if she inhaled any gas or smoke?'

'The fire crew told us an oven blew up. They got her out fast – a neighbour saw the fire and phoned in straightaway. There was a lot of smoke though.'

I struggled to sit up, but pain stabbed through my chest. A nurse stepped forwards and pressed me gently down on the trolley. 'The fire was under control when we left,' the other paramedic reassured me. 'You just concentrate on getting better. We'll try to look in on our way out.' They strode off together, bright spots of diminishing yellow.

'Do you know where you are?' the doctor asked me. Then, 'Do you understand what I'm saying?'

I focused on him with difficulty. He had sandy stubble and grey cheeks, as if he hadn't slept for a long time. Kind eyes behind thick glasses. I said, 'I'm getting there.'

The nurse giggled. 'He come from Liverpool. Six month I study in London, I am not understanding him at all.'

I didn't know doctors could blush. I wanted to tell him it just felt strange to hear English again, but talking hurt. 'I'm in hospital,' I said.

'Do you remember what happened?'

I thought I remembered an explosion. Flying pieces of brick. Something bright blue. Then nothing until the ambulance. 'No,' I said. 'It's all confused.'

'Well, some initial memory loss is normal after a bang to the head. Can you move your arms and legs for me? That's good. Now push against my hands.' But as I tried this my chest filled with pain, so that I gasped.

The doctor asked the nurse curtly for scissors to cut through my top. When he lifted the ruined material away he frowned, as if at something unexpected. He ran his fingers along my exposed ribs like an afterthought, still frowning. 'You may have some fractures,' he told me. 'We'll take a look, but normally they heal on their own.' He turned to the nurse, shifting politely to Serbian. 'She's going to need a chest X-ray as well as a head scan. And let's do an arterial blood test. There's no definite history of smoke but we don't want to take any risks with her lungs.' He looked down at my ribs again. 'She's extremely thin. Tell them to check her iron and potassium levels, too.'

The nurse started to wheel me away but the doctor put his hand on the rail of the trolley. 'Is there anyone we can call for you, Laura?' He took in my wedding ring. 'Your husband?'

Tiny fragments of that morning's events came back to me. *Safe*, I thought. *Not shot.* 'He's out of town.'

'Perhaps another family member?' the doctor persisted. 'Or a friend?'

My head ached too much to think anymore. I told him, 'I've no one to call.'

The head scan was normal, and so were the oxygen levels in my blood. The X-rays showed up two fractured ribs. 'You've been lucky,' the doctor from Liverpool assured me. Even so, he kept me in for observation. I heard him arranging this on the phone. 'Everything seems okay,' he said, 'but she's in a lot of pain from the rib fractures and she doesn't have anyone at home.' He lowered his voice. 'She also looks a bit unkempt. Yes, very low BMI. I'd like to keep an eye on her for a day or two.'

The nurses roused me every hour that night, shining torches in my eyes and making sure I knew who and where I was. In between I lay and listened to the breath and purr of the hospital, conscious even in the dark of the bone-whiteness of everything. Sheets and ceiling. It reminded me of that other ward, the one in Coventry, and I felt a woozy panic, blurred by drugs. My head hurt so badly I could barely breathe.

I woke properly at six, when a nurse turned on the lights. He checked my pulse and temperature and gave me more painkillers for my ribs. The woman in the bed nearest mine complained that someone had lost her shoes, and the nurse said he would keep his eyes peeled. I imagined a sickening unblink, like skinless grapes. I imagined him tweezering off whatever membrane stops the eye-fluids from oozing out.

Some time later he brought me a card that said TOAST – EGG – PORRIDGE. I ticked PORRIDGE and got a lukewarm bowl of it. Ate hungrily, surprising myself. A motherly woman came round with the tea trolley. 'Do you take sugar, sugar?' The tea was grey but I drank it anyway. Then I drowsed a bit and dozed a bit, until I was woken by laughing nurses.

'He's the new consultant,' one of them was saying.

'Call that a consultant?' the other scoffed. 'Looks more like an orangutan to me.'

I couldn't see these nurses because they'd closed the curtains around my bed. The curtains were a dusty blue, the colour of robin eggs. They had a harsh, tired smell, like old TCP.

'How do you feel this morning?' said a half-familiar English voice. I looked up. It was the grey-skinned young doctor from Liverpool. His stubble had grown darker and his scrubs weren't ironed. If anyone looked unkempt, I thought. I'd been hoping for the orangutan.

'I want to go home,' I said, trying to sit up. Yesterday's pain stabbed through my chest. With it came a memory of liver-spotted hands and bright blue eyes. Ana. Timor.

'Home?' the doctor said, as if I had suggested a herbal remedy. He compared the chart at the foot of my bed to something in the folder he was carrying, a slim manila flap-over with my name on it. 'I'm fairly happy with you from a head injury point of view,' he admitted. 'But those ribs won't make it easy to manage alone for the next few days.' He frowned at me. 'What I'm more worried about is your weight. You're very malnourished. I'd like to have a dietician take a look at you.'

I frowned back. The nametag on his chest identified him as Mark Lucas. 'For an Englez, you speak very good Serbian,' I said.

'Well, my mother was from Belgrade. I grew up in Merseyside, came here for a year. Which language would you prefer?'

'English is fine. I'm Bosnian, but I grew up partly in Coventry.' The similarity in our histories made him feel like a friend. 'Look,' I told him, 'I don't need to see a dietician. I need—' I trailed off. Zvezdanka Street. The explosion. How long did I have before someone at the Embassy found out? Those men would be round again. They would go into every room this time, find all my things. 'I need to leave,' I said. 'Please.'

Dr Lucas sat down on a plastic chair beside my bed, holding the folder on his knees. 'Can you tell me why you're in such a rush?'

195

'Not really.' I bit my lip. 'I just am.'

He wrote something down on a page in the folder – I saw the squiggle of a question mark at the end. 'A new country can affect people in ways they don't expect,' he said. 'Are you feeling okay in yourself?'

I didn't answer. What was there to say?

Dr Lucas took off his glasses and polished them with his sleeve before putting them on again. He couldn't have been much older than me. 'Can you remember what you were doing before the accident?' he asked. 'I'd like to get a clearer picture of what happened.'

'I was cooking.'

His eyebrows went up. 'Do you cook often?'

'It runs in my family,' I told him, offended by his scepticism. 'My brother's a chef, and my father owns a restaurant in Croatia. Right before the explosion, I was making sarma. They're stuffed leaves, you probably know them. Also halva, for dessert, and Bosanski lonac – that's a Bosnian stew.' A feeling of discomfort crept over me, gone before I could identify it. I said, 'I had the oven on a long time. The gas can't have lit properly.'

Dr Lucas pushed his glasses higher up the bridge of his nose. He seemed puzzled. 'Was all this food just for you?'

'It was for a celebration,' I said. Now I'd started talking, I was finding it hard to stop. 'There are things I haven't told you. Some of them are politically sensitive but I think I should be allowed to tell a British doctor.' I lowered my voice, even though we were speaking English, so the patients and nurses outside the curtains wouldn't hear. 'My husband is a civil servant. He's working as a Political Advisor to the British Army. In fact, he just helped to catch a war criminal.' I looked more closely at his face. 'What's wrong?'

Dr Lucas said, 'Are you talking about General Mladić?' When I didn't answer, he massaged the grey skin under his eyes. 'It sounds strange,' he pointed out cautiously. 'The army. A war criminal. Are you sure it makes sense?'

'But it's the truth.' My voice rose. 'Every word is true.'

'Try to calm down for me, Laura.' His hand moved to his bleeper.

As vividly as if it had appeared in front of me, I saw that white ward in Coventry. Syringes of fluid. Chalky pills. I couldn't stand it – not again. 'There's a way you can check,' I said. I took a panicky breath. 'My husband's Head of Section is called David Focket.' Dr Lucas's hand paused on his bleeper. 'I'll give you his number.' I forced myself to speak calmly. 'He'll confirm what I told you.'

I'm sure he thought he was humouring me. I must have looked a state: thin as I was, and ragged, with my hospital gown and untidy hair. But he found a piece of paper and lent me his pen. I wrote down the switchboard number for the Foreign Office, then Dave's extension. Thank god I remembered it. 'Phone him now,' I said. 'Please.' So Dr Lucas fetched the cordless phone from the nurses' station. He was too tired to be working, for a fact. He looked ready to fall asleep on his feet. Anyway, he made the call.

When he got through to the switchboard, a look of boyish surprise came over his face. He said, 'I'd like to speak to David—'

'Focket,' I said.

'Focket, on extension 406.' He listened. 'I'm calling from the Bel Medic Hospital in Belgrade, on behalf of Laura Quin. There's been a gas explosion at her home and she asked me to contact Mr Focket. She says her husband works with him.' He put his hand over the receiver. 'She's trying him now.' Then he dipped his head to listen. 'Yes, I see,' he said. 'Please do. Yes. Goodbye.' He held the phone to his chest. 'David Focket isn't at his desk. She's left him a message.'

I said, 'He exists, though. You do believe me now?'

Dr Lucas nodded slowly. 'The Foreign Office. My word.' Outside the blue curtains, a voice yelled his name. He jumped up. 'I've not finished my ward round! I'll come back this afternoon.'

Long after he rushed out, I lay staring at the spot where he'd stood, listening to the faint, sea-like seethe of the ceiling lights. Dave would know I'd stayed on in Serbia. But it had nearly been so much worse. Dr Lucas found it hard enough to believe that my husband was part

197

of the hunt for Mladić. If I'd mentioned the ghosts, all rational conversation would have been over between us. I tried to think through what this meant, but my mind felt clogged, gritty. All I could think about was a woman on my ward in Coventry who'd been sectioned. Her hands and legs were tied to the bedrails. She was screaming. White saliva flew out of her mouth and a bit fell on me.

My head started to hurt again. I shut my eyes but memories throbbed dangerously behind my lids. Flames and blue eyes and spit.

CHAPTER 32

I don't know how long I slept. I woke to find Big Dave beside my bed, reading from the folder containing my hospital notes, which the doctor in his hurry had left behind. Seeing me move, he put the folder down on a side table. 'Laura,' he said, with a warmth that did not reach his eyes. 'How are you?' He held up a bunch of pink lilies, producing them from behind his back, like a magician.

I took the flowers silently, wincing at the pain in my chest, which I didn't want him to see. 'Your fire made it into a local paper this morning,' Dave went on, without any more niceties. 'Apparently, the gas in old ovens doesn't always catch light. The pressure builds up, and then boom.' A jumping muscle in his throat revealed the effort it was costing him to keep his voice low and pleasant. 'When your doctor phoned, I put two and two together. I had a colleague go to Zvezdanka Street. He packed some fresh clothes for you, by the way. I've got them in a bag. And he also found these.' He placed my phone and its charger neatly on top of the medical folder, along with my purse. Then he sat down in the chair by my bed, his excess flesh spilling over its plastic edges. While I had got thinner, his girth had increased, as if my lost pounds had flocked to him. 'Someone will collect the rest of your belongings later,' he said. 'Now, why aren't you in England?'

I was finding it hard to think straight. 'It isn't Adam's fault,' I told him, determined at least to make this clear. 'He thinks I left.'

'I'll decide who's at fault,' Dave said crisply. 'Adam is due in Belgrade at two o'clock. I'll debrief him before I fly back.'

I clutched the lilies. Suddenly my ribs were making it hard to breathe. 'Does he know I'm in hospital?'

'I've told him you're stable. Naturally he's worried about you.'

The thought of seeing Adam was overwhelming. I tried to

marshal all the small, practical things he needed to know. 'Visitors are allowed until eight o'clock. He needs to be here by then, or they won't let him in.'

'I'll do what I can.' Dave fixed his eyes on a lily petal that had got crushed between the mattress and the rail of my bed. 'None of this is ideal,' he said, with heavy irony. 'Next time you blow up government property, you should phone our helpline for partners whose spouses are away. You shouldn't have a doctor contact me.'

And you shouldn't barge in while I'm asleep and read my hospital notes, I thought. Aloud I said only, 'I have concussion. Do we need to go on talking?'

He laced his fingers together. For a big man, he had unexpectedly small hands. 'It can wait until London, I think. You and Adam are booked on a flight in two days' time.' There was no pretence of offering me a choice about this. 'Say nothing else to your doctor,' he warned me. 'Do you understand?'

'My passport—'

He smiled thinly. 'I don't have it on me. I'll give it to Adam.'

I levered myself up in bed, fighting the pain in my ribs. 'I'd like you to leave now.'

Dave glanced again at Dr Lucas's folder, where it lay on the side table. 'Well,' he said. 'I'll see you in London.'

Once he had gone I lay back in bed, my chest searing. It crossed my mind to open the folder, to see what he had read. But there was no point. Dave hadn't any use for the details of my head injury and broken ribs, he was just a professional busybody who couldn't keep his fingers off private information. I took a ragged breath. My husband was on his way to Belgrade – in a few hours I would see him. If only I knew what I wanted to say.

Later that morning, a nurse fetched a vase for my lilies. She made a fussy little rigmarole of arranging them, filling the ward with their funeral parlour scent. Hazy with painkillers, I found myself wondering if Adam would bring me a flower, the way he used to do.

A white one with the woody smell of strawberries from the patch in front of Mladić's farmhouse, or a musty, spotty one from the rows of beans. I was too tired to examine what such a gift would mean to me. Since the accident, I couldn't reach the end of a complex thought.

Lunch was chicken with mashed potato and peas. It was nothing like the colours and savours of Sara's early cooking: cream and mince oozing out of smoky peppers, sausages bursting with cumin and cinnamon and sweet red paprika. I ate it so as not to give Dr Lucas an excuse to keep me. Also, because I was hungry. I did feel it was doing me good.

The tea trolley came and went before I found the courage to turn on my phone. When I dialled my answer-machine, a reproachful automated voice said, 'You have – seventeen – new messages.'

The early ones were from the Vice-Dean of Belgrade University.

'Where are you?'

'Call me.'

'Call me at once!'

Then, 'I am calling' (stiffly formal) 'to say you have been struck off our teaching register.' A pause. 'What went wrong, Laura? If you want to talk, you know where to find me.' Another pause. 'Drop in anyway. Reassure me you're not dead.'

I erased those messages, which were painful to me, even though I should have known they were coming. I felt the weight of a loss – of something unfinished, or not finished in the way I would have chosen.

The later messages were mostly from Tata. 'Why aren't you answering your phone?' 'You know I hate these machines!' 'I'm worried about you!'

There was nothing from Adam.

In the hospital, time passed slowly and sometimes seemed to stop. At four o'clock I rang his mobile. It went straight to answer-machine. I also rang our old house on Zvezdanka Street, but no one answered. At five o'clock Dr Lucas made another ward round. He did the tests I was used to by now and frowned at my ribs. 'Are you eating well?'

I said, 'As well as I can. It's hospital food.'

He nodded seriously. It was hard to make him smile. 'I'm sorry I missed Mr Focket.'

'It's not a great loss. You left a folder here.'

'Your medical notes.' His face flushing, he tucked the folder under his arm. 'There'd be no end of trouble if I mislaid those.'

I wanted to say, Go home and sleep. You look worn out. Instead I said, 'My husband will be here any minute. May I leave with him, please?'

Dr Lucas sighed. 'If it's before my shift ends, I'll have them bleep me. I put you on a forty-eight-hour care plan, in case of late complications to your head injury. I'd rather keep you here for one more night.'

After he had gone, the nurses drew the blue curtains back. 'He'd have let me go home,' the woman in the nearest bed told me, sorrowfully. 'Only they can't find my shoes.'

Over the next few hours, I rang both Adam's mobile and the apartment on Zvezdanka Street several times, to no avail. I couldn't believe Dave would keep him this long. At seven o'clock the dinner trolley made an entrance. I resigned myself to another hospital meal. All I remember now is the soup. More peas.

The last visitors left the ward at eight. So I was stuck here for another night. And Adam was – who knew where?

After a while, I sent Tata a text.

There was a small explosion at home, and I'm in hospital. I'm fine but my head aches. I love you. L.

Two minutes later my phone rang. 'Moja duša! Što se dogodilo? Kako si?'

I said, 'English, please, Tata.' It would give us more privacy.

'Are you okay? What happened? You did not phone for such a long time!'

'I'm fine. I have some broken ribs and a headache, that's all.'

'Is Adam with you?'

'No.'

There was a pause on the other end of the line. 'My soul, have things gone wrong between you two?'

I said, 'I don't know.' Words like torn muscles, fractured bones. 'He's been away for a long time. He got back this afternoon, but he didn't come to see me.'

'When do you get out?'

'I think tomorrow.'

'You want to visit? It's hot here already. Good for – how do you say, recuperies?'

I held the phone close to my ear. Dubrovnik was dust and sunlight. A noisy, dirty city that never stopped to think. I'd drink plum brandy and it would be like drinking nothing, swallowing empty space. But Dave had given Adam my passport. He had demanded my presence in London. I said, 'I need to sort some things out first, Tata.'

He sighed at that – pent up, theatrical – and I waited for the explosion, but what he said was, 'Can I tell your brother that you're in hospital? We've spoken on the phone. He's worried about you.'

I hesitated. Tarik and I hadn't talked since my wedding, but that was my fault: he'd tried to get in touch and I had pushed him away. My old instincts of caution and distrust no longer made much sense to me. We had been so young when things went wrong between us. It was all such a long time ago. So I said to Tata, 'Yes. Okay.'

We talked a little more, then I told him I needed to sleep. I lay back on the pillow and put my hands over my face as the ward quietened round me. I imagined Adam in a British Army truck, the strawberry beds and sunflower fields of Lazarevo fading into the dust behind him. But that truck should have got to Belgrade hours ago.

Perhaps it had crashed and he was dead. Perhaps he had lost his memory and was wandering in a forgotten village, uncertain of his name. Those would have been sufficient excuses.

CHAPTER 33

Early the next morning, I was visited for the last time by Dr Lucas. His stubble was on its way to a full-blown beard.

'Won't they let you go home either?' I said.

He frowned. 'I went home yesterday. That's how I missed your husband.' He took off his glasses and fiddled with them. 'He's not here this morning?'

'No.' I saw no reason to tell him that Adam hadn't come in last night. I didn't want him to know I had no one to look after me, or he might not let me leave.

'I'm discharging you,' he said. 'But if your headaches get worse, or you notice any flashing loss of vision, come straight back in. And Laura, I think you should discuss your diet with a GP.'

'Tea and porridge,' I said. 'You can't fault me.'

Maybe he didn't know how to smile. 'I brought a leaflet on head injuries for you,' he said. 'Travel safely.'

'Never mind him,' said the nurse at the desk, once he'd gone. 'He's always grumpy in the morning.'

In the privacy of the blue curtains, I took off my hospital gown and put on the clothes Dave had brought for me, since Dr Lucas had scissored through my old ones. Then I gave the lilies to the woman in the next bed and hoped they found her shoes. I almost started laughing as I signed the papers the nurse gave me. But that was just nerves. Really, I had nothing to laugh about.

Outside the hospital I stood very still and breathed in deeply, until the smell of car fumes and cigarette smoke forced the memory of antiseptic from my lungs. I didn't know what hotel Dave's secretary had booked for me and Adam and I had no intention of asking. This morning I'd found my scissored clothes folded neatly on a shelf beside my bed and had taken from my jeans pocket the key to my old house. Even if someone discovered me there, it could hardly make things worse.

A taxi drove me to Zvezdanka Street. After it had gone, I stood outside the building for a long time, preparing myself. But when I opened the front door, no one was there.

I walked over a small pile of circulars and junk mail, and on through the wreckage of a kitchen that now opened into the living room. The firemen's hoses had left puddles and there was wet ash everywhere, flakes and crumbs of it, like some monstrous dinner party gone awry. Glass from burst windows crunched on the floor, plates and pans had been knocked down and broken or blistered by the fire. The black stains on the three remaining walls looked like a language left by tongues of flame, like ancient writing.

So much had been lost in the explosion. The map of the Balkans was gone, and also the photos on the wall. Though this was fortunate, as they would have been hard to explain. I imagined the map unfurling off the table, seas and rivers sailing through the air, sunflower seeds scattering and soybeans rolling. I imagined the singed photos borne upward and Mladić's face floating for a moment above the ruins of the feast, his eyes on fire, his jug ears burning in towards his skull.

The oven itself was remarkably undamaged, though the door hung broken on its hinges. Smears of colour had burnt darkly onto the hobs – all that chopped tomato, all those green peppers and onions. Five months of scrimping, struggling, making do. I bit my lips tightly together. I would think about it later.

Leaving the kitchen, I went upstairs to my bedroom. The drawers had been wrenched open; sleeves and trouser legs were hanging out. At first, I thought it was the work of the man Dave had sent here. But I was almost sure that some of Adam's clothes were missing – a couple of old T-shirts and his most comfortable pair of jeans. When I went into the bathroom, his cut-throat razor was out on a shelf, its blade spotted with shaving foam. That could mean only one thing. I sat down abruptly on the edge of the bath, my arms folded over my sore ribs. He'd been and gone.

But why?

I would think about that later, too.

Downstairs, in the ravaged kitchen, I made a pot of chicory coffee. I felt strange and empty, still half-concussed, perhaps. For hours I wandered aimlessly through the house, drinking the bitter coffee and touching the broken things. When it got dark, I turned on the lights in every room. I wanted to make it clear I was home.

All evening I watched for a wisp of cigarette smoke, the edge of a headscarf passing through a wall. But it was Adam who came.

CHAPTER 34

He rang on the doorbell instead of using a key. He had grown a beard. Apart from that he looked the same. Desperately unsure of what I felt, I took a step towards him. He smelt of the churchyard, which he must have crossed. Rain and earth and wet grass.

'Wait,' he said. From his jacket pocket he took an old newspaper photograph of Mladić – blackened at the edges and scarred by flames. He said, 'I found this under the kitchen table. I came here to pick up some clothes.'

He'd been back just two days. Who was the god of chance and underwear? That god hated me.

'I worked out what you were doing,' I whispered.

Adam was staring at me as if he'd never seen me before. As if I had scales. He said, 'If Dave had found this...' What he did next took me by surprise. He tore the picture in half, then in half again, and then he dropped the pieces on the doorstep and brought his foot down on top, stamping and grinding them under his heel until the charred and fragile paper was reduced to unidentifiable scraps. As he kicked the ashy remains to one side, breathing hard, a motion-sensitive light came on next door and illuminated us both in a harsh white glow. 'Bloody hell,' he said. 'Should you be out of hospital?'

I said, 'I was discharged.'

But he wasn't listening to me. 'Dave saw something your doctor wrote on your file. "Psychosis. Question mark."'

The colour left my face. I felt it go, felt it draining away. For a moment everything stopped. My heart. My breath. The turning earth – skewered on its axis. I said, 'Dave had no right.'

'He's going to revoke my clearance.' Adam rubbed his hand over his hair, a sign of agitation so familiar that for a moment it felt like nothing had happened – no time had passed at all. 'Is it true? Are you ill?'

I shut my eyes. 'I'm Bosnian. You were chasing Mladić – I couldn't just leave.' In the light behind my lids and lashes, I saw Timor holding a ladder steady for me. I opened my eyes quickly. 'Look,' I said, 'I wasn't dancing naked on the pavement.'

Adam blinked at that. I even thought I saw a trace of his lopsided smile, there and then gone.

'Come in,' I said. 'Please.'

I stepped to one side, out of the emaciating light. But he looked past me, at the chaos of the hall with the brick dust on the floor, and at whatever histories were passing through the mirror, whatever memories were drifting smokily along the walls. He said, 'It's too late.'

'We can't just give up.' I had tears in my eyes; I could feel them smarting.

Standing in the doorway, his feet on the charred fragments of Mladić's face, he said, 'I think we already have.'

It was the finality in his voice that got to me, more than his words themselves. I couldn't think of a single meaningful thing to say, so I said again, 'Come in. At least let's talk.'

He shook his head. 'I'm going back to my hotel. We can talk on the plane.'

'You're leaving me *here*?'

'Just don't use the oven.' For the second time, he nearly smiled at me. He dug into his jacket pocket, brought out an envelope. 'Ticket,' he said. 'Passport. The flight leaves tomorrow, at noon.' Then he turned, his shoulders hunched, and walked back down the drive. This time he didn't stop.

I watched until he was out of sight. 'Fuck you,' I said softly. Then, still softly, I shut the door.

I went back to the burnt-out kitchen and stood there for a long time, just staring at the mess. I felt hollow. Skinned. Eventually I climbed the stairs and opened the door to the bathroom. There was his old cut-throat razor on the shelf above the sink. The bathtub with its rust spots. I ran both taps. When the tub was full, I took off my clothes and lay down in the water. My hair floated darkly, slick like weed. I could see the paleness of my breasts and my narrow wrists, the bumps that were bones, the grey-violet veins.

Psychosis, question mark.

Dave had gone to Adam armed with Dr Lucas's suspicions. And Adam had come here to find the house smashed and torn apart like an outward sign of inward disaster, a perverse sacrament. In his absence our marriage had skidded towards chaos. But what felt as painful to me, as dismaying, was the loss of my guests – my ghosts. Sara. Hasan. Marija. Ana. Timor. That long seance was over.

As the bath cooled, I began to feel as if I was standing above my own body, looking down on myself. The floating tips of my hair were familiar to me, and when I touched my face it was clammy, the way I remembered Mama's face. That razor was just across the room, with its half-moon blade. I could put the edge to my wrist and the blood would rise up in long dashes and dots; it would run down my wrists and spill itself in the water. Red, pink, curling, gone.

I got as far as stepping over the edge of the bath. Then the pocket of my jeans chirruped and shook. Clumsily, with soap and water streaming from my hair, I crouched down to extract my phone. The message was from Tarik. My brother wrote to say that Tata had called him, and he, Tarik, had a spare room. 'I think you might need a place to stay,' he wrote. 'I'm here if you do, little sister.'

Back in the tub, I drew my knees up to my chest. My face was stiff with tears. But I thought of Mama again, her glazed goldfish stare, and I thought: I am not going to die in a bathtub in Serbia.

Rising from the water, I wrapped myself in a towel. And I walked wet-footed out of the room.

BOSNIA

2011

CHAPTER 35

I phoned Tarik at eight o'clock that same night. Then I filled two suitcases with clothes and ordered a taxi. I left a note of my brother's address on the kitchen counter for Adam. I also left my rings: the plain wedding band, and the little bird with its blank, garnet eyes. I twisted them off my finger quickly, before I could change my mind.

When my taxi arrived, I got the jam jar out of the cupboard above the oven. I was glad that paper money had survived the fire, though I would have preferred the heft of coins. Nuggets, ingots: something I could hold onto. Or jewels, to sew into the seams of my coat.

The taxi driver wore a Zoran Tošić football shirt. He helped me stow my cases in the boot. The setting sun was glowing on the brutalist apartments opposite as we pulled out of Zvezdanka Street, and Radio Belgrade was broadcasting on Partizan's latest defeat. Tošić punched the wheel in despair. I would have liked to punch something. Or someone.

No more of that.

At the airport I exchanged my ticket to London, tomorrow, for a ticket to Sarajevo, tonight. The woman on the check-in desk went out of her way to be helpful. I think she assumed it was a family emergency. Why else, said her sympathetic face, would I choose Bosnia over England?

Everything after that was quiet and purposeful – the rituals of passport control, the climb up the metal staircase to the plane. On the runway the left wing crept along behind my window like a pursuer, neither closing in nor giving up, and as we rose lumberingly into the night I surrendered to the temporary peace of transit – to the in-between.

An hour later, I was standing on Bosnian soil for the first time in twenty years. Butmir airport during the siege had been no man's land, a lethal cradle of barbed wire and dirty snow. Everyone knew someone who'd braved the desperate race across the tracks. It was said you had an equal chance of living or dying – lovers and mothers shot by Serb snipers.

Outside the terminal, a squally rain started to fall as I joined the crowd at the taxi rank. You can't mistake a Sarajevan taxi. Rosary beads and dried rabbit's feet dangle over the dashboard, a spot of devotional bet-hedging, and there's always a cloud of menthol cigarette smoke. This one was a battered Volkswagen. It crawled slowly east, past the north edge of the steep and beautiful Mojmilo Park and the south edge of the Grbavica Stadium. As a child I'd sledged on the park's slopes; I'd seen my first professional football match within the stadium's spaceship-grey walls. But it didn't feel real to me yet. Nothing ever looks familiar in the dark.

At last we drew up beneath a tower block that loomed skywards in concrete chiaroscuro, a rain-slick Escher. Tarik must have been watching for me because as the taxi drove off he was at the front door, kissing me on both cheeks, picking up my suitcase. I had forgotten how tall he was. My wiry, dark-haired brother, whom I hadn't seen since my wedding – and before that, not for nine years. 'Remember how in Coventry we lived on the first floor?' he said. 'Now I'm on the ninth.'

I smiled at him. 'You're going up in the world.'

Inside the apartment block, there was a porter behind glass who winked at us and a smell that made me think of mice. The lift was broken so we took the stairs, Tarik pausing once or twice to rest the cases. I was clutching my ribs by the time we reached the top.

He unlocked the door of his apartment and I got an impression of whiteness before he opened another door. 'It's only a boxroom,' he said. There was a futon on the floor and a rail of empty clothes hangers. It felt restful. Serene. When I crossed to the window and pulled up the blind, the whole of Sarajevo stretched out below me

– headlights and rear lights threading the roads. Stars lit the black sky. I put my hand to my face and found it wet with tears.

Tarik came to stand beside me. 'When I have my own restaurant,' he said, 'it's going to be this high up.'

'My marriage failed,' I told him quietly. 'I don't want to talk about it. I just need you to know.'

He put his hand on my shoulder, and for a while he said nothing. That felt like kindness. Then he said, 'I'm glad you decided to come.' He gave my shoulder a professional squeeze. 'Little sister, you always were a stick insect, but this is ridiculous. Have you had any dinner? I've got dough rising in the kitchen if you're hungry. I keep chef's hours,' he added. 'Late to bed, late up.'

So although it was gone midnight he made lahmačun, spinning the pizza base on his hand until it was thin as card, smothering it in minced lamb and tomato paste and olive oil. He got out a bottle of red wine and we opened it in the kitchen while the lahmačun was cooking. 'It feels strange to be drinking with you,' he said. 'I still think of you as eight years old. Fishing for dace in the Miljacka.'

Those fish, wavery and elusive under the water. Staring into the wine that remained in my glass, I said abruptly, 'Is Mama's grave here?'

'I looked for it, but they can't have identified her body. I went to the Ministry. And I asked our old neighbours. I'm sorry.'

'It's not your fault.' With an effort, I met his eyes. 'Tarik – do you think there was something wrong with her?'

'She had depression.'

'It was more than that. She saw things other people couldn't see.'

Tarik shook his head. Not denying this, just thoughtful. He poured us both another glass of wine. Carefully, as if it was a question he'd been waiting twenty years to ask, he said, 'What did she look like, when you found her?'

I turned away from him, caught off guard. 'Bloody,' I said. But then I said, 'Happier.' It was true. Her face had been tranquil, as if nothing more could touch her.

The pinger went. Tarik slid the lahmaču out of the oven, bubbling and yeasty, and led the way to a room that contained a blue sofa, a bookshelf and a framed poster of a black square. For a while we were silent, eating. Paper napkins, pots of drinking yogurt on the table: it was how my family had always done things.

At last I said, 'Do you remember the night I got taken to hospital?' I picked up the wine bottle but my hand was shaking too much to pour it. 'I mean, when I fell off the roof?'

'Of course I do.'

'I saw Mama. That's why I fell.'

He set down his knife. 'You thought you saw her.'

'No.' My fingers worried at each other, nail digging into knuckle. It was hard to say out loud. 'What if you look up, and there's an old Bosnian woman standing in your kitchen with a coffee-pot in her hand? Or a six-year-old boy and a kitten?' Tarik watched me intently across the table. He made himself very still, really listening. I said, 'What if your world splits away from other people's? At the time it doesn't seem wrong. But you cut yourself off from everyone. You barely eat.'

My brother smiled, ever so slightly. 'Speaking as a chef, that's the worst possible thing.' He poured me some more wine. 'I don't think wrong is the right word, little sister.' He was being very careful with what I had told him, very protective of me. 'I sort of like the sound of your visitors. And I know people who take acid – hell, you know I've taken acid – to see the world differently.'

'I wasn't *on* acid,' I said. My hands jerked so that I knocked the table and wine spilt from my glass, the dark red seeping across the wood. 'Sorry,' I said. 'I'm sorry.'

Tarik fetched the box of paper napkins and pulled out a few to wipe down the table. After a moment he said, 'You think they were really there? The old woman and the boy?'

'Not in the normal sense,' I said. 'They were ghosts.'

At first he didn't say anything, just went on sopping up the red wine. Then he said, 'They weren't upsetting, though. You didn't feel threatened.'

216

'Only their stories were upsetting.' I twisted a napkin in my hands, very close to tears. 'I almost died. I need to sort this out.'

'Hey,' he said. 'One step at a time, okay? What you need now is sleep.'

That was true, at least. While I took the plates to the kitchen, he fetched a towel for me, a thin one that smelt of green wood. I watched him fold it over the clothing rail in my room and turn to go. 'Tarik,' I said. 'What if—' I swallowed. 'What if I'm a danger to myself?'

'You aren't.'

I picked up the towel and hugged it to my chest. 'How do you know?'

My brother looked down at me, his grey eyes the colour of smoke. 'I've got confidence in you, little sister. If you'd wanted to die, you'd be dead.'

CHAPTER 36

That night in Tarik's apartment I slept anxiously and lightly, affected in my sleep by birds and police sirens, and drunks on the street nine floors below. I woke late, and there was a moment of calm before memory came back to me. Sarajevo first. Then everything else.

In the kitchen, my brother was frying eggs. 'Coffee,' he said, when he saw me. I watched him set out two cups and heap a teaspoon of Nescafé granules into each. Next he began to pour the cups half full of cold milk, ready to top them up with boiling water. Mama used to make instant coffee like that – lukewarm and grainy.

I moved from the doorway, careful of my hurt ribs. 'You're a chef,' I said. 'Shame on you.' Opening his cupboards, I came across a traditional coffee-pot, long-handled and made of copper. I found a jar of ground coffee beans in the fridge. The stove was gas: flames flaring up, humming down. I looked round to see Tarik smiling at me.

After breakfast, he left for work and I got dressed. Then I went out to buy a newspaper. Mladić's story was on page four.

War crimes suspect to be tried at Hague

At least we had done that. I walked further and further from Tarik's apartment – through Kovačići, Grbavica, Marindvor, past steamed-up cafés and statues with eroded noses. Outside the National Museum was an ironic monument to a can of ICAR beef. I stopped beside it, remembering Tata's fury about the food drops in the siege. 'Call this international aid? A dog wouldn't eat it.'

Under Skenderija Bridge, two war amputees pleaded for spare change in heroin voices. The drug had robbed them of undertones, stranded them forever on one note. I followed the Miljacka downstream. By now I knew where I was going. *When a shell killed a person outright, they filled the hole in the pavement with red resin.* It was Ana who told me that. And it had, and they had. At the foot of the bridge that led to the brewery, resin was splashed in ragged petals on the asphalt where Mama had died – brighter and lighter than blood.

Kneeling down, I put my hand in the very centre of the rose. It wasn't a grave but it was something. Tears came to my eyes and I blinked them away. She was part of the rising city now. She was etched into its pavement, buried under its walls.

A van backfired and a flock of pigeons flew up in noisy alarm. I walked on through streets the colour of burnt sugar, where dogs slept in doorways and coppersmiths hummed to half-familiar tunes. Tram bells rang out periodically.

Sometimes I thought I saw Ana. Or the back of Timor's head, or Hasan's chicken-wing elbows. Well, you can't trust anyone. That's all. You can't even trust your own brain if it makes people up.

When I got to Tarik's flat, I opened a new blister pack of painkillers. The pills were small and white and I swallowed two of them with lots of water, as Dr Lucas had told me to. I don't know why crouching down felt important when I was crying. After an hour my phone rang. On the eighth ring I answered it. I was bracing myself for Adam, his wounded fury. How dare you? Where are you? Instead, Tarik's voice said, 'Had a good day?'

'I went for a walk,' I told him.

'With broken ribs?'

'A doctor in Serbia gave me Vicodin.'

'Never tried it,' Tarik said cheerfully. 'Take a couple more, little sister, because you're coming out tonight. Café Illyria, at seven o'clock. Call a taxi.' Before I could say anything, he hung up.

Café Illyria was on Riba Street, not far from the stone ruins of Baščaršija, the old bazaar. The north end of the street was narrow and grimy, darkened by shop awnings on both sides. Outside the building, a faded sign showed a clenched fist, like the ones on medieval tombstones. Inside, the ceiling was low, every table was full and there was a homely smell of grilled meat and baked bread. I took a steadying breath and went up to a girl who was folding napkins – a skinny teenager with pistachio-coloured hair. 'I'm Tarik's sister,' I said.

'Welcome!' She smiled widely. 'I'm Nina. Tarik's in the kitchen.' She gestured behind her, a white napkin flapping in her hand. 'Go in! Go in!'

The kitchen was a small room, full of steel and steam. Strong odours of potato and cabbage bubbled up from big pots. As I entered, a waiter passed me with two plates held high in the air, saying 'Pardon!' as he turned sideways to go out. My brother came over with steak juice on his hands and a white cap on his head. He hugged me tightly, his fists bunched up because of the juice. 'Want to see where I work?'

I hung back, self-conscious, but trying to make a joke of it. 'Is this a good idea, Tarik? I have a history with kitchens.'

He laughed and indicated a white apron. 'You won't blow up this one. Put that on before you meet my boss. Hey, Boris! My sister Laura!'

The man named Boris wiped his red face on a towel before turning away from a work bench covered in lethal and delicate cooking equipment: a two-handled chopper for herbs, pasta cutters edged like pinking shears. 'Welcome!' he said, leaning over his stomach to greet me with three wet bristly kisses, cheek to cheek to cheek. 'All this time Tarik has been hiding you!' He had his sleeves rolled up and a tattoo of a demon bulged on his bicep. I liked him instinctively.

'Ćevapčići, table six!' the waiter shouted through the door.

For the next twenty minutes, I watched knives halving onions and cutting chunks of red meat; the processes of cooking, steaming, plating; the two tense, competent chefs. 'How long have you worked here?' I asked Tarik.

'One year,' he replied, wiping his forehead on his sleeve. 'The café has been around much longer – Boris set it up after the war, as an arts centre, and his daughter Nina helps out now.'

'I run a place where everyone comes,' Boris told me. 'We have Bosnian food and Bosnian music, but we get Croats, Slovenes, even Americans – we get all kinds of people here.'

When the seven-o'clock rush in the kitchen was over and most of the diners were tucking into their main course, Boris beckoned me to his bench. Here he laid out ingredients with his big hands, telling me where each one was sourced: dark slices of smoked beef from Visoko, aubergine sauce from Tuzla, smooth white squares of Travnički cheese. 'Try one of these,' said Tarik, coming to my side with his hands cupped full of fine-skinned tomatoes and holding them out so I could breathe their earthy smell. At once our childhood burst over me: the vegetable stalls of Markale market, the tables laden with peppers and lettuces and runner beans. I felt as if a secret and ravenous homesickness might finally be sated by these tokens of field and sun.

'When do you eat?' I asked Tarik. 'Can I sit round a big tray of burek with you all, like in films?'

'Patience, little sister. All will be revealed.'

A few minutes later, the green-haired girl, Nina, came in through the door. I noticed she had a limp – a sparrow-like hop. 'Table's ready,' she said.

Tarik laughed at my expression. 'I'm taking the night off.'

'You can do that?'

Boris winked at me. 'I work like two men, you will see.'

'Go on,' Tarik said. 'I'll catch you up.'

I undid the tags of my apron and ran a hand over my hair. Back in the café, Nina led me to a table at which a woman was already sitting. I had a swift, outsider's impression of slimness and messily cut brown hair; then she turned round in her chair and I said, 'Roisin!' and we were hugging each other and laughing and both talking at once.

'It's so lovely to see you! I thought you were still touring Europe!'

'I just finished. Honey, you need to put on some weight – I can feel your shoulder blades under your shirt!'

'I'm working on it,' I said. 'How are you *here*?'

She coloured slightly. 'I swapped numbers with Tarik at your wedding. I'm meant to be singing in Cambridge tonight but I pulled a sickie – I'll fly back tomorrow.'

People at nearby tables had begun to stare at us, so we sat down. Nina brought us a bottle of wine. 'On the house,' she said. 'Don't tell my dad, he's a tight-fisted bastard.'

When she had gone, her stiff, birdish gait oddly beautiful, Roisin filled our glasses up to the brim. 'I sent a whole bunch of emails,' she said. 'What's the story? You and Adam—'

'We broke up.'

'I'm sorry.' She looked at me closely. 'You don't want to talk about it?'

'Not tonight.'

'Okay, but listen – whisky, sofa, anytime.' A compassionate, subject-changing shrug. 'Tarik told me you broke a rib?'

'Two ribs,' I said. 'I think he wants to try my Vicodin.'

She looked at me, and we both started to laugh: sudden, helpless laughter, the kind that hurts your stomach. Tarik came out of the kitchen while we were still laughing, and Roisin rose, to be kissed on both cheeks. There was a grease-spotted menu on the table but he swept it up. 'Our house, our rules. Boris is already cooking.'

Roisin poured him some wine. 'May the road rise up to meet you,' she toasted us. We clinked glasses. After that we drank in awkward silence, no one quite sure what to say. The first course came as a relief. For Roisin there was a creamy soup; for me snails, in a red pepper sauce that was one of Tata's specialties. 'Try one,' I told Roisin.

She looked uncertainly at the picks and tongs. 'I feel like Julia Roberts in *Pretty Woman*.' Nevertheless, she extracted a snail with

222

aplomb and placed it whole on her tongue. 'Oh,' she said, meeting Tarik's eyes. 'Oh wow.'

He grinned at her. 'Do they not eat snails in Paris?'

'The bankers do,' she said. 'We barely had enough money for baguettes.' She turned to me. 'Paris was the last place we went on tour. Our keyboardist fell in love with a Frenchman, so I've got half a band at home and a Cambridge bedsit on mates' rates if I look after her damn cat. So much for The Vagrant Revolution. What about you, my love? Are you staying in Sarajevo for a while?'

I glanced at Tarik. 'I want to. But I'd need a job.'

'Of course you're staying,' he said. 'We'll work something out.'

Roisin reached for the wine again. 'I'm job-hunting too.' She winked at me. 'I found a Tudor farm museum in Sussex that's advertising for a miller's wife. They provide the costume.'

I touched the slight dent on my ring finger. I no longer wanted to be a wife. But jobs in Sarajevo were hard to find: here the tram drivers had engineering degrees; the chestnut sellers on the street corners were chemists. To Roisin I said only, 'I can see you in a corset.'

She swirled her wine. 'I'd rather marry a baker than a miller. I like nice buns.'

I said, 'That's a terrible joke.' But I did laugh.

For the main course, Tarik had ordered a sharing platter of the mixed grill: skewered lamb, pljeskavice that look like flattened burgers, chicken wings and legs and breasts. 'No Michelin stars here,' he joked to Roisin. 'Bosnian food is comfort food.'

She laughed. 'Last time I went to a posh restaurant was a disaster. Remember that comedian, Laura? He was working in London on Valentine's Day, and I took the train to King's Cross wearing nothing but lacy underwear and a long coat. Only he'd booked dinner without telling me, and my train was late, so he hustled me into a cab, talking cricket with the driver all the way there because the driver was Pakistani, and I kept hissing, "Sweetheart, listen." But would he? The taxi pulled up right outside the restaurant and a doorman helped me out of it, so suddenly I was in the foyer, millionaires and orchids all over the place, with not a stitch on, and a waiter in a tux behind me saying ever so politely, "Madam, may I take your coat?"'

'And then?' demanded Tarik.

Roisin picked up a chicken leg. 'I'll leave it to your imagination.' She grinned at him. 'I'm not saying another word.'

When we finished that course, Boris himself came out from the kitchen with our desserts. He wore his chef's apron, and the bulge of his stomach paraded before him. Other diners turned openly to stare. 'Beautiful ladies!' he said to me and Roisin, offering us spoons as if they were roses. 'Chocolate soufflé,' he announced, setting a plate down in front of me. 'It is fallen purposively,' he went on, in English, for Roisin's benefit. 'At end of cooking I move up very close to heat. Taste is more – how do you say? Intense.'

'An Icarus soufflé,' I said, and Tarik laughed. Of course he did. He was the one who first told me that story – the boy and the wings and the wax and the sun, and the dazzling, catastrophic plummet.

For him there was cream cake, a childhood favourite. For Roisin a trio of miniature portions. 'You think I'm indecisive?' she said.

Tarik raised an eyebrow at her. 'I think you want a bit of everything.' He turned to me. 'You eat up,' he said. 'A thin sister is bad for my reputation.'

It would be easy to forget the things we ate, and what we talked about. But I remember it as an occasion so remarkably precious that I was able to laugh on a night I had thought laughter impossible. An Icarus laughter. Frail as a feather. Bright as a flame.

CHAPTER 37

During my first week in Sarajevo, there were times when I felt close to real happiness, getting to know the city again. There were also long hours when I felt alone. Those were the times when everything was grey and cats howled on the rooftops, when I wrapped my arms as far as they would go around my own body, as if my fingers could press my shoulder blades back in.

At a loss for what to do, I began to roam the suburbs. I saw blocks of flats that had stood for twenty years without walls or roofs, and ash trees that staked a tenant's claim to empty houses – branches growing out of broken windows, roots pushing under shell-pocked walls. Sometimes I bought newspapers. I read these eagerly at first, then with increasing frustration. As Mladić's slow trial sank to the back pages, it seemed to me that Bosnia had gained nothing: the country's future looked no less bleak. And everything else looked unlit. Bloodless. Dreary. Crabbed.

I was regaining weight, that was one good thing. But I didn't feel like myself. The painkillers made me clumsy; I bruised my arms on the frames of doors and broke Tarik's plates. 'I can't even walk in a straight line anymore,' I complained to Roisin when she phoned from England. She said, 'So zigzag.' She always could make me laugh.

Tata also rang frequently. 'Are you eating well?' he said. And at the end of the week I found an answer-machine message from Adam: a noise like the start of a word as he opened his lips, then a quiet sigh and a click as he hung up. I sat on the floor for a long time, looking at my phone. But I didn't ring him back.

In the afternoon I walked down to the river. The brackish water bobbed with coke cans, used condoms and dreams. As I stood looking at it, I remembered Timor calling me a vila. Run away with me, he'd said. Then I remembered a phrase William Littleton had once used. Dreams and visions. At first I couldn't think what it meant, then I did: it was how they'd solved codes at Bletchley Park. Perhaps that was what the ghosts were – dreams, visions, unravelled threads of my own mind. Even so, I still missed them. I was sorry they were gone.

When Tarik came home from the café that night, I was curled up on the sofa with the jobs section of *Oslobođenje* scattered angrily around me, and for good measure *The Sarajevo Times*. 'No joy?' he said, when he saw what I was doing.

I pushed away the crumpled pages. 'Not unless I learn to drive a bulldozer. I've got six euros left in the world.'

'Stop worrying, little sister. You've got me.'

'How long for?'

Tarik looked at me and coloured. 'Don't judge me by the past,' he said. 'I quit coke eight years ago. I've been different since then.' I felt horrible at once. I didn't trust myself to speak. Tarik reached for the bottle of wine we had left unfinished the night before. 'Nina's going to university soon,' he said. 'Boris will need someone to replace her at the café.' He poured two glasses. 'It's just answering the phone and doing the box office for weekend gigs, but it would tide you over till you found something else.'

I could feel my heart rising. I had liked the café – its unswerving faith in the arts, and its staunch Bosnian identity. 'Do you think Boris would have me?'

'I'll talk to him.' Tarik sat down beside me, pushing my feet away to make room. I smiled at him, wryly – *Thanks*, and he shook his head – *It's nothing*.

The day I went back to Café Illyria, it was pouring with rain. One of the warehouses on Riba Street had become a building site. The atmosphere was tribal, leery. Men in hard hats stopped talking and stared at me as I went past. I folded my arms across my body and hurried to the café.

On the billboard outside was a poster for tonight's band:

GROUCHO AND THE PLATYPUSES, in rain-swollen ink. As I went through the door, I breathed in the smells of hot flatbread and potato from the kitchen. Then I took the stairs down to the basement, where Nina sat at a desk, plugged into an iPod and twitching with music. She popped out her earpieces. 'Doors open in ten minutes,' she said. 'C'mon, I'll show you round.'

I followed her sparrow-hop into a room with black walls. Groucho and the Platypuses were warming up. 'We are the future,' they crooned. Their lead singer had a voice like tyre-tracks in syrup.

'They're good!' I said to Nina. Resolutely unimpressed, she flicked her green hair.

When the audience began to arrive, I took money and handed over tickets while she pointed out regular customers. 'Mr and Mrs Tomić,' she told me, as an old lady in a headscarf approached on the arm of her husband, who wore a grease-spotted necktie. They were arguing loudly.

'For you, it's okay,' Mr Tomić said. 'You are deaf. The last concert here, I covered my ears.'

Mrs Tomić shook her head. 'I'm not deaf. Your ears are too big.'

A pair of teenage girls followed them, with rain-spangled hair, and then a whole family of Montenegrin tourists in plastic ponchos. I would grow to love the buzz of evening gigs at the Illyria. That first night, though, I was worried by small change and schoolgirl maths, grateful when the music started. Nina and I sat at the desk, a flashlight under her chair in case of fire. The songs came through the door not muffled but softened.

In the interval we helped behind the bar upstairs, which had a homely squalor, the old wood grooved by decades of elbows. Along the length of it were cracked leather stools and big-bellied men with dirt under their nails. The ones who carried hard hats came from the building site down the road. Mr Tomić asked me for plum brandy and a glass of white wine for his wife. 'The music, it's not bad,' he said. 'Young people today dance like goblins.' The teenage girls snickered, leaning against the wall and downing diet cokes.

At the end of the night, Boris told me, 'The job's yours if you want it.' He was wiping a damp cloth over the bar. 'You can say no,' he went on. 'My daughter finds it as dull as Hades.' But I said yes before he finished talking. He poured out some shots of walnut liqueur and we sat down at a table to drink it; just him and me and Nina, at first, and then Tarik joined us, drying his hands on a tea towel.

'Okay?' my brother asked me. I nodded, grateful to be part of this community and of Boris's warm aims for it: fat-bellied Boris, who seemed to get everywhere in spite of his bulk; arts director, chef, barman and bouncer, as the need arose. Tonight, he kept getting up to serve beer to the builders who still lingered – a group of Bosnian Serbs from Banjaluka, reluctant to face the rain-ridden night. 'Let's find some hot Sarajevan pussy,' one of them said. Another man sat on his own, staring at me. A skinhead with a folded, blueish scalp, like old bedsheets, he reminded me uneasily of the soldier Ana had once called a chetnik. Even his hand, wrapped round his pint, was tattooed with the same four C's. Само слога Србина спасава – *only unity can save the Serbs.*

As Boris poured a final round of liqueur, a cat entered noiselessly through an open window. It saw us and hesitated, feral, ribby, and missing bits of ear. 'Ratko!' Nina said, scooping the cat up in one hand and dropping it in my lap, from where it sprang, hissing, back to the windowsill. 'Dad names all the stray kittens after war criminals,' she told me. 'It's because we can never catch them.' The skinhead glanced up. Nina rubbed her leg, the stiff one, and I found myself wondering if she had got that injury in the siege. When the war ended she would not have been more than a baby – which didn't make it impossible.

I said, 'We caught your cat's namesake,' and I saw the skinhead scowl. Ratko Mladić was on trial for crimes against humanity, but some people still saw him as a nationalist hero. 'I hope he rots in the Hague,' I told Nina. 'I hope they lock him in a cell so deep he never sees daylight.'

She spat on the floor. 'Fuck him. I want to get on with my life.'

Her father said, 'Clean that up, you animal.' He put out his big hand and cuffed her green head, gently.

They were good people, although they weren't at all what I was used to. They were louder and brasher. Unwistful. Alive.

CHAPTER 38

From then on, I was at the café from ten until five, and on Friday and Saturday evenings. I had Mondays off. Nina was right: there was not much for me to do. All morning I sat in the basement, waiting for the phone to ring and leafing through the introduction to a book of Bosnian folk tales I had found in Tarik's apartment – the very one I had taken from Sarajevo, in fact, all those years ago. My brother was a source of wonder to me. I remembered him on cocaine, pit-eyed and clumsy. Now he moved deftly in tight kitchen spaces, at ease as fat spat in frying pans and water bubbled in saucepans, although he had scars from old burns on his hands and once, Boris said, he had lost an eyebrow when a stuffed pepper caught fire. Tarik confirmed this, laughing in his quiet way. For years I had thought of him as someone who was always leaving. Yet he had come back here first.

What was I saying? Oh, the folk tales. Yes. I was pursuing an old ambition, though slowly, painfully. I wanted to regain my ease with words – to be able to translate with clearness and precision. But for the moment I was just noting down anything that caught my attention.

Ukrainian archaeologists found outlines of waterbirds carved in the earth at a 3,000-year-old cult site.

A bracelet from NEOLITHIC Poland shows a woman's arms raised like wings and a swan or goose on either side of her.

At her wedding feast, a magical Russian princess hid the dregs of her wine in her left sleeve and the bones of her swan meat in her right sleeve, and later, as she danced, a lake appeared that was full of white swans.

On busy nights I helped in the bar, where elderly men nursed beakers of plum brandy, and if there was a gig I ran the box office. To the performers I was mostly invisible, though once or twice I found myself slipping out to the chemist's before the doors of the Illyria opened, to buy them cough sweets, and halfway through the night they might ask me for something else, with the politeness of urgency. A safety pin. A hairclip. They were caught up in their work. I admired that.

At closing time, Boris and Tarik would turn up the lights and begin to stack the chairs. I still got tired easily, so I sometimes went home by myself. But the building site down the street looked menacing at night, a dark sore, and Tarik worried if I walked alone through Baščaršija, where two people had been mugged in the last month. So mostly I waited for him.

One Saturday a local secondary school rented out our basement to rehearse a play by Safet Plakalo, the famous Sarajevan writer. I sat at my desk as the students flung down bags and scripts, their teacher trotting behind them – a bright-eyed old man, his body the shape of a shrivelled pear. 'We don't need one hundred voices,' he scolded them. 'Stop making noise!' Behind his back they rolled their eyes, or put their fingers round their throats and stuck out their tongues. After an hour or so, I got myself a pot of coffee from upstairs, and on impulse a pen and paper. For a while I did nothing more, just watched the old man darting forwards to lay his hands on ankles in inverted benediction, to hold wandering feet in place. When things went badly he spoke curtly in Bosnian. 'From the beginning!' he said. 'Again!'

You are the only one who can never see yourself except as an image. That's true, though it wasn't Plakalo who wrote it. I think it was Roland Barthes. So perhaps the stories we are most drawn to are the ones that show us images of ourselves? As the morning went on, I found myself writing about vilas. In my book of folklore they flickered incessantly between women and fish or waterbirds, revealing a doubleness that was sometimes outside – ragged wings, a glittering tail – and sometimes inside, a hidden "tale."

At one o'clock the old man stopped the rehearsal for lunch. I realised that writing had absorbed me utterly, for hours. 'Hurry!' his pupils told each other, grabbing their sunglasses and phones.

'Just take care!' he shouted after them, as they passed me on their way upstairs. 'Wait for the green man if there is no zebra!'

An hour later they came back to rehearse a kolo dance, stripping their shoes and socks off under the mounted gel lights. 'If I get a splinter in my toe, I'm going to sue,' one girl grumbled. 'It's stupid. Traditional dances and stuff.'

Accordion music formed the backdrop to my writing all afternoon. The smell of sweat and dust rose up from the stage floor. Tiredness tugged at my concentration but I persevered, fighting it off with pot after pot of coffee. '*One* two,' the old man shouted, '*Hop* hop, *hop* hop.' The boys lifted the hems of their T-shirts to wipe their faces; the girls tucked them into their bras or tied them at one side in a knot. A giant of a teenager spun the splinter girl, her brown hair whipping out behind her, and he was so big and she so small that she looked weightless in the air; his hands just touched her waist and she was flying – knees bent up behind her, laughing on a high-pitched intake of breath.

The students put their socks and shoes on again at five o'clock. 'If you eat in Boris's café, remember for a tip you make a circle,' the old man warned them, as they raced past me.

'A circle?' I asked him.

'A round number.' He laughed. 'I don't know why I teach them kolo. To me, Sarajevo is the city of art. But all they want is to be American pop stars.' I was struck by the truth of this. At the same time, I'd seen his students forget about their I ♥ BRITNEY T-shirts and surrender to the magic of the traditional dance.

I stayed late in the café that evening to type up my article. When it was done, I sent it to *Balkanista*, an online English and Slavic arts magazine that Nina sometimes read. I signed myself Laura Guska. That, not Quin, felt like my real name.

I got an email from the magazine's editor a week later. 'We'd like to publish this,' he wrote.

That night at the café, Tarik opened a bottle of wine to celebrate. Boris and Nina sat down to share it with us. The skinhead with the nationalist tattoo was back at his table, I noticed; some of the builders from the local site had become regular visitors to the café. They got very drunk, and Boris had already thrown two of them out. 'Better to retreat with honour than advance in disgrace,' he'd warned them. 'The morning is wiser than the evening.' Now the skinhead was signalling for another beer, but Boris acted as if he couldn't see him. Like any good barman, he had a talent for that.

At first we talked about my article, then about the latest issue of *Balkanista*. The editorial claimed that staff at The National Museum in Sarajevo hadn't been paid for several months. 'There's no money for art,' Boris said. 'Foreign Aid poured in after the war, so the churches look very nice, and the mosques. But now? Nothing.'

Nina smacked down her glass. 'The West should make Serbia pay.'

I said, 'Bosnian art is good enough to pay for itself.' I'd been thinking about this a lot, lately, watching music and theatre thrive at the café. 'The West is never the answer,' I said. 'Look at the Hague. Mladić claims he's sick, and at once the Dutch stop his trial and take him to hospital, a man who caused the deaths of a hundred thousand people.'

Across the room, the skinhead met my eyes and drew his index finger across his throat. I stood up, startled and angry, and he stood up too, pushing through the crowded tables towards the exit.

'What's wrong?' said Tarik.

I opened my mouth to explain, but then I hesitated. The man really did have exactly the same blueish shave and crude tattoo as the Serb nationalist ghost. Could that be why no one else had noticed his obscene gesture? What if I pointed right at him and they still saw nothing? I felt my face drain of colour. 'Nothing's wrong,' I said, sitting down.

Once the wine bottle was empty, Tarik went off to clean the kitchen while Boris ushered people to the front door. Nina started to wipe down the tables. 'I'll finish up,' I told her. She blew me an air kiss, making a henpeck sound with her lips as she left the room.

I took a seat at the empty bar to think things through. There was no way I was going back to hospital. But I couldn't risk slipping into that other world again – not when I was starting to find my place here. So, I would have to get rid of the skinhead on my own.

Balkanista

June 2011

Vila. By Laura Guska.

The Balkan vila is a water spirit, a cousin to the Russian rusalka, and, more distantly, the Greek siren. Her name also shares an etymology with the Old Norse *veior* (hunt) and the Avestan *vayeiti* (she pursues, frightens).

Vilas are the souls of girls who died young. This can make them cruel: they drown noisy shepherds or turn them to stone; they steal horses, destroy crops and tangle fishermen's nets. In the medieval Serbian poem "The Building of Skadar," a vila demands the blood sacrifice of twin children or a faithful wife before she'll permit the city walls to rise.

At best, the vilas of epic verse lack interest in human affairs. They hold hands in closed circles and fall asleep easily. When Prince Marko, the great Serbian hero, begs his sworn sister for help in a fight, she rebuffs him. "Didn't I say, dear, didn't I warn you never to start quarrels on a Sunday?"

Yet the most ancient rituals see vilas as a life force. In Romania they live all winter in the dark eddies of deep rivers, but when peasants make pastries shaped like birds, then the water spirits turn into woodcocks and it becomes spring. In Slovenia they dance in human form through rye fields, singing, and the crops ripen beneath their feet. And if any Slavic girl throws flowers on a lake at midsummer or pours wax in a saucer of water at midwinter, her future husband will be revealed by a vila.

In folklore, as well, more hopeful patterns arise. A puny Bulgarian boy frees a vila who is stuck in a bush and becomes the strongest man in his village. A Macedonian shepherd picks leaves to shield three sleeping beauties from the sun and is followed home by more sheep and goats than he can count. Most magnificently, a Bosnian merchant offers refreshment to a troupe of dancing girls and they leave enough gold behind them to pay for the building of the Buzadžija mosque.

These "white" vilas are all local spirits, existing in relation to a specific community. They sustain its most delicate balances, weighing in on the side of the poor, the young and the good-hearted. They give the gift of futures.

CHAPTER 39

In July, at the café, we had comedy and a Sevdalinka band. In August, a poetry slam. By September, the trees beside the Miljacka had turned the colour of autumn and my walk into work became a chaos of competing smells: roast chicken, corn on the cob, a market stall selling hot cider. Once I saw the skinhead leaning on the counter of this stall. As I went past, he gestured obscenely with his middle finger and drew it across his throat again. I renewed my resolve to put him out of my mind.

Even in summer, the basement of the café had sustained a seeping chill. Now it was truly cold. Tarik brought mugs of hot coffee down from the kitchen. When old Mrs Tomić turned up one night in a rabbit-skin stole, a little ragged round the edges, I coveted it fiercely. Only the performers seemed unbothered by the temperature. They stood on the stage in yoga pants and exercise bras to wake up their vocal cords, bub-bubbing and *aeiou*ing, noises like whale song rising from deep in their chests. Their strange rituals became a backdrop to my writing, as did their coughs, which I heard when they took cigarette breaks outside the café. I worried about how much they smoked – they were so young. Although Boris said, 'Let me tell you, don't work with old actors. We had a Bulgarian *Lear* once. The king kept taking out his false teeth and Gloucester pinched Nina's bum.'

Balkanista had published two more articles of mine. The first was a review of Amina Hadžić's maze-like new novel, set in the Balkans of the seventeenth century – a half mythical, half modern world, where men looked at their blood under microscopes and their stars through telescopes, and the uncharted edges of every map pulsed with dragons and sea monsters and pirate kings. The second was a follow-up piece about the scarcity of Bosnian literature in

237

British bookshops. If I translated Hadžić, I wrote, would the English read her? Or was all they wanted Swedish noir?

My birthday fell on the first Monday of October, when the café was closed. Tata phoned at breakfast. Afterwards I said to Tarik, 'Can you cook the rabbit dish we used to make? Roisin will be here in time for supper.' She'd rented a room in Sarajevo for a week, and I couldn't wait to see her again.

'When does her plane land?' Tarik asked, with a self-consciousness that made me look at him closely. But I said nothing for now. We went to the meat market near Markale to find a rabbit, breathing in the winter smells of smoked venison and ham. It had taken me some time to get used to eating properly again, but now I loved the Bosnian meals we cooked together at home – unapologetically fried and doused in wine. Tarik served up enormous portions that spilt over the edges of his oversized plates. In their excess, their hospitality, they reminded me of my first days with the ghosts.

Roisin came at six. Tarik was making long lengths of pasta, rolling it out and twisting it round a wooden pin. 'It's like watching a magician take ribbons from thin air,' she told him, mockingly, but also admiringly.

While the pasta was drying, he jointed the rabbit and I tore handfuls of rosemary and thyme. Roisin took up her guitar to tune the strings. 'So, what next?' Tarik asked her, when we sat down to eat. 'Do you think you'll stay in Cambridge?'

She shrugged. 'I doubt it. People there are very highbrow. I'm not really into books.'

'That makes two out of three of us,' he said, smiling at me.

For dessert, to counter the heaviness of pasta and meat, I'd cooked a fruit tart. Voćni kolač. 'Some things just sound better in Bosnian,' said Roisin. 'Jagoda, for instance, is a lovely word for a strawberry.' Over coffee she prowled Tarik's shelves. '*Foods of the East. Spices and Herbs.* Do you only read about cooking?'

'Sit down,' he told her. 'You don't like books, remember?' He refilled our cups. 'Jagoda,' he said. 'Where did you learn that?'

She laughed. 'My mum was a hippy. She still has long silver hair. We used to go on camping holidays in the Balkans, jump off cliffs naked. Ima li kamenja? Are there rocks?'

'Možeš li mi posuditi donje rublje?' Tarik said promptly. 'Can you lend me some underwear?' Roisin threw a cushion at him.

I left them to it and went into my bedroom to check my phone. I wasn't sure if Adam would remember my birthday; he was good at putting things out of his mind. But there was a missed call from him. Without letting myself wonder what I was doing, I pressed redial. Six rings. Then the click as he picked up.

'Happy birthday,' he said quietly.

'Thank you. How are you?'

'All right.'

'I'm sorry about the plane ticket.'

'Yes. Well, Dave didn't fire me.'

'I needed to come home.'

There was a crackle on the line. After a moment, Adam said, 'The Lyons have a baby boy. He's called Daniel. Peter says it's Biblical. As in den.'

I smiled, though of course he couldn't see that. 'How is Peter?'

'He's fine.'

For a few minutes, we said other unimportant things to each other. There was no fight or anger in either of us – that's how I could tell it was over. Only the details were left. The house, the money. The things lawyers handle. In the end, I said, 'I have to go.'

He said, 'Be safe, Laura.'

'You too.'

I really meant that. Adam will always be important to me. He is part of my life, because he was in its first pages. But he belongs in Whitehall, with David Focket. It's different for me. Bosnia is where my blood comes from.

My birthday wound up in a grungy bar, where Roisin had heard about a blues jam. She sang, of course – her hand on the pianist's shoulder, her voice in the bassist's ear. That's just how she was. Tarik lent on a pillar and watched.

When her song was over, she came and sat on the edge of his chair, then in his lap. He put his arm round her. 'I'm tired,' I said, after a while. 'I think I'll call it a night.' They offered to walk home with me but I told them to stay.

Baščaršija was alive with wintry cheer. Bars were glowing and glittering, and couples stumbled about, buying hot nuts. On impulse I detoured past the café. I had my key with me and I thought I would just sit for a while. I wanted the dark. As it was a Monday, the post was on the floor. I picked up two businesslike envelopes and a third one with my own name handwritten on the front. It had a Bosnian postmark. A stamp depicting a brown bear.

Dear Laura Guska (it began)

I am Sarajevan poet, and I am hoping to find translator for my new anthology. I am liking very much the way that you are writing for *Balkanista* magazine. How do you say in English lirski? Lyrical?

One of my poems is about vila – I send it now for you to read. Do you speak Bosnian language? You write about translating Hadžić, so I think perhaps you do.

In hope of your responses,

Ivan Tabak

I turned the airmail paper over in my fingers. Ivan Tabak. Three years ago, I had heard him lecture at St John's College in Cambridge. I'd planned to go back and talk to him, but instead I had met Adam. The strangeness of his letter coming to me now was hard to credit. A proof positive of the intricate magic of our lives.

CHAPTER 40

Tarik came into the kitchen early the next morning, while I was making a pot of coffee. 'Things are looking up,' he said, when I told him about Ivan's offer. Though I noticed that he also glanced behind him, as if his mind was on his bed.

'Coffee?' I offered. My brother had never liked mornings.

'Thanks,' he said. 'So, can I read this letter?'

I was just starting to explain that I had left it in the café when Roisin appeared, wrapped in his dressing gown, a bit pink-faced. 'Hi,' I said blankly.

'We didn't—' She blushed. 'It got late.'

'Are you *blushing*?' I said.

Tarik mumbled something about grabbing a shower. 'You have this,' he told Roisin, pushing the cup of coffee I'd made for him into her hands.

'Coward,' she called, as the door shut.

I picked up my own cup. 'He likes you.' I was torn between amusement and concern. How she felt wasn't at all clear to me. She had always flitted between musicians before; she got over one and under another.

Now she leant against his kitchen counter, his dressing-gown sleeves swamping her hands. 'I like him too.' Pushing back the sleeves, she took a sip of coffee. 'Jesus, this would wake the dead! Do you mind, Laura? Say now if you do.'

'I don't mind,' I said slowly. That was true, up to a point. She was only here for a week. But if that didn't worry them, why should it worry me? The future was capable of surprises. I had my own evidence of that.

Ivan had included an email address at the top of his letter. I wrote back that same morning. In my reply I proposed sending him a

241

translation of the poem he had sent me. If he didn't like it, he had only to say so.

I read that poem many times over the next week. It began with a vila dancing on the banks of the Miljacka, laughing, blue with cold. Under her feet, town halls, theatres and museums grew up like blades of spring grass. 'She danced,' I wrote. But Ivan had written plesala je. It's a supple verb; 'dance' is firmer, so my vila seemed more pronounced, heavier-footed than his. What might she do instead? Skip, waltz, twirl? My crossings-out and pencillings-in brought me to what, in Sarajevo, we call ceif – a state of consciousness that comes out of beloved rituals, like making a pot of coffee or lighting a fire.

When I emailed Ivan my final version, Boris advised me to include my phone number because many Sarajevans did not have regular access to a computer. He also asked if he could see the original poem, but I told him I'd taken it home.

Three days later, Ivan phoned. 'I like the way you translate me,' he said. Not *hello*. As always, I heard the Sarajevo accent with pleasure – the cut-off final syllables, like a knife had come down. 'We speak English!' he said, doing so. 'Best I think in English about English translation.'

He told me he was a lecturer at Sarajevo University, where he taught Slavic literature and also a small writing class. Right now, he was visiting friends in America. 'We have argued about one of your words,' he said. 'Why did you not translate vila?'

I had taken a long time over that decision. 'She belongs to Sarajevo,' I pointed out nervously. 'She *needs* to sound un-English.'

'Yes!' Ivan said. 'I think so too.' He asked me if I was willing to translate the whole anthology and offered a flat fee. And he'd be home by November, so perhaps we could meet up then?

From this point on, Ivan's poems took up most of my time. I admired the funny and bleak way he wrote about the war, but it was not without problems for me.

242

> To the sniper in the Jewish Cemetery:
> Don't shoot before I finish my cigarette.

Later in this poem he *ti*-ed the sniper – using the intimate form of *you*, which no longer exists in English, to make a quiet point about killing neighbours. And he was also fond of unyieldingly local words.

> Now, hiding in the woods,
> We eat squirrel meat
> Where once we used to picnic.

Mezetluk literally means going out for a snack with friends. My first try was brunch, but it felt too trendy, and I liked the open-air cosiness of picnic, in contrast to the hostile woods. So I wrote words down and crossed them out, and sometimes it felt like the poems were bending to me, and other times like they were pushing back.

All through October, rock bands and comedians continued to turn up at the café. One night it dawned on me that we should do a recital – a public reading would help us sell copies and might even attract a western publisher. But when I ran up to the kitchen to share this idea with Tarik, he looked at me doubtfully over an armful of curly-leafed kale. 'It's not that easy, little sister. All our weekends this year are booked up.'

'We could move one booking,' I argued. 'The aim of the café is to support the arts.'

My brother dumped the kale in the sink. 'Boris's first aim is to make money,' he said sensibly. 'Look, I'll see what I can do.'

When I went back to the kitchen a few days later, ready to argue my case, Boris met me at the door. He never cancelled a booking, he told me with pride, but he was willing to open the basement on a weeknight, so long as I took responsibility for all the arrangements and publicity. 'Thank you!' I said, and hugged him, all bloodstained apron as he was, and sweat-spiked hair.

He laughed. 'Don't thank me yet. It's going to be a lot of work.'

From then on, I was not only a translator but an events manager too. I sent out a press release. I argued down quotes for the printing of posters and fliers. 'Cheap as chips,' Ivan insisted, when we spoke on the phone. 'That is what you say in England, yes?' It had become a cheerful doctrine with him that I could pull miracles out of my sleeves. Although much less sure of this myself, I was determined not to let him down.

The evening before he was due home from America, I told the cider drinkers and kebab eaters on the south bank of the Miljacka, 'There's a poet doing a recital at Café Illyria next Wednesday.' Swallowing my nervousness, I said, 'He's Sarajevan – very talented.' I pressed my newly printed fliers into their hands. Then I walked on through the dark shadows of Baščaršija until I reached the café.

CHAPTER 41

I drove to Sarajevo airport at six o'clock on Sunday evening, having borrowed Nina's car – to save Ivan a bus ride, I said, but really I was just impatient to meet him. His flight was delayed, so I waited nervously by a currency exchange booth, holding a homemade sign with his name on it.

At last a voice behind me said, 'I am arrived!' and I looked round to see the man I remembered from that long-ago lecture, resplendent in red corduroy trousers and a mustard-yellow shirt, and beaming all over his sleep-creased face. 'Tourists, they queue,' he scoffed. 'I say to them, move over! Bosnian poet coming through!' He shook my hand, since everyone knows from film and myth that it's a British thing to do, then he leant forwards to kiss me on both cheeks. He had a soft moustache, waxed to pointy tips.

'It's great to meet you,' I said, in Bosnian, as we walked out of the airport.

'English!' he told me. 'Only English while I am with you!'

The car park was noisy with American backpackers. 'Do you think the air hostess's breasts were real?' they asked each other. 'You can't fly with fake breasts, man. They pop!' Ivan seemed hardly aware of them. He had been travelling since dawn, he said, with a stopover in Istanbul. Nonetheless, he asked if I could drop him at the university, where he needed to sort out some papers. In the car he nodded against the passenger door, not quite asleep, as the suburbs of Hrasno and Grbavica slid past. 'Have you always lived in Sarajevo?' I asked him.

He shook his head, his smile deepening the creases under his eyes. 'My life, it is unusual.' He told me he'd studied in America, but came home to get married. 'She was special person,' he said. *Was*, I noted. Not *is*. They'd lived together on the outskirts of Sarajevo, near

245

Mojmilo Hill, and he had been a university lecturer until the war, when he was forced to become a soldier. 'I do not talk about those days anymore, except in my poetry,' he said, looking out at the lights of Grbavica. 'I just try to teach young people to read our literature, perhaps one day to write it. I think this is important. They don't get job. They have no voice. In our country,' he ended softly, 'it is a bad time to be young.'

He had that small moustache he twisted when he was out of words.

The next morning I woke up much earlier than usual. Sideways autumn light spilled across the river, creating an underwater world of glowing cranes and scaffolding. Ivan was outside the Illyria when I got there, smoking and rubbing the sleep from his eyes. His shirt this time was pale blue with silver stripes. 'Bad habit,' he said, putting out his cigarette when he saw me.

The café was closed on Mondays, so we had the place to ourselves. I took some chairs off a table near the bar and we sat together all morning, drinking pots of black coffee and reading out his poems. *Your* poems, Ivan called them. At first, he often reverted to Bosnian. 'English!' he told himself, smacking his forehead. Gradually he sank into the foreign language, but he found it effortful. After a few hours he proposed a break. He chain-smoked rollies as we strolled up Riba Street, lighting the second from the butt of the first. The bitter smell reminded me of the homegrown tobacco the ghosts had used on Zvezdanka Street.

'Two,' Ivan told a Roma girl in charge of a streetside grill. Handing over a coin, he received in return the charred cobs of corn. 'I miss food from home when I am in America,' he explained, passing one to me.

Biting into the black and yellow kernels, I remembered the first poem he'd sent me – the one about cornfields springing up under the feet of a vila. I told him of my struggle to translate *plesala je*. 'All vilas dance,' I said. 'Have you noticed that?'

We were in the heart of the old town now, outside the Gazi Husrev Beg Mosque. Ivan put another cigarette between his lips. 'For water spirits, dance is a hard and joyful thing.' He reached into his pocket for a match. 'Do you know the German fairy tale about this?'

I said, 'Remind me.'

A pigeon flew past us. Ivan raised his arm to fend it off. 'Once there was a mermaid who loved a prince,' he began. 'So she went to a witch and bought some feet. The witch told her every step she took would be like treading on a sharp knife. But she walked all the way to the royal palace, and when she got to it she danced for the prince.' He broke off at that point. Perhaps he had forgotten the rest of the story. Or perhaps for him it ended with the mermaid dancing before the human court – beautifully, ignoring the blood that spilt from her feet and turned the bottom of her shoes bright red. It seemed a long time before he spoke again. 'My wife used to read this to my son,' he said.

A son, I thought. And I imagined a black-haired boy on a sofa, curled up yawning and sleepy against the past-tense wife. 'How old is he now?'

'Too old for fairy tales.' Ivan moved his hand as if to dispel a phantom, and I caught again the haunting aroma of his tobacco.

'May I?' I asked him.

He passed me his cigarette. While I smoked, the light changed colour. Big raindrops fell individually, one on my arm, my neck, my leg; then it was raining really hard, and as we ran towards Riba Street it started hailing, the hail coming down so fast it looked like the world was made out of dots.

'Sarajevo!' said Ivan. In the café he doubled over to catch his breath, his elbows on his knees, water dripping from both ends of his moustache. 'Always too much weather!'

That night I asked him to supper with Tarik and Roisin, but he said he preferred to go home. Since the war, he said, he had tried to live quietly, or else he got headaches, terrible migraines.

Under his flamboyant clothes, I sensed he was a very private man.

CHAPTER 42

On the second day of his visit, Ivan met me outside the café at noon, wearing a sky-blue coat with yellow elbow patches. He had one of his headaches and asked rather tersely if we might go to the Celtic Pub. He could cope with white noise, he said, but it would be easier if it was in English. I agreed at once. As we set off up Riba Street, I stopped briefly at a kiosk to buy *The Sarajevo Times*. In the arts section I showed him the advert for his recital tomorrow.

CAFÉ ILLYRIA

An Evening With
Ivan Tabak

LOCAL POET READS FROM
EXCITING NEW COLLECTION
(BOSNIAN AND ENGLISH)
14.12.11 – 2100 h.

There was also a short review of his work, which called him the cream of Sarajevo's poets, a fresh voice, Bosnia's brightest and best. I completely agreed. But it struck me how all these metaphors had to do with flavour or light – as if the attraction of talent lies in our greed to consume it, our desire to see it burn.

At the bottom of the street, outside the building site, I saw the skinhead again. This dismayed me because he had not appeared for weeks. He flicked open a knife and began to peel an apple, letting the skin fall to the ground. When I looked back, he pointed the blade at me.

In the Celtic Pub, girls with stick-and-poke tattoos drank Cola Zero with a side of chips, while paunchy alcoholics slunk up and down to the bar. We found ourselves a table and Ivan took out a creased notebook. Working through the rest of the anthology took us almost the whole day. Then we talked about what he would read the following night, in the café. I liked the poem about the dancing vila. He wanted to end on one called "Hope."

'Is not a poem so much as a list,' he said, turning to it. 'I ask my students what helps them survive dark nights of the soul.'

I said, 'For most people in Sarajevo, it's probably coffee. Or fried food.'

He laughed. 'Chicken kebab.'

I admitted I'd never eaten a Sarajevan kebab, and he said at once that he knew the best place.

'She wants every filling you have,' he told the woman behind the counter of a tiny shop in Novi Grad, twenty minutes and a crowded bus ride later.

I took the paper bag she held out to me, smiling warily.

'Taste it now,' Ivan urged me. So I did, and it *was* good. Hot, salty meat in grilled bread, oozing with spicy red pepper sauce.

We left the shop to eat by the Miljacka, which was low in its banks here, slipping darkly towards the city centre. Ivan had bought a handful of Preminger beers. He knocked the tops off on a rock with practiced deftness, each bottle spurting out a creamy froth. A mist was creeping down from the mountains and the lights on the cranes were haloed in red. He pointed to the nearest one. 'Sarajevo! Destroyed into existence.'

'I like that.'

'Yes?' He gave a wave of his hand. 'It is yours.' I laughed, and so did he. But then he said, 'Best translators are authors too. I mean it. Some day you must write your own story.'

'I wouldn't know how to start.'

'How it starts doesn't matter. What matters is how it ends.'

For a while we were both silent, occupied by the beers and kebabs.

When Ivan had finished eating, he squatted on his heels beside the Miljacka, cleaning his hands in the slow-moving river. 'Can I say something else?' he asked me.

'Of course.'

'Stay in Sarajevo. I do not talk about forever, but stay at least one year. I want your help.'

'My help?' I repeated blankly.

Shaking off the water, the bright drops falling back into the current, he explained that two of his former poetry students were hoping to publish a dual language anthology. 'I hope for them an international profile,' he said, smiling at the outrageous splendour of that. 'Also, I have novelist friend you must meet – he is looking for English translator. I know you think you are not ready, but opportunity is like tram. If you don't jump on, it will go past.'

I gazed into the dark flow of the river and let myself imagine translating more Bosnian writers into English. Organising readings at Café Illyria, arranging interviews for *The Sarajevo Times*. Ivan's offer felt like more than fate: it felt like providence. Looking up at him, I said simply, 'Yes.'

'So it is deal,' he said, beaming at me. He held out his hand, in that most English of gestures. 'Plans we can make today, tomorrow,' he said. 'Whenever you want.'

Neither of us said much as we walked downstream. The Miljacka was equally quiet beside us. After a while Ivan turned south, onto Gatačka Street. The name was familiar to me, but I couldn't think why. Gradually I became conscious that Ivan's breathing was laboured. He was moving stiffly, as if in pain. 'Headache is back,' he explained. He walked on in silence for a while. 'I slept only two hours last night,' he said at last. 'I have terrible nightmares, so I do not like to sleep.'

I said, 'What are your nightmares about?'

A cyclist rode past us, ringing a bell. When the sound had died away, Ivan said, 'My son was on a sledge, in the war. A shell hit him. My wife, she killed herself.' He spread his hands, a gesture that both expressed and curbed an old grief. 'I wrote my first poem about him. I called it "Hasan."'

I said, '*Oh.*' Suddenly dizzy, I sat down on a garden wall.

Ivan sat down next to me. 'Perhaps these things are not to be pronounced,' he said.

But I caught his hand and pressed it. 'They are to be pronounced,' I told him fiercely. 'I'm sorry about your wife. I'm sorry about Hasan.'

I said goodbye to Ivan outside his house. Then I rushed home to Tarik's flat. There I searched online until I found his poem.

You lay on the snow, a smashed angel.

It was about my Hasan. I felt sure of it. Sara's husband was called Ivo – that could be a nickname. She had even told me he was a lecturer.

My first thought was a sort of wild excitement. I wanted to run back to Ivan's house and pound on the door – to tell him I'd known his best friend, his neighbours, his wife and his son. But my next thought came to me in Roisin's sensible voice. You probably read his family history on the internet, Roisin would say.

Well, I searched for hours and couldn't find it. Perhaps it was there once, and the web page had since been removed. Perhaps the ghosts were only stories that I spun around the poet Ivan Tabak. His revelation felt like a fold in the fabric of things. But perhaps it was not.

CHAPTER 43

I spent the morning before Ivan's recital handing out flyers in Baščaršija. That afternoon we set up the café. We started at three o'clock, to be in good time. Boris and Tarik laid out chairs. Nina hummed into a microphone. I put candles at the edge of the stage so that small yellow flames would glow and twinkle. After a while, Tarik said, 'When do we meet this poet of yours?' and I explained that he had a headache. He was lying down in his house, in the dark, I said, trying not to worry. But worry swamped me. At about six o'clock, I left the café and walked to the pharmacy near the cathedral, on the excuse of buying my poet some paracetamol. Breathing in the dry, medicinal air above the shelves, I tried to think calmly. Tarik, Nina, Boris: had any of them met Ivan, even in passing? I could not recall a single time.

Outside the pharmacy, the air had the porridgey smell of unfallen snow. Ivan Tabak was flesh and blood, I reassured myself. Roisin and I had met at his lecture in Cambridge. But could I have imagined his letter? His poems? His return from America to Sarajevo?

There was a bar up the street from the pharmacy that had a decorative barrel outside. I might have sat on the edge of it forever, my mind swarming with doubts, if that Serbian skinhead had not blundered out of the bar's front door. He stopped there, sucking on a cigarette, swaying and leering at me. Just the smoke he blew out troubled and hazed his edges. Ivan had *spoken* to me. He'd drunk my coffee. But then, so had the ghosts. In spite of the cold, I found myself sweating. An audience of fifty people was due at Café Illyria in – I glanced at my watch – one hour, to hear a poet who wasn't in Sarajevo read from a work that didn't exist. I had advertised this event in a newspaper; I had sent tickets to four literary agents. I had taken stark leave of my senses.

252

I went on sitting there as the night turned terrible: the smogged-out stars rose, and the pale tumour of moon. I sat until despair froze through my thin coat and made my fingers sausage-red and numb. Then I got up. I needed to go back to the café and confess that Ivan Tabak was not coming – not tonight, and not ever. There was nothing else to be done.

I dragged my icy feet through Markale market, where the tables were stripped bare. I was dimly aware of shadows shifting behind me, someone who stumbled and muttered. When I looked back, I saw the skinhead. There was a bright thing glinting in his hand. All the anger I felt at myself and my ruined plans rose inside me, and on an impulse of furious grief I span round and lurched right at him. I was braced for the deference the ghosts used to show solid objects – the way they would melt around or through them. Not sharpness. Not hairy flesh. So I will never forget the surprise on his face, nor the sour, beery smell as we slammed together. His knife nicked my wrist as it clattered to the pavement, and the blood that welled out of me was dark and hot and undeniably real. He grabbed my throat, his thumbs pressing so hard it felt like I was drowning. But I got my knee up into his groin, hard, and his grip loosened enough for me to writhe away and start running – spurred on by the sound of him staggering behind me for the awful seconds it took to burst out into Fra Grge Martića Street.

A pair of Christmas shoppers swore as I pushed past them. Without hesitation I shouldered my way into the crowd outside Moj Café, jostling against a high-heeled woman on her phone. 'Watch yourself,' she said. Only then did my heartbeat start to slow down. My wrist was bleeding where the skinhead's knife had caught me, but the cut was not deep; worse was the way I could see his thumbprints on my throat in the café window. I pulled up my coat collar to hide the red marks, like splash burns from scalding water, or like grotesque lipstick kisses. The couple at the nearest table stared at me through the glass. That was enough to make me turn away and walk quickly down the street, breaking into a run as I passed the building site. I didn't stop until I reached the Illyria's familiar front door.

Only once I was inside, voices babbling up from the basement, did I allow myself to think the word *knife*. The word *stabbing*. I had nearly become a statistic of the Baščaršija backstreets. My legs suddenly shaky, I sank down beside the coat-stand in the hall. I stayed like that for several minutes. Just crouched there, breathing, on the floor. Then I stood up and made my way downstairs.

Nina was on the door, or rather she was closing it behind the last two ticket-holders. She pantomimed wiping sweat off her brow when she saw me. 'Where have you been?' she hissed. 'We're about to start!'

I said, 'Ivan?'

'On the stage.'

Pushing past her, I slit open the door. I saw the audience peering out into the candlelit darkness. The shine of Ivan's orange shirt. 'My name is Ivan Tabak,' I heard him telling them. 'If you ask me later, I can sign it on your napkin, or some such thing. No problem.' I heard them laugh.

Nina tapped my shoulder. 'Tarik is saving you a seat,' she whispered.

'You take it,' I whispered back. 'I want a moment on my own.'

I saw her start to protest, but I put my finger to my lips and gave her a tiny push, and she tiptoed through the door on sparrow-feet, her green hair glowing.

'Plesala je,' Ivan began. His low voice came through to the box office where I sat with a cut on my wrist and bruises on my neck. I had made a big mistake – I was less in control than I'd thought. But I had lived to tell my tale. Or my tail, that old joke.

At last Ivan began to recite his final poem, the one about hope. In a moment he would say my name, and I would go out into the flickering lights, the whistles and claps. I would take his hand. And I would look towards my future.

ACKNOWLEDGEMENTS

In any language, *thank you* is my favourite thing to say.

This novel began to unfurl when I moved to Bosnia to help put on a performance of Shakespeare's *Twelfth Night*. To all the friends who shared their homes, memories, advice and recipes, and especially to Dejan Čokić, Goran Knezović and Ilija Pujić: this book wouldn't exist without you. Any mistakes are mine alone. *Hvala.*

The stories of strangers are an incredible gift. To the pawnbroker at the Grbavica bus stop, the history student who joined me for a cup of coffee in Baščaršija, and the artist at Vrelo Bosne who spent a summer afternoon teaching me about water spirits – a very special thanks.

I owe so much, as well, to Andrew Garrod at Youth Bridge Global, for taking a chance on an inexperienced co-director, to Jessica Swale and Alex Payne, for showing me the ropes, and to Boro Todorović and Dzenan Catic, for patiently teaching me Bosnian.

Dancing on Knives took over a decade to bring into the world. My agent Joanna Swainson and the team behind the Mslexia First Novel Award gave me self-belief when I needed it most. And the women who run Honno Press are fairy godmothers, one and all. Rebecca Parfitt, Lynzie Fitzpatrick, and Gemma June Howell: *diolch yn fawr.*

Perhaps the most magical thing about writing is finding your tribe. Many fateful years ago, I stumbled upon the best group of writer-friends I could possibly hope for: generous, bracing and brilliant. Bobby Darbyshire, Julia Rampen, Ellen MacDonald-Kramer, Eden Carter Wood and Emma Bamford, I love you all.

Finally, I'm so grateful to everyone who has celebrated milestones with me or helped me back to the path when I lost my way. Victoria Rowlands, Becca Coker and Anna Dempsey: I'm lucky to have you in my life. And Peter and Margaret Rush, you've been there for every story I've ever told. Thank you.

AUTHOR'S NOTE

The war in Bosnia began in 1992, when I was nine years old. Living at the time in a tiny Surrey village, I knew nobody from the Balkans. However, my parents' lovingly chaotic house has always been open to everyone, and especially those newly arrived in England. Perhaps that's why the television footage of besieged Sarajevo – the bombed buildings and displaced families – impressed me so vividly. I was just starting to understand how fragile a thing *home* can be.

Twenty years later, I moved to Bosnia to work for Youth Bridge Global – a charity which uses theatre to bring together young people from divided communities, encouraging friendship and collaboration. For those interested, there are stories and photographs, as well as some ways to support future projects, on the website: youthbridgeglobal.com. As a theatre director, I lived in the beautiful medieval city of Mostar, where the walls are still scarred by bullet holes, jobs are hard to find, and ethnic tension persists. It was here I began to imagine the novel that would become *Dancing on Knives*. Most of the people I met had lived through the war, and all were acutely aware of its ongoing impact on their lives. I wanted to explore that long shadow.

After I left Mostar I spent a summer in Sarajevo, researching and writing. Of all Bosnian cities it is the most cosmopolitan, which felt right for Laura, giving her a past that cuts across individual ethnicities and religions. The people I met were generous in sharing their memories with me. A library-dweller by nature, I am also indebted to a wide range of books – from histories and works of social anthropology to war dispatches and personal memoirs. Most important to me were Tom Gjelten's *Sarajevo Daily: A City and Its*

Newspaper Under Siege; Ivana Maček's *Sarajevo Under Siege*; Barbara Demick's *Besieged: Life Under Fire on a Sarajevo Street*; *In Harm's Way* by war reporter Martin Bell and Marko Attila Hoare's *The History of Bosnia*. The Bosnian war poems in the anthology *Scar on the Stone*, edited by Chris Agee, offer moving insights into life under fire, and Laura quotes from one of the most beautiful: 'Some of the Secrets are Out' by Hamdija Demirović.

Collectively, these are the influences that inspired the ghost stories in my novel. However, *Dancing on Knives* is a work of fiction, not biography. For this reason, I invented for Laura an imaginary home in Sarajevo: Gnijezdo Street. "Gnijezdo" means nest. It felt fitting for a girl whose surname – Guska, or "goose" – recalls the birds of passage that flee their homes in the harsh winter but return with the spring.

According to legend, ghosts seek vengeance or justice, and I chose to hang my story on the long-delayed capture of Bosnian war criminal General Ratko Mladić in 2011. I drew on descriptions by journalists who encountered him during the war, and on the transcripts from his seventeen-month trial at the Hague. His bullying pride and unrepentant prejudice rose from those pages in a way that was brutal but illuminating. Almost everything he says in my novel – from his anger about being helped to walk 'as if I am a blind man' to his hate speech about Muslims – comes from his own mouth. It felt extremely important not to add to his words.

My account of Mladić's arrest is also based on published facts whenever possible. His tactics on the run are well-documented, though the informer Bojan Lepović is my own invention, as is the retired British civil servant, William Littleton. Where details remain classified, I have constructed a narrative from reports and rumours in news coverage at the time, and from what's known of methods used to capture similarly high-profile war criminals –

notably, Saddam Hussein. Significant Western involvement in the discovery of Mladić seems probable. The Bosnian president, Bakir Izetbegović, publicly thanked the British Secret Services for their support. Mladić himself is reported to have asked his captors, 'Which one of you is the foreigner?'

For five years after I finished *Dancing on Knives*, I thought it was too quiet a book to interest publishers. A Bosnian ghost story about a war the West had all but forgotten? Then, in May 2022, came *Black Butterflies* – Priscilla Morris's gorgeous and haunting novel set in the siege of Sarajevo. There is a place, I realised, for books that invite us to reflect. Three months earlier, Russia had invaded Ukraine, creating war in Europe again. With a new sense of urgency, I revisited the manuscript of *Dancing on Knives*, setting off a chain of events that led to it being longlisted for the Mslexia First Novel Prize and accepted for publication by Honno Press.

It's still a quiet novel. Nevertheless, I hope it can be a reminder that the consequences of war aren't over when they stop being front page news. For those from Ukraine, and now Gaza, even peace – though longed for – will not be an ending: the legacy of conflict is for life. My book acknowledges that. But it also explores how a sense of community might be rebuilt. In *Dancing on Knives*, the poet Ivan Tabak's determination to give young people a voice reflects the quest of Youth Bridge Global's artistic director in Mostar, Ilija Pujić.

Stories cannot undo the past, but they may bring hope.

ABOUT HONNO

Honno Welsh Women's Press was set up in 1986 by a group of women who felt strongly that women in Wales needed wider opportunities to see their writing in print and to become involved in the publishing process. Our aim is to develop the writing talents of women in Wales, give them new and exciting opportunities to see their work published and often to give them their first 'break' as a writer.

Honno is registered as a community co-operative. Any profit that Honno makes is invested in the publishing programme. Women from Wales and around the world have expressed their support for Honno. Each supporter has a vote at the Annual General Meeting. For more information and to buy our publications, please visit our website www.honno.co.uk or email us on post@honno.co.uk.

Honno
D41, Hugh Owen Building,
Aberystwyth University,
Aberystwyth,
Ceredigion,
SY23 3DY.

We are very grateful for the support of all our Honno Friends.